SILVER OR LEAD

MAFIA FOR HIRE
BOOK 1

DARCY HALIFAX

Published by Paladin Publishing

Silver Or Lead
Copyright © 2023 by Darcy Halifax

Cover design by: Covers by Aura
Editing and proofreading by: Messenger's Memos – Fiction Editing
Services
Formatting by: Darcy Halifax

SILVER OR LEAD

MAFIA FOR HIRE
BOOK 1

DARCY HALIFAX

DEDICATION

Welcome to the world, Darcy!

I dedicate the dick-rot to you, Kelly. Thank you.

CONTENT GUIDE

Please be advised that Silver Or Lead contains content that some readers may find triggering.

This is book one in a dark(ish) romance with a guaranteed HFN (it is book one of a completed duet).

There is no bullying or violence between the MCs.

For a full list of triggers (to avoid spoilers here), please head to my website and search under Content Guide.
Content Guide

CHAPTER ONE

The dark hood over Angela's head was suffocating. Every breath felt thick, and her heart pounded furiously to make up for the lack of oxygen. Or so it seemed. A good deal of her racing heart was from pure terror.

It seemed ludicrous that just ten minutes prior, she had been getting into her car in the parking lot at the hospital where she worked as a surgeon, and now she was rolling around in the trunk of a stranger's car with her hands bound behind her back and a hood over her head. It wasn't her first time in this kind of predicament, and she reminded herself that she *could* breathe through the thick fabric. So, she ordered herself to take one measured breath in, then exhaled slowly. She repeated the action three more times before she was able to breathe with more ease and wonder just how she had gotten into the situation.

A group of three men had walked over to her, and her well-honed spidey senses flared to life. But, like an idiot, she ignored them when one of the men spoke politely.

"Excuse me, are you a doctor?" the man questioned.

Angela confirmed that she was indeed a doctor, then the man grimaced and said, "I'm really sorry about this."

He moved with lightning speed, wrenching her hands behind her back at the same time as a black hood was pulled over her head. She had gotten a few kicks into some shins before she was shoved into the trunk of a flashy car.

Now, here she was, being driven to a second location like a victim. But she wasn't a victim. She never would be again. Which was why, when she felt the car slow down and eventually stop, she tucked her feet underneath her in preparation for the trunk to open.

She strained, listening to the sound of the doors opening and closing, followed by some muffled voices. She quickly looked down, shaking her head vigorously and dislodging the black fabric. She gasped, blinking and trying to see anything at all. But there was nothing but her in the surprisingly large space. When the trunk opened suddenly, she pushed up from her knees, ramming her head into the chest of her nearest abductor. He grunted but didn't go down.

"Shit! Grab her!" the man yelled.

She found herself in the arms of not one but two men as she was hauled bodily out of the car. They continued to carry her — swearing all the way as if *she* was the problem — across what looked to be an underground parking garage. It was large, with polished concrete floors and dozens of vehicles. Unfortunately, she was unable to get a good look at any license plates before she was loaded into an elevator.

The man she had rammed into grabbed her jaw, forcing her to look at him. "Will you calm down? Nobody's going to hurt you," he said.

Angela yanked her head back. Her skin was already crawling from the unwanted touch. "Like I haven't heard that before. Fuck you!" she snarled at him.

He shook his head, stepping back and not saying anything else. She watched the numbers on the elevator go up and up until the doors finally opened on floor fifty. She was finally placed on her feet as the men dragged her from the elevator, down a hallway with closed doors, and into an open area with couches. She took in every detail she could, from the soft-gray walls to the plush carpet beneath her feet. She realized she was in a very expensive building, and the underground area must have been a private garage.

"Hey." Her abductor clicked his fingers in front of her face. "I'm going to untie you because you're going to need your hands. Don't try anything stupid, Doc," he ordered her.

Angela had no intention of listening to him, but she nodded her head, feigning submission. Her right fist shot out the moment her hands were freed, striking one of her kidnappers in the throat. The large brute of a man choked, his blue eyes going wide before he bent forward and coughed. Angela took great satisfaction in the look of shock and pain on his face as he struggled to breathe. She raised her foot to kick the man's testicles into his abdomen, but a silky-smooth voice stopped her.

"Enough of that."

The words, spoken casually, held a command her body was unable to ignore. She hesitated, and it cost her dearly. The big man was up and holding her arms to her sides in seconds. She cursed her own stupidity more than anything else. *Never hesitate,* she told herself. *You know better.* "Let me go."

"Not gonna happen," her captor snarled at her, giving her a shake.

Angela ignored him, her brain working quickly. He

had a very strong grip on her arms and was standing back enough that she had no hope of inflicting damage with her feet. So she bit him instead. At least, she tried to. The moment her teeth grazed his knuckle, he swore and jumped back, releasing her from the prison of his arms. She made it one step before she was brought up short by the barrel of a gun.

"I need you to calm down, Doctor."

Her eyes flicked past the deadly weapon to the man holding it. She was sorry to find the most gorgeous man she had ever laid eyes on. It was just her luck to discover the reincarnation of *David,* only for him to be a criminal. He had dark-brown hair that was thick and wavy, tanned skin, and eyes that were several shades lighter than his hair, making them a startling and beautiful contrast. "Who are you? Why have you taken me?" she finally demanded.

"Vincenzo Romano."

Angela was so shocked that she stopped all attempts to escape. She knew the name well, even though she had never had the misfortune of meeting the man before. "Romano? The rebel mafia prince?"

He grimaced. "Call me Roman. I'm no prince," he responded.

She snorted. "No shit, you're not a prince. A killer is what you are." Angela slammed her mouth shut, cursing her runaway mouth. She knew the man's reputation. She knew he had killed his own father so he could inherit the mantel of Don of the largest mafioso in the country. His face turned hard and cold, and she saw the monster beneath the thin veneer of civility he'd had in place.

"If I am a killer, you'd do well to be a little nicer to me," he told her silkily.

"Nicer? I've been kidnapped!" Angela yelled.

"It was an emergency," Roman said, as if it absolved him of his sins. "We need your help."

Angela slammed her mouth shut and blinked. "I'm sorry. Did you just say you need my help?"

He nodded once, muscles flexing in his jaw.

Angela laughed. She couldn't help it. The way his eyes narrowed dangerously told her it wasn't a welcomed sound. "Your goons tossed a bag over my head and locked me in the trunk," she reminded him when she had herself under control. "I'm not helping you with shit."

He took a deep breath, as if striving for patience. "I regret the means—" he began, only to be interrupted by a man running into the room.

"Roman! He's getting worse," the man said, looking scared.

"Bring her!" Vincenzo Romano commanded before sprinting out of the room.

A strong grip on her upper arm forced her to walk across the corridor and into a room that looked suspiciously like an infirmary or a doctor's office. The crime boss was standing with his back to her by a hospital bed. The goon dragged her closer, and her medical side took over. She shook off the hand holding her and moved toward the man on the bed. He was young, perhaps in his early twenties, and incredibly pale. He was also unconscious, and his breathing was labored.

"What happened?" she demanded, beginning a visual triage.

"He was shot," Roman told her, frowning down at the man. "It was a through and through. Our usual physician patched him up and assured us he would be fine. About an hour ago, he began to have trouble breathing, and his blood pressure dropped."

Angela listened to the explanation, checking the man's heart rate with two fingers against his inner wrist. Finding his pulse rapid, she moved her gaze down, lifting the sheet. His chest was bare save for a dressing on the right side of his abdomen and some alarming bruising spreading out from beneath the bandage.

"How long ago was he shot?" she asked, rolling the

man carefully onto his side. She noted another dressing on his back, slightly higher than the wound on his front. The bullet clearly had not traveled straight.

"About ten hours," Roman replied.

Angela's head whipped up. "Ten hours? Are you the ones responsible for the bullet-riddled bodies brought into my ER over the last day?" she demanded.

She didn't have all the details, but there had been some kind of shootout on the streets—a turf war or something. And the hospital had been slammed with patients. Two men had died before making it to the ER.

Roman's face remained blank as he crossed his arms over his chest. "How he was shot doesn't matter. Just fix him."

Angela shook her head. "It doesn't work that way. I don't have x-ray vision. I can't see what's going on inside of him. He could have internal bleeding, broken ribs that caused a bone shard to puncture a lung or enter his bloodstream . . . anything. Call an ambulance."

"We can't," Roman stated.

"Then take him to the hospital yourself," Angela insisted.

"We can't do that either," Roman told her.

Angela glanced at him. "Because you'll be arrested." It was a statement, not a question.

"Because it would end in more bloodshed," Roman

corrected, frowning down at her from his considerable height. "That's why."

"And because I made them promise not to take me."

Angela looked down, finding the young man awake. His eyes were a startling blue in direct contrast to his dark-brown hair and eyebrows.

"I'm . . . Luca," he said slowly.

"Luca." Angela's smile was strained. "I'm Dr. Angela Hawthorne. I'm not going to sugarcoat it; you look to be in critical condition. You need to go to the hospital."

"Can't . . ." Luca said. Only this time, his words were more gasp than anything else.

"Don't speak, *mio fratello*. All will be well. I promise," Roman vowed. He smiled at Luca, setting down the hand he had been gripping tightly. He nodded once to the man hanging onto Luca's other hand on the opposite side of the bed, drawing Angela's attention to him.

He looked older than Luca, perhaps in his late thirties. He had brown hair that was pulled back in a messy bun, and his dark-brown eyes were red-rimmed. He kissed Luca's hand tenderly and gave a strained smile. "Rest, okay?"

Luca nodded, his chest rising and falling rapidly. "Love . . . you."

"I love you too," the man replied, brushing Luca's sweaty bangs off his forehead.

It was clear they were a couple. *And a cute one at that,* Angela thought. Despite the circumstances, she didn't want to see that love die. Luca needed more medical intervention immediately. She cleared her throat, digging deep for her usual compassionate bedside manner. "Excuse me, mister...?"

"Salvatore. Just Salvatore. I'm Luca's partner. Please, help him," Salvatore all but begged.

"I can't. Not here. I'm sorry," she answered honestly. "If you want him to live, you need to get him to a hospital." She hoped he would listen more than Luca and Roman.

"If *you* want to live, you better get to work."

A familiar *snick* accompanied the words, and Angela stiffened. She turned to find herself at the wrong end of Roman's handgun once more. Her eyes flicked to his caramel ones, finding a coldness that spoke of a man who was not bluffing. She smiled regretfully at Salvatore and Luca before stepping back.

Roman watched her with narrowed eyes. "What are you doing? Save him," he commanded.

"No," Angela replied succinctly.

The look on Roman's face was one of complete shock for a second before it morphed into pure rage. It was a look she was very familiar with, and she braced herself for a blow. But it never came. Instead, she found herself with a muzzle of a gun pressing painfully into the center of her forehead.

"I said, *save him*," Roman repeated with quiet deadliness.

Angela met his eyes once more. "And I said *no*."

"You took an oath," her original kidnapper pointed out from beside Roman. He was looking just as frustrated and murderous as his boss. "That's a thing, right? The Hippocratic Oath?"

She shrugged. "Sure. I took an oath. But not to you."

The gasping breaths of the young man behind her were the only sounds in the room for a few heartbeats. She did her best to ignore the dying man. But it was hard. Very hard. Still, she would not yield. She had done so in the past, and it had cost her more than a few bruises. Cuts, bruises, and broken bones were easily healed in the grand scheme of things. But her mind, her *soul*—those things were much harder to repair. She refused to feel them shatter again.

Roman ground the cold metal deeper into her forehead, no doubt leaving a mark. "Are you really prepared to die for the sake of pride?"

Angela raised her chin as much as the gun would allow. "It's not about pride. It's about power. You seem to think you hold all the power in this room because you have that gun. But in actual fact, *I* am the one with all the power. If you want me to save that man, you'll apologize," she told him. "You'll get that gun out of my face. And you'll get the fuck out of my space."

"Roman, please," Salvatore practically sobbed when Roman didn't immediately move.

Roman stared at her for another tense second before his thumb pushed the safety back on the gun with practiced ease. He lowered the weapon to his side and swallowed audibly, taking a step back. "I apologize for the way you were brought here. I apologize for your treatment. Please, will you help my brother? He's innocent."

Angela maintained eye contact for a heartbeat longer, seeing the pain and fear hidden in the depths of the eyes that also held death. They tugged at something inside of her, something she couldn't—and *wouldn't*—name. Turning away, she said, "Nobody is innocent. Not even me."

Then she got to work, saving a man who probably wasn't worth saving.

CHAPTER TWO

Roman watched the woman bark orders at his crew. He nodded when they looked at him, telling them, "Get her anything she needs."

He was furious with Dr. Gaines. The older man had been their private physician for years. He was paid handsomely for his service. And his silence. Roman wasn't naïve. He knew the doctor only treated them because of the money. The older man didn't really give a shit about any of them. But that didn't mean he could put his baby brother's life at risk by doing a half-assed job.

The last twenty-four hours had been hell. His brother, who was twelve years younger than he was, had managed to fall in love with his bodyguard over the past year. A bodyguard who came with a shady past and a bunch of enemies that finally came knocking. Salvatore was usually more than capable of taking care of business. Unfortunately, his badass rep meant sweet fuck-all when it came to matters of the heart. And having a partner—a *male* partner at that—had painted a huge target on not only on his back, but on Luca's as well.

The end result of months at war with a rival crime syndicate seeking revenge had been a bloodbath on the streets. It wasn't Roman's usual style, but it was unavoidable. After killing Raz, the leader of The Razors, Roman was ready to celebrate . . . Until he saw Salvatore screaming and hugging a bloody body to his chest. Roman knew in an instant that it was his baby brother. A brother he had already saved once before, and who was the one bright spot in the dark underbelly of his life. He hadn't been lying to the doctor; Luca was inno-cent and everything that was good in the world. And Roman would do anything—including kidnapping, using, and disposing of the female doctor—if it meant his brother would live.

"This is all my fault," Salvatore said for the hundredth time. His eyes were locked onto Luca's pale face, and he had a death grip on his hand.

Roman didn't blame Salvatore. He knew what it

was like to escape a past that was hellbent on keeping its claws dug in. Salvatore was a good man. He was one of Roman's best friends and loyal to a fault. It had taken some time to get used to the idea that his thirty-four-year-old best friend was sleeping with his twenty-two-year-old brother. But in the end, he couldn't ask for a better man to love Luca than Salvatore.

"This isn't on you," Roman told him sternly. "Place the blame where it belongs—on the man who pulled the trigger." *And on the doctor who fucked up,* he added silently. Too bad Raz couldn't be killed twice. But the doctor, on the other hand . . .

"He needs surgery," the female doctor abruptly announced. She placed the ultrasound probe onto the portable machine and pushed it away with her foot. "He's bleeding internally. And who knows what else."

Roman had spared no expense when he built the Omertà complex, the high-rise building they were currently in. It was all things to him and his crew—home, business, and leisure. Which meant it was important to have a top-of-the-line private medical facility. "Then do it," Roman said implacably, looking at the beautiful woman in front of him.

Trust Abel to abduct a gorgeous female doctor, Roman grumbled silently.

Her eyebrows rose, and she looked incredulous.

"You want me to perform surgery here? Impossible."

Roman gritted his teeth, striving for patience. He couldn't believe the balls on the woman. To not so much as flinch when he held a gun to her head? Grown men couldn't boast the same. "The adjoining room is set up as an OR. It is fully stocked. If there's something you need that isn't there, tell me. I'll see that you get it."

She looked through the window into the other room. "You have a fully equipped operating room here?"

Roman nodded once.

"Who the hell are you?" she asked.

He figured it was a rhetorical question, considering he had already told her his name. Still, he answered, reminding her, "Roman. Call me Roman. Who are you?"

"I won't be calling you anything. Thanks all the same," she responded primly. She hesitated for a moment before saying grudgingly, "I'm Dr. Angela Hawthorne." Then she ordered everyone to stay out of the operating theater in order to keep it as sterile as possible and wheeled Luca away on the bed.

"Doctor Hawthorne." Roman waited until she looked over her shoulder at him. "If my brother dies . . . so do you."

She didn't respond, simply turned and walked through the double doors. He really wished it was a threat that held weight with her, but he could tell it wasn't. She simply didn't give a fuck.

"Ballsy, huh?" Abel said, stepping up beside Roman and rubbing his throat.

"That's one word for her," Roman muttered, glaring at the closed doors. He nodded to some of his men, knowing they would watch the outsider like a hawk. They wouldn't hesitate to step in if she made one wrong move.

Roman ran his hands through his hair, grumbling when his gun got in the way. He tucked it into the back of his slacks, thinking about the doctor. She was absolutely stunning. But it wasn't the long, honey-blonde hair or the full lips—or the even fuller breasts—that claimed his attention. It was the shadows in her green eyes. Shadows he was well familiar with.

She didn't lie earlier. She would have let Luca die. The knowledge enraged him as much as it turned him on. He hadn't met a woman yet who could stand up to the likes of the heir of not one but two mafia families. He wanted her. Badly. He told his cock to stand down. There was no point lusting for a woman he could very well have to kill. Even *his* kinks had their limits.

He walked over to Salvatore, who had his head in his hands. "Luca's a tough little shit. He's going to be fine," he said.

"What if he isn't?" Salvatore whispered, looking up at Roman.

Roman squatted down, gripping his friend by the back of the neck. "Then we make the world burn."

"Yes," Salvatore rasped, his hands fisting on his thighs. "We burn it all to the ground."

"How many of those Razor fuckers are still alive?" Abel asked, patting Salvatore on the back.

"Enough to release some stress," Roman assured him. He stood and held out a hand to Salvatore. "Coming? Or do you want to stay close to Luca?"

Salvatore gripped Roman's hand, allowing his friend to pull him to his feet. "I'm not going anywhere." His bloodshot eyes met Roman's. "Save some for me?"

"You got it, brother," Roman promised. "Do you think you're up for some research while you wait? I want to know more about Dr. Angela Hawthorne."

Salvatore looked longingly at the closed doors where Luca was hopefully being saved. "I can try. But Luca is the computer genius. Not me."

Roman grunted at that. Luca was their resident computer whizz. At first, he had been dead set against

Luca having anything to do with the business. He wanted his little brother to live a normal life, free of violence and danger. But Luca was determined and damn hard to say no to. In the end, he had gotten his way and was now their official technology specialist.

"I'll do it."

Roman whipped his head to the doorway. His distant cousin—the only female in his inner circle—was standing there looking like the badass she was. With red hair and hazel eyes, she was a throwback to a time when the Sicilian side of his family had married into the Irish Mafia. Maria, or Morrigan as she preferred to be called these days, was dressed from head to toe in black and looked to be carrying enough weapons to take down the government.

"Morrigan," Roman greeted her. "How are our guests finding their new accommodations?"

Her lips twitched as she made her way closer. "There have been some complaints."

Roman clucked his tongue. "How rude."

"That's what I said. I also told them you have no patience for rudeness." She smirked. Morrigan wasn't a touchy-feely person, but she still gave Salvatore a brief hug, whispering in his ear.

"I don't know," Abel said with his trademark grin. It

was somewhat strained due to his worry for Luca, but it brightened his eyes momentarily. "I think Roman could be getting better at it. You should have heard the way the doctor spoke to him. Our boy here didn't so much as twitch."

"What did she say?" Morrigan demanded, looking murderous. "Do I need to teach her a lesson in manners?"

"Down, girl," Roman said, blocking his cousin's path to the operating room. "She's in there saving Luca's life."

"Is she? Or is she in there chopping him up?" Morrigan asked flippantly.

When Salvatore made a pained sound and darted to the door, Roman frowned at Morrigan. She simply shrugged, unconcerned with his ire. He could hear the doctor's voice talking to Salvatore before his friend promised to behave and not touch anything. Then Salvatore tossed them one last frantic look and entered the room.

"Real sensitive, Morrigan," Abel said dryly.

"Whatever." Morrigan flipped him off. "Tell me what she said."

Roman snorted softly. He allowed very few people to speak to him like that, but Morrigan was one of them. And she knew it. "She didn't like being kidnapped or having a gun held to her head," he offered.

"Can't blame her for that," Morrigan allowed, opening up a switchblade to play with.

"She throat-punched me and tried to bite my hand off," Abel said dramatically. "And that's *after* she head-butted me in the chest."

Morrigan's eyes lit up. "I gotta be honest, I'm trying very hard not to like her."

Roman rolled his eyes. Abel and Morrigan had a love-hate relationship. Abel loved her, and Morrigan hated *him*. To be fair, Roman believed Abel insisted on chasing Morrigan purely because she was the only woman ever to turn him down. Abel also teased her because she was so damn serious, and he was anything but. The two were like night and day. Roman allowed the persistent bantering and threats of bodily harm because he knew Morrigan needed some lightness in her life. Not to mention the fact that she could handle herself.

"Ouch. That hurts more than my throat," Abel told Morrigan, holding a hand to his heart.

"No fighting. We just came out of a war. I'm not looking for another one," Roman scolded the pair.

"Go," Morrigan bade him. "Beat some of that

tension away. I'll see what dirt I can find on your feisty doctor."

"She's not mine," he retorted quickly. *Too* quickly, if the startled looks of his two friends were anything to go by.

"Just a figure of speech," Morrigan assured him, appraising him with eyes that missed very little.

Roman kept his face carefully blank and forced himself not to shift. The last thing he needed was for his personal assassin to learn he had an inappropriate hard-on for their captive. "I want to be updated on Luca's status every ten minutes," he ordered. "And let me know what you find out about Dr. Hawthorne."

"You're expecting there to be something?" Morrigan asked curiously.

Roman nodded once. "I'm betting on it," he stated. Then he stalked from the room, heading to the elevator and leaving Abel to risk his life by asking Morrigan out for the millionth time.

Once he was in the privacy of the elevator, he allowed his head to drop down, his chin resting on his chest for a few moments. He prayed, briefly in Italian, to any deities still listening to his sorry ass. Luca had to be okay. Because if he died, Roman knew he would be losing his brother as well as his best friend. As little as last year, he would have scoffed at the notion of a love like theirs. Now? Roman envied it.

When the elevator doors opened with a soft whoosh, Roman shook off the sentimental thoughts. He stepped out and glanced at the floor-to-ceiling windows that afforded a truly stunning view of the city of Monash. Because the Omertà complex was the heart of his legal *and* illegal enterprises, a prison of sorts was needed. His father had been into the clichéd version of dank basement torture chambers. It suited Vincenzo Romano Senior perfectly. But Roman was not his father. He offered only the best for the people at his mercy. As such, the interrogation cells were on the top floor. All four penthouse apartments had been converted into a place that made grown men piss their pants and beg for mercy.

No, Roman thought, looking around the light-filled room. *No dark dungeons for me.*

He nodded wordlessly to the handful of men keeping watch over the prisoners before striding into the center of the large space. "My baby brother is fighting for his life," he stated, eyeballing the dozen men and women chained to the concrete walls. "Who wants to fight for theirs?" When no one answered, he *tsked* and shook his head. "When I ask a question, I expect an answer."

"What are you going to do to us?" a woman with oily black hair asked. She was very pale and looked terrified.

"I'm going to kill you, of course," Roman replied truthfully as he walked closer to her. He raised her chin with the tip of his finger, explaining, "And I'm going to do it slowly because I'm feeling tense and pissy. Your boss really fucked up." The woman whimpered, and Roman let her go for now. He knew she was one of Raz's sluts and privy to everything the sick man did. Roman had no sympathy for her.

"Please, let me go. I'll disappear. I won't give you no trouble," a man pleaded to Roman's right.

Roman stepped over to the man. "Oh, I know you won't give me any trouble. Because this"—he whipped out his gun, shooting the man in the knee—"is no trouble at all. In fact, it's a pleasure."

He reached down and grabbed the man's shattered knee with his left hand. He reveled in the screams as he pulled with all his might, flesh and bone fragments rending and tearing under his strength. He thought about his brother bleeding out on the street like a common gangbanger while he pulled the man apart piece by piece. A familiar bloodlust hit him, and he reveled in the sensation of the crimson liquid coating his hands as he made his way to the next man.

As he pounded the man's face into a pulp, he surprised himself by offering up another prayer—this time that he wouldn't be forced to do the same thing to the lovely, busty doctor with the spine of steel.

Because god knew he didn't need another innocent ghost haunting him.

CHAPTER THREE

It was twenty hours later when Angela finally felt comfortable enough to leave her patient. As she suspected, Luca had been bleeding internally thanks to a nasty laceration to his liver. There was some other soft tissue damage as well, but it was the lacerated liver causing him to be critical.

It was a common enough injury to sustain from a gunshot wound, and one she had dealt with many times as a trauma surgeon. Often, minor lacerations required no treatment other than close monitoring, but Luca's was large. The liver was highly vascular, and nearly all the blood in the body had to flow through the liver at some point after being pumped from the heart. A lot of Luca's blood vessels were pulverized from the trajectory of the bullet, and it took her six hours to be satisfied she had stopped the bleeding. Although the liver couldn't be sutured in the same way other organs and skin could be, it could be embolized. And that is exactly what she had done.

He was damn lucky she had access to a fully equipped OR, including ultrasound and x-ray machines, and typed blood for transfusions. She shook her head, gazing around the clinic in wonder. It was precisely the set-up she wanted to have at the shelter she volunteered at. Unfortunately, that would take millions. She shook the useless thoughts away, checking Luca's vitals one last time. Performing an impromptu surgery after being kidnapped had not been on her list of things to do after her twelve-hour shift. But she couldn't deny being pleased with the outcome. She was a doctor to her core, and Luca would make a full recovery.

"You did good work, Doc," Abel praised from beside her.

"Yeah, yeah," Angela muttered. She barely spared the man a glance. She was absolutely exhausted.

Sometime during the long night and day, her primary kidnapper had introduced himself as Abel. Despite not wanting anyone else in the room when she performed surgery, Abel and Salvatore both insisted. She acquiesced after watching them clean their hands and arms meticulously and don a fresh pair of scrubs each. She also took the time needed to sterilize her own hands before tossing on a gown and gloves and getting to work on Luca. It was tricky to monitor his vitals as well as perform the surgery, but she'd worked with far less in the past.

"He's really going to be okay?"

Angela looked up, finding Salvatore clutching Luca's hand, his bloodshot eyes on her. Now, this man, she gave her full attention to. Salvatore hadn't left his lover's side the whole time. He had murmured sweet words and made promises, never faltering. She could respect that kind of dedication. She could also see the love he had for the man lying as still as death between them. "He has a lot of healing to do. But I'm confident Luca is going to make a full recovery," she assured him.

Salvatore jerked to his feet and rushed around the bed. He all but threw himself into her arms, squeezing her tightly. Angela patted him on the back, not having energy for much else.

"Thank you. Thank you so much," he said gratefully.

When he pulled back, Angela noted the moisture in his eyes. She summoned a small smile for the man. "I'd like to say it was my pleasure, but . . ."

Salvatore barked out a laugh, scrubbing his face vigorously. "You're all right, you know that?"

"Thanks," she told him dryly. "Now, Luca needs to stay on IV fluids to ensure he doesn't get dehydrated and to increase his blood flow to his major organs. It needs to be switched out every four hours. He also has a catheter in so he can urinate freely without getting up. I want him in bed for forty-eight hours at least."

"I can handle all that," Salvatore stated.

Angela wasn't convinced. She looked worriedly at the man who had only regained consciousness very briefly just an hour ago. She wanted to stay and make sure his medical care was followed up adequately. But she also wanted to get the hell out of dodge.

Her doubt must have shown on her face because Salvatore chuckled, saying, "Seriously, Doc. I know I haven't been a shining example of competence, but that was because of my sheer terror over losing Luca. I'm a Vet—ten years Marine Corps. I wasn't a field medic, but I'm more medically qualified than a civilian. I have administered IVs in the field, as well as sutures. Now that I know I'm not going to lose him, I got him. I promise you."

The information surprised her, and she gave him a shrewd look. She had assumed she was dealing with a bunch of criminals. He definitely had a military bearing, she mused, noting the closely cropped hair and the straight back. Perhaps she would make it out of there alive, after all.

"Now, don't look at me like that, Doc," Salvatore said, catching her gaze. "I'm no saint. I wasn't before I joined the Marines nor during active duty. And I'm certainly not now. But you have nothing to fear from me. And never will." He held out his hand, and Angela took it, shaking it firmly. "If you ever need anything, come find me."

"How about letting me go right now?" she asked, after dropping his calloused hand. "Do that, and I'll call it even."

Salvatore smiled, but it didn't reach his eyes. "Not my call."

Angela grimaced. "Of course not."

"I may owe you, Doc. But I'm Roman's man," Salvatore said seriously.

Angela watched him brush the hair back from Luca's face, placing a gentle kiss on his forehead, and wondered how many lives those hands had taken. *No more than Vincenzo Romano,* she thought, turning away to wash her hands at the nearby sink.

Roman had been in and out over the last day, staying only long enough to ensure she wasn't killing his brother. But even when he wasn't around, she could feel his gaze on her. She couldn't explain it, but she knew he was watching her. Always. As the hairs stood up on the back of her arms, Angela looked up, noting the security camera in the corner of the room. The little red light was blinking. To her chagrin, her nipples pebbled, and she swore silently. *Oh, yeah. My body knows when he's watching, all right,* she thought. It pissed her off.

Her body, which responded to very few men even in the best of circumstances, had no business coming to life around a man like Roman. She wanted to flip him off but managed to restrain herself. Thoughts of him returning to check on Luca for the first time, covered in blood splatter and what she knew was arterial spray, was a good incentive to play nice.

With her hands clean and no other way to stall, she squared her shoulders and turned around. "Now what?" she asked.

Abel stood nearby with his arms crossed in front of his broad chest. "That depends on you," he said. "I'd really hate to kill you. You saved Luca. He's very important to all of us."

"I'd hate for you to kill me too. So, we're on the same page. Great. I'll just be on my way then," Angela informed him. She walked across the room, but her shakily confident exit was ruined when two men with guns stepped into her path, blocking the door. Swallowing, she turned and raised her eyebrows at Abel. "Want to tell your boys to move?"

Abel shook his head. "Not just yet. You need to answer a question first."

"What question?" she asked warily.

He walked to a nearby table. "Silver?" He held up a pile of cash in one hand. "Or lead?" He pulled his gun from his holster, pointing it at her chest. He went so far as to remove the safety.

Angela gave him a bland look. She was getting really sick of people pointing guns at her. She stepped forward, using a finger to push the muzzle of the pistol down. "Please. We've already covered this. Your lead doesn't scare me."

Abel grinned at her. He flicked the safety back on and re-holstered his weapon. "Silver it is." Then he tossed the thick stack of money at her.

Angela caught it and looked down, finding all hundred-dollar bills. A quick estimate had her guessing it was around ten thousand dollars. She simply raised her eyebrows at him, saying nothing. Abel looked to his right, lifting his chin in the direction of another man who opened a duffel bag. He pushed it over with his foot, sliding it across the floor. When it hit her foot,

Angela glanced inside at a pile of money divided into similar thick stacks.

They think they can buy me? she thought angrily. She took a deep breath to calm her rising ire. And not only that, but her nerves as well. For all her bravado, the stress and pressure of her ordeal were beginning to catch up with her. She was going to crash. She recognized the signs. And when she did, she wanted to be anywhere but where she was.

Taking one more deep breath, she pasted what she hoped was a pleasant smile on her face. "I don't want your silver either. Just to be clear, I wouldn't so much as wipe my ass with your money." She paused, warning herself not to say anything else. But her mouth opened. "Go fuck yourself."

Abel smirked. "I'd rather fuck *you*."

Angela glared at him. He was a gorgeous hunk of a man if you liked the rough sort—which she did. But she wasn't into killers, so she raked her scathing gaze from the top of his messy blond hair to his booted feet. Then she focused intently on his crotch until he started to squirm. If there was ever a time when she wished she had laser vision, it was then; she would have fried his testicles right off his body and danced around in the ashes. Something of her thoughts must have shown on her face because Abel gulped and covered his junk behind his hands.

Saying no more, she turned and stalked from the room. She had no idea where she was, let alone how to get out, but she walked swiftly down the long hallway. She felt numerous pairs of eyes on her from the surrounding rooms and cameras that were scattered strategically in the corners. She kept expecting to be stopped, especially by the boss-man himself. He had stayed close as she worked on his brother, but he had been in and out a lot, answering calls and fielding questions. She supposed that murdering a bunch of people in broad daylight the day before came with some rather time-consuming consequences. A hysterical bubble of laughter fought its way past her lips.

Oh yeah, she thought. *I'm about to lose it.*

When nobody stopped her, she kept walking, and finally made it to the elevator she had arrived in. Pressing the down button, she waited for it to light up to signal her freedom. But it didn't. Gritting her teeth, she all but punched the button. Nothing happened. She looked up, noting a security camera above the elevator doors. She barely suppressed a shiver. She knew he was watching her. Roman. Even through the lens of a camera, she could feel his gaze. She told herself it was fear, nothing more. But the hardening of her nipples made a liar out of her.

Cursing under her breath, she glared at the camera. "Open the doors."

The camera's red light continued to blink at her, the silence making her want to scream. When her hands started to shake, she fisted them quickly, praying her body held up just long enough for her to get the fuck out of there. Or long enough for Roman to march down the hallway and put a bullet in her head himself. There was a part of her that didn't much care either way, and she hated herself for it. So, she straightened her spine one last time and gave her next order with everything she had.

"Open the fucking doors, Roman! I'm done. Do you hear me? Do you understand what I'm saying? I'm fucking done." Her words wobbled along with her chin, and moisture flooded her eyes. She closed them, denying the helpless feeling—denying the world.

After what felt like hours, a small ding sounded, followed by a soft whoosh. Angela opened her eyes, walking quickly into the elevator. She saw the ground floor button was already illuminated and made no attempt to press anything else. She stared straight ahead, willing memories—both new and old—to stay beneath the surface.

Thankfully, the elevator finished its descent, and she walked briskly through the large, opulent foyer. She ignored the staff sitting behind a tall reception desk, especially the one man holding his earpiece and talking quietly. She made it to the double-glassed doors under her own steam and walked into the night.

It would be later, as she was standing in her shower under the too-hot spray, that she would fall to her knees and begin to cry—the adrenaline and endorphins finally leaving her body. Yes, she had been badass. She'd been a boss and owned the hell out of the situation. But it was only because her fight-or-flight response was for shit.

As she rocked back and forth, Angela put her hands over her ears to block out the triggered memories, telling herself she was okay over and over again . . . How long would it take her to believe it *this* time?

CHAPTER FOUR

Roman watched the scene between the doctor and his second-in-command from the security room. He had wanted to be there when she was given the ultimatum, but he didn't trust himself. Not to stop himself from killing her—which they probably should have done—but to stop himself from tying her to his bed.

He wanted the woman like he'd never wanted anything before. It was as if her mere presence had awakened a sleeping beast. He'd been witness to a lot of beasts in his lifetime, but the lust she sparked within him scared him more than any of those other monsters. So, once he believed his brother was going to be okay, he left the hard talk to Abel, fleeing to the relative safety of his security office.

Watching her now, as she stared down the barrel of a loaded gun for the second time, his cock hardened yet again. She was a thing of beauty, bold as brass and stronger than any person had a right to be. She looked tired, but her words were just as fierce as they had been the night before. He was surprised to realize he didn't want to fuck some submission into her. No, *he* wanted to submit instead.

He recalled her telling him that *she* was the one with all the power. "And I'll be fucked if she wasn't right," Roman muttered.

"Sir?" Alaric, his night security manager, queried.

Roman waved a dismissive hand. "Nothing."

"She's feisty," Alaric commented, watching the screen just as avidly as Roman was.

"That's one word for her," Roman allowed, glancing at his phone. It had been blowing up with messages and calls, including from the cops. Luckily, Roman had the best, most ruthless attorneys on his payroll, and they were fielding all the annoying questions. As well as keeping the police at bay. He knew he would need to put in an appearance with the cops sooner or later. But he was hoping to get some sleep first.

"I'd rather fuck you."

Roman's attention snapped to the camera feed. His

friend was getting his flirt on with the prisoner. "Oh, hell no!" He growled, fists clenching tight. He wanted to reach through the screen and throttle his oldest friend. But that wouldn't be anywhere near as satisfying as feeling real flesh give beneath his hands.

Turning sharply on his heels, he strode to the door, pausing with his hand on the knob when he heard nothing but silence. It was odd. From what he knew of Dr. Angela Hawthorne, she should have been ripping Abel to shreds with her razor-sharp tongue.

Did that mean she was considering it? he wondered, his anger rising to dangerous levels. He risked a glance back and his shoulders relaxed. He dropped his hand from the handle, feeling less murderous. The look on Angela's face was enough to flay the skin and muscle from Abel's bones. It was clear she wanted nothing to do with the man.

When Angela turned and walked confidently from the room, leaving behind a hundred thousand dollars in clean money, he tracked her movements from screen to screen. His eyes narrowed, seeing the proud tilt to her head and the straight back. But there was something else. Something not quite right. His instincts were never wrong, and they were suddenly screaming at him that she wasn't as put together as she appeared.

"Boss? You want the boys to stop her?" Alaric asked, glancing up.

Roman didn't respond for a moment, weighing his options. He couldn't afford to trust that she wouldn't walk out of there and straight to the nearest police station. For one, she clearly hated his guts. But he had more important things at stake than mere business dealings or the chance of going to prison. He had many people that relied on him for their wages, their work, and their families. Plus, his baby brother was vulnerable right now and would continue to be for weeks. He really couldn't risk all of that. But . . . he had a feeling he wouldn't allow anyone to touch a single hair on her head. So, after some inventive swearing in Italian, he did the only thing he could.

"No. Tell the boys to stand down. Nobody is to touch her," he ordered.

Roman smiled when she punched the button, glaring daggers at the camera. But his humor died quickly when he noted the fine shaking in her limbs and the tiny hitch in her breath. Her eyes changed for a moment, losing their hard-ass stare, and he got a glimpse of raw fear, anger, betrayal, and a pain so deep his own breath stalled. She was more than just the top-rated surgeon, born on the rich side of town, that Morrigan had discovered from her preliminary search.

There was a world of hurt in her stunning green eyes. There was trauma. And damned if he didn't want to find out why, so he could hunt down every mother-fucker who had ever hurt her.

It was crazy. He was an Italian-Sicilian crime boss, so he was known for being emotionally charged. But the level of emotions the doctor stirred in him was just ridiculous. He had only briefly met her. And under truly shitty circumstances, at that. But it was the truth. When she told him she was done, just fucking done with everything, Roman felt the words reach down to his heart—down to his fucking soul—and rip him the fuck open. It sounded dramatic, but he didn't know how else to describe it.

He went over to the control panel to activate the elevator himself, then watched unblinkingly as it carried her down all fifty floors. Only when she was out of his building did he leave the security room. He nodded his head to the two guards stationed outside the door. The room was manned by three of his people at all times. He had ordered the pair out earlier because four people in the enclosed space was pushing it. But he was satisfied to see them slip quickly back inside as he made his way to the stairs.

He swiftly walked down the one floor to the medical suite. He ignored Abel for a moment, instead heading directly over to where Luca was sleeping. The machines and tubes attached to his brother were hard to stomach, but Roman knew they were keeping him safe and comfortable. So, he did his best to ignore them as he placed his hand over Luca's forehead. He felt warm but not feverish, and the beeping from the equipment was steady. Roman sighed, suddenly exhausted.

"He's resting comfortably," Salvatore said from Luca's other side.

Roman nodded, his tongue stuck, no words forming. This was his baby brother. Luca and dozens of other people were Roman's responsibility. They were his to protect, and he had failed.

"You didn't fail anyone," Salvatore said, crossing his arms over his chest and leaning back in his chair.

Roman narrowed his eyes at his soon-to-be brother-in-law, his hand staying on Luca's shoulder. "I didn't say I did," he answered gruffly.

Salvatore snorted, humor dancing in his eyes for the first time in days. "You didn't have to. I can read you. This wasn't your fault any more than it was mine. And you told me this wasn't on me . . . remember?"

Roman said nothing. He had failed his brother once before. Failed in his promise to his mother on her deathbed. It burned his ass that he had allowed it to happen again.

Knowing Roman well, Salvatore simply shook his head and went back to stroking Luca's arm gently. "What are you going to do about the doctor?" Sal asked. "She didn't take the money. And Abel didn't shoot her."

———

"I couldn't bring myself to do it," Abel piped up from behind Roman. "I mean, waste that sexy body of hers? Not a chance."

Roman spun around and pinned him with a cold look. "Don't talk about her like that. And if I hear the word *fuck* and her name in the same sentence again from you, you'll be shitting in a bag for the rest of your life."

Abel looked taken aback for a moment, his eyebrows raising nearly all the way to his hairline before he smirked. "Are you staking a claim?"

"I'm not staking anything," Roman refuted. "Unless it's a real stake, and it's through your annoying face."

Abel snorted, sharing a knowing look with Salvatore. "You're awfully defensive there, Roman. Did the good doctor get to you?"

Roman remained silent, running his tongue over his top teeth. He was gratified when Abel dropped his playfulness, recognizing the action for what it was—impending violence.

"What's the plan, boss?" Abel asked somberly.

"Boss?" Roman rolled his eyes. Abel was included in a handful of people who had never called him *boss*. He must have looked really pissed off. "Nobody likes an ass-kisser, Abel."

Abel shook his head, adopting the look of a kicked puppy. "Sheesh. A guy can't win around here."

Roman finally smiled. Abel was annoying as hell, but the lightness he brought to Roman's world was very much needed. "Put some men on her," he said. "Men you trust implicitly. I want her followed day and night until further notice. Make sure she doesn't do anything stupid."

"She won't," Salvatore said confidently. "I'm pretty sure that woman doesn't have a stupid bone in her body."

Roman agreed. Still, he had to be cautious. He had just allowed someone to walk out his front door who knew critical things about their lives and operation. Someone who hated them. He groaned. "I'm a fucking moron, aren't I? She's probably already at the cop shop spilling her guts."

"I agree with Sal," Abel said. "She won't talk. She worked too hard to save Luca. She gives a shit about her patients. I can tell. She won't do anything to jeopardize him."

"Of course, she won't," Roman agreed quickly. "Everyone loves Luca. But I'm positive her good work ethic doesn't extend to me. Or you."

"Me?" Abel gasped, pointing a finger at himself. "What did I do?"

"You kidnapped her. Then threatened to kill her. Then tried to buy her off," Salvatore reminded Abel cheerfully.

"Oh, well, when you put it like that . . ." Abel pouted a little.

Morrigan chose that moment to enter the room, joining the discussion. "I don't care if she's Mother Teresa incarnate. She still needs to be watched. Another chat at the end of something pointy wouldn't go astray either," she added.

"Morrigan . . ." Roman warned.

Morrigan simply shrugged. "I didn't say I was going to *use* the pointy thing. Just that it couldn't hurt."

"I'll talk to her," Roman declared. He didn't want his vicious cousin anywhere near Angela without a chaperone.

"*Talk.*" Morrigan snorted as she made her way over to Luca, sitting down beside his feet on the end of the bed. "Is that what they're calling it these days?"

Before Roman could give her a verbal spanking, she turned to Salvatore, telling him to take a shower and promising to take care of Luca in his absence. It made it hard for Roman to chew her out when she was being so damn nice. "Just . . . stay away from the lady doctor, Morrigan."

"I was going to offer to follow her for you, but I've changed my mind," Morrigan said with a sniff.

That gave Roman pause. For all her bloodthirsty ways, Morrigan was loyal and trustworthy. She was exactly who he could trust Angela's safety with.

"I'll do it, too," Abel volunteered.

Morrigan sneered at him. "What do you mean, *too?* I just said I changed my mind."

"Please. We all know you're going to do it," Abel responded, calling her bluff. "You want the night shift? Or the day shift?"

Morrigan glared at Abel for a moment before saying, "Night."

"And I'll do day." Abel turned to Roman, giving him a double thumbs-up. "All systems go."

"Fine," Roman agreed. "Thank you." He knew the pair would not only watch Angela and ensure she didn't get herself killed with her choices, but they would also protect her with their lives if it came to that.

"And you'll have that extra chat with her," Salvatore said, standing up. "For clarity's sake."

"Right. For clarity's sake," Roman agreed. He would get some downtime first, though. Because as tired as he was, he wasn't confident in his ability to not go with his first plan of tying her to his bed.

CHAPTER FIVE

ngela slept for fourteen hours straight. It hadn't been an easy sleep. Nightmares followed her, her demons snapping at her heels even as her body had shut down.

Still feeling like warmed-up pig shit, she tightened her ivory satin robe as she walked into her kitchen, where the smell of coffee already brewing finally penetrated her senses. She quickly grabbed a knife from the butcher block, spun around, and found Roman looking beautiful and deadly at her dining room table. He was holding a cup of coffee—in her favorite mug, no less.

Her heart was going a million miles per hour, and she told herself it was the fear of having someone break into her home and not the fact that the mobster looked damn fine in his black suit. "How dare you," she hissed at him, pointing the knife in his direction.

"How dare I what?" Roman raised an eyebrow, taking a sip of her coveted special-order coffee.

He looked confident and sexy. *No, not sexy,* she told herself. *He held a gun to your head two days ago, and now he's broken into your home. He's a criminal.* "Get the fuck out of here before I stab you through your cold, black heart."

Roman's brown eyes widened. "Wow. And I thought *I* wasn't a morning person." He held up her mug. "Coffee?"

"Roman . . ." she said through clenched teeth.

A groan rumbled through his chest. "Mmmm, I love the way you say my name."

Angela gritted her teeth and shook her head. "This isn't a joke, Roman. My life isn't a joke. Stay away from me."

He took one sip from the mug before setting it down. He leaned forward, resting his forearms on his knees. "I agree with you. It's the reason I'm here. To make sure you don't do anything stupid."

"I rarely do," she snapped.

"Good to know. But to ensure that . . ." He tipped his head to the duffel bag at his feet. "Take the money."

"I don't want your money. I already told your goon

that," Angela reminded him. She lowered the knife but didn't put it down, edging slowly to the counter behind her. She had a gun in the top drawer there. If she could keep him talking long enough, maybe she would have a chance to get it. "How is Luca?"

Roman's whole face softened, and he smiled. "He's doing okay. He woke up for real about eight hours ago. He won't be dancing any time soon, but he's back to his typical perky self."

Angela was genuinely glad to hear it. "That's good. I'm glad. Is Salvatore managing Luca's medical needs okay?" Her hand touched the drawer, and she told herself to keep her nerve. Roman's eyes were focused unerringly on her, like a predator. It made her tingle, but not only in fear.

"So far," Roman answered. "He's been changing out Luca's fluids and giving him pain meds and antibiotics to the minute as per your schedule." He nodded his head at her. "Thank you for taking the time to do that. It's a very thorough list."

She slowly opened the drawer behind her, slipping her hand inside. The feel of the cold metal made her heart pound. But this time, in relief. Her other arm stayed lax at her side, gripping the knife. "I'd hate to see my hard work go down the drain because you don't know how to give antibiotics."

"Luca is being treated like the treasure he is, I assure you," Roman said. He pushed himself up, looking her over from head to toe. "What are you wearing underneath that robe?"

Angela glanced down, seeing the way the satin material clung to her curves. And curves she indeed had. She was on the taller side for a woman at five foot ten, but she wasn't a stick. Her breasts were more than a handful, her waist was flared, and her thighs were toned but full. The robe was short, ending mid-thigh, and was open enough to show her cleavage.

It had been a spontaneous purchase years ago. One to make her feel sexy and powerful, and feminine. She had since purchased many more in various shades and styles because it had done the trick. But it was for her only. Not for the few men she brought home every so often. And certainly not for the man in front of her.

Looking up, she caught Roman biting his bottom lip, and she commanded herself to keep her shit together against the wiles of the dangerous man in front of her. "Armor plating," she finally replied. "I'm wearing armor beneath this."

Roman chuckled. "You're quick."

"And you're not listening to me. Get out of my home, Roman. You're not welcome. I won't say anything to anyone. You have my word. It can't be bought, so you'll just have to trust me. If you can't do that . . ." Angela shrugged. "I honestly don't give a fuck."

Roman took a step closer. "Listen here, princess—"

"Don't call me that!" she snapped. "Never call me that!"

He eyed her for a moment, his face impassive. She held his stare, forcing herself not to shake. That particular pet name brought a slew of trauma along for the ride. As a matter of fact, her stomach swirled sickeningly just hearing it from his mouth.

Finally, Roman dipped his head. "All right. How about if I call you Angel instead?"

"How about you don't talk to me at all," Angela fired back. "How about that?"

He chuckled, rocking back on his heels, his hands now in his pants pockets. "You're like a little kitten. Hissing and spitting."

She stiffened, her mouth opening in a silent snarl. "A kitten? More like a tiger." She gripped the butt of her gun and whipped it out. She leveled it at his heart without hesitation.

"Well, well, well," Roman drawled. "It seems the kitten has claws."

She tossed her knife onto the counter, gripping the

Smith and Wesson revolver with both hands. She cocked the hammer. "You think I won't?"

"Actually, I believe you will," he commented. "I recognize that look in your eyes. I see it every day in the mirror."

Roman moved closer; each step carried a lazy confidence, as if he was used to being on the wrong side of a gun and was bulletproof. He stopped when he was directly in front of her, staring at her with those caramel eyes of his. To her shock, her pussy clenched. She wanted him *bad*. It pissed her off as much as it excited her. She pressed the muzzle against his chest in warning.

"Go ahead," Roman urged her. "Pull the trigger. Do what an entire mafia empire hasn't been able to do. Kill me."

She didn't kill him.

She kissed him instead.

———

Shock held Roman immobile for a second before he groaned and gripped the back of Angela's head, tilting it to his satisfaction so he could assault her mouth. She tasted just how he knew she would—like pure sin.

Her tongue dueled with his, fighting for dominance. And their teeth clacked together as their heads moved. It wasn't the most graceful first kiss he'd ever had. But it was by far the hottest. He tightened his grip, keeping her head still so he could pull back a little. He traced her bottom lip with his tongue, groaning from the breathless, needy sound she made. The gun was still between them, and it would take nothing more than a twitch of her finger to go off. Abel, Salvatore, and Morrigan would have lost their shit at him. But his lust was overriding his common sense, and he delved back in for another kiss rather than disarming her.

Eventually, she wrenched her head back, her chest rising and falling with her rapid breaths. Her pupils were blown, and her cheeks were flushed. Her lips were swollen and wet. And her hair was a mess from his hands. He wanted to fuck her. Here. Now. But there was that look again, that vulnerable, pain-filled look that had him cursing and telling his cock to stand down. She was dangerous. In more ways than one.

"You know, I want to kill you as much as I want to save you," he confessed. "I can't have someone with your power walking around." He wasn't just referring to the knowledge she had about them, but he didn't elaborate.

She raised her chin, looking every inch a queen. "I don't need saving."

"Oh, Angel . . ." He dipped his head, running his nose along her cheek and under her jaw, placing a gentle kiss on the fluttering pulse in her neck. "You need saving more than anyone else I've ever met." He knew it was the truth.

"You're wrong," Angela refuted. "And I told you not to call me Angel."

"But it suits you," Roman told her, his gaze dipping to her ample cleavage. He swore when the ivory satin fell off her shoulder, revealing a dusky, pebbled nipple. "You're fucking naked."

Angela looked down, noting the way the robe had parted, but made no move to correct it. "And?"

He swore again, more viciously this time because her lack of action was a crystal-clear invitation. "You have no sense of self-preservation at all, do you?" he asked.

"I'm the one with the gun," she reminded him. "I'd say I'm doing okay."

"Ah, but you're not going to use it. Are you?" Roman pressed. He reached out, running the back of his hand down the slope of her breast, and stopped right above her nipple. "You're a glutton for punishment. Just like me."

"I have no idea what you're talking about," she replied. But she finally brought one shaking hand up and pulled her robe back into place.

"You do," he retorted. "I used to have the same danger-seeking habits. It never ended well," he warned. Her eyes raked over him like a physical caress, and his cock jerked hard in his slacks, precum already leaking from the tip. "Angel . . ."

She shrugged, admitting it as if it was no big deal. "It's a coping mechanism."

"The danger-seeking? I'm well aware," he promised. "Been there. Done that. I was a pain whore once, too. It helped—for a time."

Her eyes shot to his, her tongue darting out to moisten her lips. "What did you do?"

He thought about not answering, already knowing he was on shaky ground. Admitting such intimate things to a virtual stranger—one who was holding a gun, no less—was idiotic at best and deadly at worst. But he decided to push *both* their limits by reaching slowly for the button on his slacks.

He flicked it open, watching her hand remain steady even as her eyes followed his movements. He lowered the zipper, freeing his hard dick. It wasn't every day he went commando, but he was glad he had chosen to do so that morning. "Exhibit A," he said roughly.

Angela's eyes widened, and her mouth dropped open. "What is that?"

He knew exactly what she was referring to—the jewelry impaling his cockhead. "It's called a magic cross."

"Magic . . . cross?" she repeated slowly.

Roman loved the way her voice deepened. He hefted his erection, fingering the two curved bars at the end. One went down vertically through his glans, and the other was horizontal, giving it an appearance of a cross. It had been a spontaneous, youthful act back when he craved pain in all its forms. He'd received it with the piercing, that was for sure. It had been extremely unpleasant, and the healing time was a real bitch. However, he was more than happy with the end result. It felt damn good—and not just to him. His lovers always seemed more than satisfied with the added stimulation.

"Two piercings, four holes in total," he elaborated. "The shape of it is why it's called a magic cross. And no doubt because of all the *magic* it makes happen."

Angela tore her gaze away for a moment, meeting his eyes. "Really?" she asked drolly.

Roman grinned. "*Mi scusi.* I do love a good pun."

"Uh-huh," she said with a small shake of her head. "Put it away now."

"Are you sure that's what you want?" he murmured, stroking himself from root to tip. Her eyes locked onto his hand as if pulled by a magnet. "I could put it in you instead. I'll even let you keep your gun."

"And then what?" Angela wanted to know.

He shrugged, playing with the metal bars, hissing from the pleasure it wrought. "Then I leave, and you can pretend it never happened," he said, though it annoyed him a little. "Come on, Angel. Take out some of that anger and aggression you have swirling around inside of you on me. *Use* me."

"And what will *you* be doing?" she asked.

"Using *you* as well, of course," Roman promptly replied. It tasted like a lie, and he wondered why. He couldn't recall even half the women he had used and tossed aside in the past. Yet, the thought of doing the same to the doctor felt like a betrayal.

He held his breath when she reached out with her free hand, her pointer finger tracing over the ball at the end of the bar beneath his crown. She moved onto the top bar before slicking her finger with his precum. She met his eyes as she licked it off her finger, and Roman lost his grip on his control. He pulled her against him, his erection splitting her robe and rubbing over the skin of her stomach. It felt fucking amazing. And if her loud moan was anything to go by, Angel felt the same way.

He made short work of her belt, untying it and pushing the satin off her shoulders. She let the robe fall to the floor but didn't put her gun away.

Roman stepped back, looking at the erotic picture she made. All that soft, creamy skin was rounded in all the right places. Her breasts hung low due to their weight and had large dark areolas with hard tips he wanted in his mouth *yesterday*. The dark steel resting against her dimpled thigh was just inches away from the neatly trimmed thatch of dark hair between her legs. She was magnificent.

"Well? Are you just going to stand there?" she taunted when he didn't move.

Muttering in Italian, he picked her up and moved her to the closest flat surface. It wasn't a horizontal surface, but the wall next to the refrigerator would work just as well. He shrugged out of his suit jacket and unbuttoned his shirt, taking some care to place them on the kitchen countertop; he had a meeting in an hour and didn't want to have to change beforehand. Then he let his pants drop to his ankles. He jacked his cock a few more times before stepping in close. The feel of her skin against his own had him groaning, and he took her mouth in a savage kiss.

Angela tightened her hands on his shoulders as much as the revolver would allow, giving as good as she got. She rubbed against him shamelessly, and Roman wondered if he would embarrass himself before he even got inside of her. He cupped her breasts, squeezing the heavy flesh before leaning down and taking a hard tip into his mouth. He sucked hard, hollowing his cheeks, gratified when Angela moaned and raised one of her legs to wrap around his hips. The action caused his dick to rub along her clit, and he felt wetness there already.

Straightening up, he gripped her thigh tightly with one hand, using his other to delve into the depths of her pussy. "Fuck!" he snarled. She was hot, tight, and wet.

"Ugh!" Angela shouted out, grinding down onto the two fingers he'd speared her with.

He had to be inside her. *Now.* "Are you on birth control?" Roman asked gruffly.

Angela looked at him as if she didn't understand what he was saying. "What?"

"Birth control," he repeated. "Are you on it? Because I want to feel this tight cunt gripping my cock bare. I'm not interested in anything between us. I'm clean. Are you? Don't lie to me about this, Angel," Roman warned.

She shook her head. "I would never. I'm on the pill. Have been for years. And I get tested every six months at work. I don't have anything."

"I don't either," Roman promised. "Do you believe

me? Answer me, Angel," he demanded, tilting her chin up when she remained silent. "Do you believe me?"

"Yes," she gasped, riding his hand.

"Good," he stated. He removed his fingers, wiping them on his dick to add some slickness, then he tilted her hips to his satisfaction and pushed into her in one smooth stroke.

The feel of her body opening to his—*accepting* his—made his eyes cross. There was some resistance—she was tight as hell—but the glide was smooth, thanks to her wetness. Running his hands over the back of her thighs, he fingered the crease where her ass met her legs before squeezing her sweet cheeks. He hiked her up, urging her to wrap her legs around his waist. He did his best to ignore her wiggling hips and gasping moans until she obeyed him.

When she was wrapped around him and pressed completely against the wall, he gripped her hips and pulled back until just the flared head of his cock remained in the inferno of her pussy. He locked eyes with her. "Look at me. Keep your eyes open," he demanded. "I want you to see who's fucking you. I want you to know it's *me* giving you the best fucking of your life."

It took a few seconds and two deep breaths before

Angela obeyed. When she did, she smirked at him. "Promises, promises."

Roman grunted, leaning forward to nip at her lips. "You just have to push, don't you?"

"I can't seem to help it," she admitted. "You bring out the worst in me."

"The worst?" he questioned, driving back into her and forcing her body against the wall with a slap. Her scream was music to his ears. "Or the best?"

Angela didn't answer him, but he didn't hold it against her. As he continued to pound into her, he found himself incapable of speech as well. Her body gripped his to perfection, and he made sure to tilt his hips just right so his magic cross hit her sweet spot with every hard thrust. He loved that she didn't hold back, squeezing him with her thighs and scratching at him with her hands. She used her weight to shove herself down as much as his restraining hands would allow, clearly chasing her own pleasure. She was doing just as he had suggested and using him. But she did obey him, keeping her eyes on him the entire time.

He increased his tempo, slamming into her over and over again. Sweat dripped from his forehead onto her tits and he leaned down to lick it off. "Fuck!" he swore when Angela pulled roughly on the hair at his nape. He ground his hips against hers and dug his fingers into her ass, never breaking his rhythm.

The moment her release hit, her internal muscles clamped down so viciously on his cock that she damn near forced him out. He grunted, not having that at all, and pushed back in roughly as far as he could go. The tight fit had his eyes nearly rolling into the back of his head, and his own release charged up his shaft. He came with a roar, his dick spurting inside of her. His tempo was completely ruined by the sheer pleasure pulsing through his system, as well as the grip her body had on his. So he ground his pelvis against hers instead, adding pressure and friction to her clit.

"Ugh! Oh my god!" Angela yelled, tossing her head back and squeezing her eyes closed. She panted and moaned and swore and screamed her way through her own orgasm.

Her beautiful face was a sublime mix of pleasure and pain and held so much shock that Roman wondered if she'd ever experienced such a release before. Or perhaps she didn't *want* to, he thought, his heart beating a mile a minute even as his dick gave one last kick of cum. The way her jaw was clenched, and the solo tear that escaped her closed lashes had him thinking it was the latter.

Because that tear made him want to pull her close,

instead of setting her aside, he lowered her legs from his hips and pulled out the moment he could. He steadied her with a hand to her elbow when she wobbled a little, receiving a glare for his efforts. Still, he didn't let her go until he was positive she could stand on her own two feet.

She made no effort to cover herself, and she was still holding that damn Smith and Wesson revolver in her right hand. He could feel wetness high on his shoulder blade and realized the metal had dug into his skin hard enough to cut him. Some part of him wished it would scar. Which was madness. *But it is what it is,* he admitted. He had long ago stopped lying to himself. Living in denial had caused him and his family too much pain.

Bending over, he picked up Angela's robe and held it out to her. She looked at it for a moment before taking it from him silently. She shrugged into it, pulling it closed and hiding her luscious body. But not before he saw some of his cum dripping out of her sweet hole and adding to the slickness on her inner thighs. A growl rumbled in his chest. He wanted to clean her up with his tongue. But that would be far too risky. He already felt a possessiveness over her he had no right feeling. Discovering what they tasted like together would be too much.

He finally noticed that she had yet to say anything, and he frowned, looking down at her. Her face was hidden from him by that wild hair of hers. He raised his hand to tuck it behind her ear, hesitating when she flinched. His frown deepened. He didn't like that reaction at all. In fact, it made him want to kill. "Are you okay?" he asked, stepping back and giving her some space. "Did I hurt you? Was I too rough?"

"I'm fine," she replied quickly. She raised her head and rolled her eyes. "You didn't hurt me, Roman. I can handle a good fucking. I certainly have before."

His teeth slammed together, and his eye twitched. The thought of her with another man was infuriating. Instead of dragging her back to his cave, he strove for politeness. "I was just checking."

"No need." Her voice was clipped. "I think it's time for you to leave."

His immediate reaction was *hell, no.* But that just wouldn't do. He had that meeting to attend, after all. He pulled his black slacks up, tucking his semi-hard dick in as he carefully zipped. It was uncomfortable with his cock still wet. He buttoned his white dress shirt from the bottom to the top, covering the large tattoo he had on his chest. She had made no mention of the skull nor the colorful flowers, but she stared at it now. When she didn't ask about it, he knew he had stalled long enough. Finally, he picked up his jacket and folded it over his forearm. Then he stared at her.

Angela gestured to the front door of her one-bedroom loft apartment. "If I find you in my home again without an invitation, I'll use this." She waved the gun at him. She met his eyes boldly, all hint of tears vanished. "Consider yourself used, Roman. I never want to see you again."

It was too bad for her he liked the sound of his name on her pretty lips too much to ever let that happen. He didn't care about the crap he'd said about using one another.

Striding to the door, he paused before leaving. Though he believed she wouldn't go to the police, another reminder wouldn't go astray. "Keep your mouth shut about Luca. I'm warning you. Don't betray me, Angel. I've built my empire on the bodies of traitors. I'd hate to add yours to the pile."

CHAPTER SIX

"I can't thank you enough, Dr. Hawthorne."

Angela turned to the older woman, looking down to accommodate her much shorter stature. "How many times have I told you to call me Angela? And you are very welcome. I only wish I could do more. But with my hours at the hospital . . ."

Sister Philomena smiled. "Angela. You do more than enough. I wouldn't be able to keep this place open if it weren't for you."

Angela returned the smile, albeit with a hint of sadness because she knew it was true. Lighthouse Resource Center was a not-for-profit charity offering resources to all those in need in the community. It was run by the wonderful nun in front of her with the help of a few of her Sisters, and some volunteers like Angela.

The center offered help to the homeless, those running from abusive situations, LGBQT+, employment assistance, and much more. It was more than just a shelter. It was a true beacon of hope for those in need—no matter their age, race, or creed. It was a wonderful establishment and sorely needed in such a large city. In fact, Monash needed at least a dozen more. Unfortunately, the Lighthouse struggled enough to stay afloat as it was. Wishing for more centers was a fruitless dream.

Angela donated her time a few days a week. She saw men and women, teenagers and children, who couldn't afford formal medical assistance. No matter the time of day or night when she arrived, she always had a line waiting for her. It broke her heart. As far as she was concerned, access to healthcare was a right, not a privilege. But you wouldn't know it based on the number of people she saw every week. She had just spent one hour giving a sex education talk to some local teenagers, followed by another hour helping Sister Philomena install a new basketball hoop in the recreation hall. Now, she and the nun were standing in the office looking down at the heavy duffle bag filled with money.

Angela cringed a little as she zipped the bag back up. She did her best not to feel like a hypocrite for teaching sex-ed when she herself had unprotected sex with a stranger just a month before. What's more, she was using the money Roman left on the floor of her apartment—something she had sworn not to do. But over the last month, she decided to use the money for something worthwhile. Just because she wouldn't so much as burn it if she was freezing to death didn't mean it couldn't help others. So, here she was, handing over a hundred thousand dollars to a nun. She trusted the Sister implicitly and knew the funds would be used for the greatest good. But still, she found the act a little cringey.

"Who did you say this was from again?" Sister Philomena asked.

Angela cleared her throat, looking over the woman's head. "A silent donor."

"Ah," Sister Pip nodded, her eyes twinkling. "Well, be sure to thank him or her on behalf of Lighthouse."

Angela smiled, not telling the older woman that she had no plans to ever see Vincenzo Romano again. She *had* seen him a handful of times over the past month. It was impossible not to when she had spent so much time at his obnoxious skyscraper in the middle of the city. But she rarely spoke to him. She was civil—as civil as possible given the circumstances of him threatening her life and then screwing her against her kitchen wall. But that was it.

The day after making the biggest mistake of her life with Roman, she put on her big girl panties and marched herself into the foyer of the Omertà complex. There, she demanded to see Luca. Abel was the one to come down, grinning like an idiot and welcoming her as if they were long-lost friends. Then he escorted her up to the medical suite, where she did what she considered was her duty and followed up with Luca's medical care until she was satisfied he was on the mend. That involved returning to remove the catheter and then the stitches, and of course, making sure he had enough antibiotics and pain medication. And then there was the physical therapy and rehabilitation advice.

All in all, it had taken the better part of the last month. But with Luca up and about, practically back to his old self, she no longer felt obligated to attend to him. However, she *did* find herself in an unexpected predicament. She liked Luca. Somehow, the young man had wiggled his way into her heart. Roman's younger brother was a fun, vibrant guy with a quick wit and a playful side that she had discovered she desperately needed in her life.

She didn't know when it had happened, but she had no friends. None at all. Sure, she had colleagues that she occasionally joined for drinks and with whom she could share how her day went. But a friend she could call in the middle of the night when she was feeling low, or someone to talk to about the latest episode of *The Bachelor*? She didn't have that. And the saddest part was, she couldn't remember the last time she did.

Her past had a lot to answer for. She knew that. It made her reserved and unwilling to trust. It made her want to stay in and live alone—and only venture out for work. And she had been totally fine with that until Roman and his merry band of criminals had kidnapped her. Now, Luca and his partner, Salvatore, were putting her isolated life into stark contrast. And she realized she wanted what they had. Not the illegal stuff, but the family.

The family that had your back, no matter what. And if she was being honest, knowing there was someone who would literally kill for you held a certain appeal. She had been let down—*destroyed*—by the people who should have cared for her the most. And yet, here was Roman and his organized crime syndicate, showing her what *real* family was. It was wild. And something she wasn't ready to admit to anyone, least of all the man himself.

The sex with Roman had been the best and worst of her life. Sure, it was the greatest male-induced orgasm she'd ever had, but it also caused a ton of guilt and shame. What had she been thinking? She hated the man. He and his goons had taken her from safety and flung her into their violent world. After the shit-storm of her younger years, she felt safe and insulated —if a little lonely—in her life. And then Roman had to come along, urging her to use him and his magnificent dick. A dick that had the most erotic piercing she'd ever seen—let alone *felt*. The whole thing was extremely unfair.

"I'll see to it that the money is deposited into the Lighthouse's accounts appropriately," Sister Philomena said.

"Of that, I have no doubt," Angela assured her. She helped her pack the money into the safe before walking outside with her. "What do you think you'll use it on first?"

"Oh, I have no idea," Sister Pip said, hands going to her cheeks. "There's the roof that needs repairing in the men's sleeping quarters, a new stove needed in the kitchen, not to mention the walls that need to be replaced because of rot. And food is always needed."

"Sounds like you have *plenty* of ideas," Angela said, placing a hand on her arm. "In fact, it doesn't sound like it will do everything you need."

"It's incredible!" the nun enthused. "Truly, Angela,

such a large sum of money is a miracle. It will help so many."

Angela smiled, so happy to see Sister Pip excited. She worked tirelessly for others, even though she was well into her eighties. She was compassionate, patient, and the least judgmental person Angela had ever met. She embraced everybody with open arms. She was also very candid and rather feisty for a nun, with a humorous side and a heart of gold. As far as Angela was concerned, the nun needed to be protected at all costs. "I'm so glad," Angela finally replied.

Sister Pip reached up, patting her on the cheek in a maternal way that had Angela blinking back tears. "You're a good girl."

She wondered if the nun would still say that if she knew Angela had allowed a criminal to bang her against the wall with his metal-tipped dick? Her cheeks heated. And, to her mortification, so did her core. One would think someone with her history would have a hard time with sex of any kind—let alone the kind that left bruises on hips. And there was a time when that had been the case.

It had taken a lot of therapy and a lot of hard work to gain her power back. And to achieve the healthy relationship she now had with her sex life. That's not to say that she slept with every hot mafia boss she found—

she didn't. But she also no longer denied herself the pleasure nor the release that could be found in sex that was her choice.

"Whatever are you thinking about?" Sister Pip asked. "You're looking very flushed."

"Nothing," Angela replied quickly. "Just thinking about the rest of my day. Busy schedule."

"You work too hard," Sister Pip chided.

"It feels that way sometimes," Angela admitted. She looked around the dilapidated ex-orphanage, seeing all the things that needed to be done. "But it also never feels like enough."

"I understand. You're a giver, Angela. It's a blessing to the world, but oftentimes not so much of a blessing to you. Why don't you let your friend do something special for you, hmm?" the nun suggested.

Angela frowned in confusion. "My friend? Who do you mean?"

"Why, that handsome man leaning against that truly lovely machine over there." Sister Philomena pointed to the man and the flashy car Angela hadn't yet noticed. "I've seen him a few times recently. I'm happy for you."

Angela's frown turned to a scowl when she took in the tall, muscled blond man. "It's not like that," she said quickly, dispelling any misconceptions the nun might have about Abel and her.

Sister Pip chuckled a little. "It never is, dear. Thank you again. I'll see you on Friday."

Before Angela could correct her again, the Sister was already walking off. Gritting her teeth, Angela made her way over to her unwanted visitor. Abel was leaning against his red Ferrari with his ankles and arms crossed. Angela wanted to punch him in his smug face. "This is the most conspicuous car in the world. Why do you insist on following me around in it?"

"This is my baby," Abel proudly replied, running his hand over the curve of the bumper. "I would never betray her by driving a different car."

Angela rolled her eyes. "Of course, you call it a *she*," she muttered.

"You seem grouchy today," Abel pointed out with cheer.

Angela tossed him a filthy look. "Gee, I wonder why."

"I don't know why. Would you care to tell me?" Abel offered innocently.

Angela strove for patience. It was a rare commodity whenever this particular man was around. "It's been a month, Abel." She couldn't believe she was on a first-name basis with her kidnapper. "Why are you still following me?"

"Boss's orders," he replied easily.

"Well, your boss can take a long walk off a steep cliff," Angela said with a raised chin.

Abel's slow smile was sexy and knowing. "He'd love to hear you say that."

Angela made no comment. Because she knew exactly how Roman would react to such a comment. It would be as annoying as it was exhilarating. Shaking her head, she turned on her heel. "This has been fun, Abel. But I'm out."

"Wait," he called. "Can you take a look at something for me?"

He began to unbutton his shirt, and the last of Angela's patience snapped. She fished in her purse, quickly retrieving her pepper spray. Pointing it at Abel's blue eyes, she let it fly.

"Argh!" Abel screamed. "What are you doing?! Stop it!"

She watched, more than a little satisfied, when the criminal in front of her went down to one knee, his eyes streaming with tears. "That's what you get for being a pervert. And in broad daylight!" she scolded him.

Abel rubbed his eyes with the heels of his hands. "Fuck!" he yelled. "You are one brutal female. No wonder Roman is so obsessed with you. You're his perfect match."

"I beg your pardon?!" Angela exclaimed. She had never been more insulted in her entire life.

"I was only going to show you this weird spot I have," Abel whined, his bloodshot eyes still streaming tears as he climbed to his feet.

Angela's mouth dropped open. "Are you serious? You want medical advice?" She couldn't believe her ears.

"You're a doctor," Abel pointed out, looking pitiful.

"You kidnapped me," she reminded him.

Abel looked pained, planting his fists on his hips. "When are you going to let that go?"

"Let it go? *Let it go?!*" Angela repeated shrilly, taking a step forward.

Abel held up his hands, warding off her advance. "Whoa there, Doc. No need for more violence. I apologize, okay? I was desperate. When Roman told me to go and find a doctor, I took the first one I found."

"Did you ever consider *not* kidnapping anyone?" she asked sarcastically. "Maybe asking them to help?"

Abel shrugged his heavy shoulders. "Honestly? No. I was so worried about Luca. Besides, asking for things isn't really my way."

"Why am I not surprised?" Angela muttered to

herself. She silently warned herself not to continue the conversation, but she couldn't help asking, "What *is* your way?"

Abel held his hands out in front of him and made two fists. His impressive biceps bulged as he admitted, "Smash."

"Great." She rolled her eyes. "I was abducted by the Hulk." Abel laughed, and she was annoyed at the quick recovery he seemed to have made from the pepper spray. His eyes were still red, but they didn't seem to be burning him anymore. "And now I'm apparently being stalked by him."

She noticed Abel and his ostentatious car the same afternoon she had sexed up Roman. After a long shower, disassociating under the spray long enough for her hot water to turn cold, she ventured to the store. Abel didn't even try to be subtle. He honked his horn at her and even had the audacity to wave his gun around. She was a little worried about his mental stability, if she was being honest. But she completely ignored him that day, and every day since, other than to offer him the occasional cup of coffee. She was a sucker—sue her.

Seeing him outside her apartment on her way to work so early in the mornings caused her to feel bad, and she had taken him a to-go cup a couple of times. But that didn't mean she liked him. And it certainly didn't mean she wanted him to follow her around forever.

"I'm not stalking you. I'm watching you for your own good," Abel quickly retorted.

Angela looked at him drolly. "My own good, huh?"

"That's right." Abel shot her a serious look this time. "So you don't do anything stupid. I'd hate to have to tell Roman you went to the police."

"It's been a month," she pointed out frustratedly. "I haven't so far."

"Things change." Abel shrugged his heavy shoulders. "Though I happen to believe you won't do the dirty on us. Not after spending so much time making sure Luca recovered perfectly. Plus, you've used the money Roman blackmailed you with."

Angela huffed. "Firstly, of course I was going to make sure Luca was okay. He became my patient the moment I worked on him. And, as much as I hate to admit it, your boss was right. Luca is a sweetheart."

Abel grinned. "Luca is the best. He's the annoying little brother everyone never knew they wanted. The best thing Roman ever did was find him and raise him."

Angela was curious about what Abel meant by *finding* Luca. She did know Roman, from twenty-two years old, had raised Luca from the time he was ten. Luca was chatty and spoke about his big brother as if he hung the moon. Angela thought it was sweet, and she was happy for the young man. But given that she knew Roman was more likely to hang human beings than the moon and the stars, it was difficult for her to reconcile Luca's hero worship with Roman's reputation.

"Secondly," Angela began, finally getting back on track. "I realized there *was* something more than ass wiping that your blood money could be used for."

Abel looked over her shoulder at the Lighthouse Resource Center. "I've seen this place a few times driving past, but can't say I knew much about it. I did some research after I followed you here so often. It's a worthwhile cause."

Angela huffed. "What would you know about worthwhile causes?"

Abel pursed his lips, clearly insulted. But what got to her was the flash of hurt in his eyes. "Not everything I do is illegal, Angela. I'm more than just an abductor of women," he pointed out quietly.

It felt very much like a reprimand. And it worked because she felt immediately guilty. She sighed, her shoulders drooping a little. She found words to be a wonderful offensive, as well as defensive, maneuver. But her quick wit and extensive vocabulary also made her a bitch. "I'm sorry," she said.

Abel immediately perked up, smiling at her. "All good."

She could only shake her head in wonder. Abel was like a big dopey puppy. How he mastered being scary and serious half the time was astounding.

"Now, as I was trying to show you before . . ." he broke off, unbuttoning his shirt halfway. "What do you think?"

She thought he had a mighty fine chest. It was hairy but not Chewbacca-level hairy, and it was heavily muscled. It didn't hold a candle to Roman's, however, whose chest was more finely muscled, like a swimmer or a dancer. Roman's abs were chiseled and he was toned to perfection—not an ounce of wasted skin on the man.

The tattoo covering his chest from pecs to abdomen was a surprise. The skull not so much, but the vibrant display of flowers in orange, purple and even pink were a shock to discover. It looked like he had a flower garden on his chest with a skull buried amongst the petals. It was beautiful. She wanted to trace it with her tongue.

"Uh, Dr. Hawthorne?" Abel interrupted her lusty thoughts. "You still with me?"

She looked the man up and down. "Not even on your best day, Abel."

Abel snorted. "You're funny," he told her. "It's cutting, and it hurts," he added quickly. "But it's funny. I like it."

"Great," Angela responded dryly.

"The spot," Abel prompted. "It's itchy as hell."

Now that she wasn't focused on his incredible pecs, she saw very clearly that the man had a rather large red blistered spot in the center of his chest. It was chicken-pox. She had no doubt about it. She couldn't count the number of times she had diagnosed it over the years. But where would be the fun—or the revenge—in simply telling him that? "It looks like an STI," she said instead.

"STI?" he repeated, looking at the spot.

Angela nodded solemnly. "Yes. As in, a sexually transmitted infection."

"What?" Abel went pale before her eyes. "But no one has polished my knob for weeks! And never without protection," he exclaimed.

"I don't know what to tell you, Abel. It looks very much like dick-rot," she told him seriously. "If not treated immediately, it will progress to your balls. They'll become puss-filled sacs instead of happy sacs and will eventually fall off."

"I don't believe you," Abel declared, crossing his arms over his chest.

She shrugged. "Since when has belief made anything more or less of a fact? Google it." She turned and walked away, tossing over her shoulder, "Good luck."

"Wait! What's the treatment? Angela! Angelaaaa!" Abel bellowed.

She kept it together just long enough to get into her car. Then she burst into laughter. Was it cruel? Maybe. Did she care? Not in the slightest. Let the clueless Hulk with the red-rimmed eyes waste his day googling dick-rot.

She was sure it would yield some very interesting results.

CHAPTER SEVEN

Roman had just finished a phone call with his attorney when Abel barged into his office. He looked pissed off and was puffing, apparently having stormed his way through the building until reaching his destination. Roman sat back in his chair and waited patiently for whatever Abel had to say. Such entrances were not uncommon.

Abel marched his way to Roman's desk, slamming his hands onto the polished wood. "You need to kill her."

Roman's heart skipped a beat and he sat up straight. "Explain," he demanded, knowing Abel was talking about Angela.

"She did something horrible. Something there is no coming back from," Abel explained, his blue eyes wide.

"What the fuck?! Did she go to the police? Why?" Roman demanded, launching from his chair and striding around the table. "What did you do?"

Abel's head snapped back. "Me? What makes you think *I* did something? It's that woman's fault, not mine."

"Because she seemed quite happy to ignore me and my threats for the past month, that's why. Something new must have happened," Roman stated.

It was the truth. It was one month to the day since he had really spoken with Angela. He had been shocked when she showed up wanting to check on Luca. He was counting on never running into her again. But she sashayed her pretty rump into his building almost every day for a week after that first time. And then every other day for the following two weeks. It was only in the past five days that she stopped showing up in his foyer. And that was because Luca was up and walking around, and pretty much back to normal. She no longer had a reason to be here.

If he was grumpier than usual the last few days, it had nothing to do with the fact that he missed seeing her face on his security cameras. He wasn't proud of the way he watched her every move when she was in his building. It made him feel desperate. But she went full ice queen on him the first time he tried to thank her for returning to follow up with Luca, and he'd be damned if he would tolerate that type of attitude. So, he asked Luca to find a way to send the security feeds directly to his phone, and he followed her from afar.

Over the past month, the number of times he got himself off in his private bathroom was borderline ridiculous. The worst part was, it wasn't anywhere near as satisfying as it should have been. Because now he had Angela's sweet pussy to compare his pleasure to, and his hand came up short. Very short.

He didn't want to admit that sex with Angela was the best of his life. For one, it wouldn't be happening again, which meant he was doomed never to feel the same pleasure. For another, it had been far more intense than simply great sex. Her body, her face, her *heart*, all combined to make it an *experience*. A life-changing one. Which could have been wonderful, but was actually terrible due to the circumstances.

"Well? What happened?" Roman demanded again.

"She didn't go to the cops," Abel said, and Roman was instantly relieved. "She—" was as far as he got before he was interrupted by the office door being flung open again.

"Have you told him yet? You promised you would wait until I could be here to witness it," Luca said as he walked in, followed by a hovering Salvatore.

"You know about this?" Roman asked Luca. He was shocked because Luca seemed to have forged a good relationship with the doctor. Perhaps even a genuine friendship. But then, he wasn't surprised. His brother had that effect on most people. He was irresistible.

Even to a jaded ex-military bodyguard who was raised in a brutal crime family, Roman thought, looking at Salvatore. His old friend had a stupid smile on his face as he gazed adoringly at Luca. The man was head over heels in love and Roman was pleased to see it.

Luca covered his mouth and giggled. His brown eyes sparkled with mischief as he nodded his head. Roman relaxed a little more. Luca wouldn't be that carefree if real killing was involved. Which meant Abel was being melodramatic. Again.

"Wait until you hear this," Luca said, rolling his eyes at Salvatore when the other man gently pulled him over to the couch, insisting he sit. "I'm fine, Sal."

"Yeah you are," Salvatore replied with a wink and a grin.

Roman rolled his eyes and Abel gagged, but the two men ignored them and shared a sweet kiss. Luca tired easily and wasn't up to any heavy lifting, but he was basically fully recovered. And he owed it all to Angela. To think he could have lost his brother for good . . . Roman shook his head. The rage and pain such thoughts caused, reminded him he still had his old doctor to deal with. Dr. Gaines had been his guest for the past month. Roman had largely ignored the older man, but knew he couldn't do that indefinitely.

When Luca and Sal finally parted, Luca grinned at Roman. "Angela told Abel he had dick-rot and his balls were going to fall off."

As Salvatore and Luca laughed, and Abel look disgruntled, Roman lost his cool. Again. "Why was she looking at your dick?" he yelled at Abel.

Luca's mouth snapped closed, and his eyes widened. "Whoa, easy there."

Roman looked down, realizing he had palmed one of his knives and was now holding it tightly by his side. He shook his head a little, marveling at the woman's ability to get under his skin so easily. He was known for his cool, calculating demeanor. Yet, here he was, pulling a knife on one of his oldest and dearest friends. He acknowledged the stupidity of it, but he didn't put it away. "You were saying?" he invited Abel.

Abel held his hands up. "She didn't see my cock. In fact, she maced me."

That gave Roman pause. "She what?"

"She sprayed me with pepper spray. Burned like a bitch," Abel said, rubbing his eyes.

Roman looked closer, noting some residual redness

along Abel's lower lashes. "Why exactly did she feel the need to do that?" he inquired, finally pocketing the blade. He needed to remember that Angela could take care of herself. She had proven it time and time again in the short time he had known her. What's more, it wasn't his place to get insulted on her behalf.

"I simply asked for medical advice," Abel explained innocently. "I have these spots . . ." He yanked his shirt down a bit, revealing numerous red and white spots on his chest. "I wanted her medical opinion."

Luca snorted, leaning back against Salvatore. "It's chickenpox. Hardly the end of the world. But Angela told him it was an STI and he was about to lose his most prized possession."

Poor Abel looked so horrified that Roman couldn't help laughing. Sal and Luca joined in. Abel, however, did not. He looked very indignant.

"It's not funny!" Abel shouted. He shook his finger at all of them. "That woman is a menace."

"She's wonderful," Luca corrected.

Roman couldn't help but agree with both of them. "And this is why you want me to kill her? Because she lied about your dick falling off?"

"Yes. I can't think of a better reason to," Abel said, cupping his junk. "Can you?"

Roman considered that. Abel kind of had a point.

"Well, it could be a new record. I was about to pay Dr. Gaines a visit. I don't think I've ever killed two doctors in one day before."

Luca glared at him. "That isn't funny. I swear, you three and your records. I wouldn't mind if they were normal. But they're positively morbid."

"Babe, are you saying you're not proud of me for gutting the most men in a seventy-two-hour period?" Salvatore asked in mock outrage.

Luca shoved his lover. "That is exactly what I'm saying."

"What about my record of burying the most amount of people alive in the one grave at a time?" Abel asked. He turned to Roman. "Do you remember how hard it was to stuff four people into a hole and cover them up with dirt? I had blisters on my hands for weeks."

"I remember," Roman said. "Your whining is why I invested in a small excavator."

"You're all sick," Luca informed them. "Can't you find a healthy hobby?"

"Says the man who hacked into WITSEC last night to discover the new identity of a witness so Morrigan can assassinate him," Salvatore said, tickling Luca on the back of his neck.

Luca laughed, pushing Sal away. "It's hardly the

same thing."

Roman agreed. It was likely semantics to some, but it was a degree of separation they all agreed would always be there. Luca had never killed anyone, and if Roman had his way, he never would. Even in situations like the witness, Luca was given all the details, and he had the final say about whether he would use his computer skills to essentially send someone to their death. When Luca said no, Roman respected it. The instance of the witness was a private contract Roman had taken for Morrigan from a father looking for the murderer of his beloved daughter. Luca had taken one look at the file and agreed to find the asshole's new identity. Morrigan was out executing him as they spoke.

"And what do you mean, killing two doctors in one day? I thought you were letting Dr. Gaines go," Luca said with a frown.

"On the contrary. I have him scheduled for decapitation after lunch," Roman responded mildly.

"Roman. Not funny," Luca scolded.

"Do you see me laughing? His negligence almost cost you your life," Roman fired back.

Luca sighed and stood up. "He made a mistake."

"One that almost killed you," Roman pointed out, not moved in the slightest by his brother's doe eyes.

Luca moved in for a hug and Roman wrapped his arms around him, being careful not to squeeze too tightly. His eyes met Salvatore's across the room and a wealth of understanding moved between them.

Luca pulled back, saying, "You've had him locked up for a month already. It's time to shit or get off the pot, big bro."

Roman snorted humorously. Dr. Gaines was locked up on the top floor. But not in any of the interrogation rooms, nor was he chained to the wall in the main area. He was imprisoned in what amounted to a fancy, private cell. He had his own kitchen and bathroom, a bed and a sofa. He even had a TV.

Roman had gone back and forth on what to do about him for the past month. On the one hand, he had been a good doctor to them for the past ten years. As good as a doctor was when they took money for looking the other way. He was greedy and self-centered, with a nasty gambling habit. One Roman secretly continued to help feed. Sometimes money wasn't enough to keep a man loyal. But addiction? That won every time. Roman simply ensured the doctor took a few heavy hits every couple of months, making Roman's money very much needed, which kept the doctor's mouth firmly shut. It was known within certain circles that he was their physician, so it also guaranteed the man some protection.

Overall, Dr. Gaines had done a decent job of patching up their hurts. He was trained in general medicine and not a surgeon, let alone a trauma surgeon like Dr. Angela Hawthorne. But he had been sufficient to diagnose concussions and stitch knife wounds. Unfortunately, he had become complacent over recent months. And misdiagnosing Luca had been the final nail in his coffin.

"I'll speak with him now," Roman told Luca.

"Great." Luca smiled winningly. He held out his hand to Salvatore, who allowed himself to be dragged to the door. But he did hesitate on the threshold.

"Need me?" Sal questioned.

Roman shook his head. "All good, Sal. Go with Luca." Salvatore raised his chin in response, leaving the door open behind him as he trailed Luca. Roman was already standing, so he figured he'd take his brother's advice. "I'll head to the top floor now."

"I'll come with you," Abel offered.

"Are you sure? You're sick," Roman said.

Abel rolled his eyes. "It's just some spots. They're itchy and look to be spreading. But that's it. I don't feel sick."

Roman shrugged. "Fine." He didn't know much

about chickenpox, just that it was usually a childhood illness. He made a mental note to google it later.

They rode the elevator in silence, Roman watching as Abel scratched his chest and arms. He spoke briefly with the men stationed outside Dr. Gaines's door before knocking once to announce his presence. Opening the door, he found the older man sitting on the couch watching reruns of *MacGyver*.

"Your services are no longer needed," he stated, getting straight to the point.

Dr. Gaines jumped up, looking panicked. "Please, Mr. Romano. I've been good to you. Loyal. I—"

"You have been," Roman interrupted, uninterested in begging. "Which is the only reason why you're walking out of here today."

"You're letting me go?" Dr. Gaines asked, shocked.

"You're free to go. *But* . . ." Roman added, staring at the older man. "You are *not* a free man. And you never will be. You will always be *my* man. Do you understand?"

"Of course, Mr. Romano. I would never betray you," he said quickly, looking so relieved he could yet cry.

Roman was unmoved. He was also unconvinced. "Here are the rules. You never speak about what you have seen and heard over the years. You remain loyal even though you are no longer our physician. You do not so much as mention my name. If anyone asks you about me, you contact me immediately." He stared at the doctor hard. "You've seen what I can do. You don't want to be on the receiving end of that."

"Of course. Of course!" Dr. Gaines practically yelled. "Thank you. Thank you, Mr. Romano. I didn't mean for your brother—"

"I'd not mention Luca if I were you," Abel advised, glaring at the man from his impressive height.

Dr. Gaines gulped, pushing his glasses further up his nose. "Right. My apologies." He looked between Roman and Abel. "What happens now?"

"You retire," Roman stated. "You move to an island and chase women half your age. And you never speak about me to anyone. Ever. I'll be watching you."

Roman turned and left before he changed his mind and throttled the doctor. Abel closed and locked the door, following Roman over to the huge windows. The glass was one way. His prisoners could see out, but nobody could see in. It was also soundproof and bullet proof. He found it added to the mental stress of his prey —being able to see outside but gain no help.

"Contact Scott and Iain for me, will you? Inform them they'll be taking an extended vacation," Roman said, watching as a helicopter grew bigger in the distance. He wondered if it was heading to the hospital and if Angela was about to have a very busy day.

"Lucky them," Abel commented, making a note in his phone. "Will do. And Morrigan?"

"She'll be taking an all-expenses-paid vacation in about three months herself," Roman admitted, turning to Abel.

"Ah, I thought so," Abel replied easily enough.

Roman was glad he didn't need to explain. Someone like Dr. Gaines was too much of a liability to be allowed to retire in the traditional sense. Scott and Iain would follow him closely for a few months, then Morrigan would make sure the good doctor suffered from a tragic drowning accident as he snorkeled on the reef or something. He wouldn't keep his final decision from Luca, but he also wouldn't volunteer the information. Knowing his brother, he likely already knew what the outcome would be. But he'd had to at least try to talk Roman out of it. It was just his way.

All the men and women he employed had their strengths. Some, like Abel and Salvatore, could be relied upon to perform every role within his empire. But some, like Morrigan, had very specific talents. She had come to him from his mother's family, trained by his maternal grandfather to infiltrate and incapacitate the enemy. Roman didn't approve of the techniques used, nor the young age at which Maria had first been indoctrinated as the family's assassin.

When he killed his father and renounced his family, Maria came to him for work and protection. She wanted out of the family as much as he did. Recognizing her skill, as much as her need to escape the circumstances she was born into, he readily agreed. She adopted the name Morrigan and chose not to reside in the Omertà complex with most of his crew. He didn't mind. He knew she was loyal. As far as he was concerned, she had been forced to do enough things. Now it was time for her to make her own choices. Besides, she was lurking around the building more often than not anyway.

"How is the lovely Morrigan?" Abel asked. "I haven't seen her for two weeks."

"Still not interested, I'd wager. But I'd like to see you ask her out again," Roman added with a grin. Three weeks ago, Abel brought Morrigan a bunch of flowers he had no doubt stolen. Morrigan lit them on fire.

Abel crossed his arms over chest, looking miffed. "Women are so touchy these days."

Roman snickered a little. "Have you ever thought it could be you and not them?"

"Ridiculous," came Abel's prompt response.

Roman grinned and shook his head. Abel's ego was

a thing of beauty. His head was so big that Roman often questioned how he could walk through average doorways.

Abel itched at his thigh, swearing softly, before looking back up. "Now that Dr. Gaines is out of the way, what are you going to do about the new job opening?"

Roman had thought about that. In fact, he had thought about little else for the past month. It was one of the reasons why Dr. Gaines had remained his guest for so long. Making a final decision about *him* meant making a decision about *her*. "I'm going to ask if a certain mace-happy doctor would like the job."

Abel gaped at him. "You're dreaming. There's no way. She hates you more than she hates me. And that's saying a lot considering she just threatened my balls with puss."

Roman scowled at his friend for a moment before adopting a superior look. "Luckily for me, I'm not you. I know just where to strike when it comes to women."

"The booty?" Abel guessed.

Roman snorted. "No. See, this is what I mean. You're useless." He shook his head, tsking. "I'm refer-ring to the heart."

Abel's frown was disapproving before he adopted a more neutral expression. "You plan to seduce her? For real?"

"What if I did?" Roman asked, watching Abel closely. His friend shrugged his heavy shoulders, turning to look out the window instead of replying.

Abel always had something to say, which is how Roman knew Abel had feelings for Angela. He couldn't blame him, but Roman didn't like the fear that spread in his chest. Fear that Angela might have feelings for Abel in return. After all, they had been spending a lot of time together, what with Abel following her. Plus, she actually talked to Abel when she visited Luca. Unlike her cold shoulder act with himself.

"I don't think you should," Abel admitted, facing Roman once more. "She's a good person who has had something bad happen to her. She's not like us, Roman."

"You mean *bad* people who occasionally have *good* things happen?" Roman's jaw clenched and his heart began to pound a little faster. Abel's eyes ran over his face, and Roman knew his friend could read him. They were too close for him not to see the anger in Roman's eyes.

"You're not a bad person, Roman," Abel told him, moving closer and placing a hand on his shoulder. "In fact, you're the best person I know. Well, used to. The doctor may have you beat." He grinned, giving him a shove.

Roman rocked back on his feet but regained his balance quickly, the tension leaving him as he relaxed. Abel didn't like her. Not like *that* anyway. Roman could tell the difference. "I don't mind being second place. For once," he added with a smile. "But you'll be happy to know I wasn't referring to seducing her heart."

He didn't mention he had already seduced her body. He hadn't mentioned the sex to anyone. And seeing Abel's reaction just now confirmed he had made the right decision to keep it private. His loyal friend was likely to punch him in the face if he found out. He continued, "You mentioned she donated that hundred large to a shelter?" Abel had messaged him the moment he saw Angela carrying the familiar duffle bag into the Lighthouse Resource Center.

Abel nodded. "That's right."

"That's her soft spot. That's where I'll hit her," Roman stated. He'd been trained to identify weakness and then exploit it to achieve his goals. This time would be no different.

CHAPTER EIGHT

Angela's pet project is a pit, Roman thought as he walked around the grounds of the old orphanage.

The location was good—prime, even—from a business perspective. But it was practically falling down in places. Not to mention all the graffiti. Saint Andrews had been a boys' home fifty years ago, before being vacant for at least ten. Luca had given him a lot of information about the center, as well as the nun who ran it.

Sister Philomena was an active and vocal member of the community, acting in service from the time she was twenty-one. She was now eighty-eight and showed no signs of slowing down. Luca had warned him that the nun was well-loved, including by Angela. So that was where Roman intended to start. He had yet to meet a woman he couldn't charm—holy or otherwise.

"Excuse me, can I help you?" an old female voice came from behind him.

Roman stiffened for a moment, surprised because he had not heard her approach. He turned, smiling warmly at the nun who watched him politely—and shrewdly. Roman's smile dipped a little. The woman in front of him may have been devoted to the church and the community, but she was no one's fool. Roman looked around, noting they were alone. He knew Angela was on the grounds somewhere. Abel had followed her here just thirty minutes prior. Salvatore had accompanied Roman, but he was waiting in the car. Not that he was happy about it.

Roman rarely went anywhere on his own, even though he was more than capable of looking after himself. But he had a lot of enemies, the worst being his family. And Sal, Abel, and Morrigan were very protective of him. Each acted as his personal security whenever was out in public. But he wanted to talk to Angela on his own. He didn't want his annoying and observant friends to discover he had slept with her. Plus, it would be the first real conversation with her since the mutual orgasms.

"Forgive me for trespassing," Roman said with a

charming smile. "I was just looking for a friend. I believe she volunteers here."

"We have lots of volunteers," the nun replied serenely, offering no further information.

"I'm glad to hear it. I do hope my recent donation will be put to good use." He looked around, taking in the cracks and the dreary atmosphere. "It looks like you could use a few more donations."

"Oh, you're the silent donor?" She moved closer, placing her hand on his arm. "Thank you very much. I am Sister Philomena, the manager here you could say. I guarantee the goodness of its use."

Roman patted her hand. "I believe you. It's lovely to meet you, Sister Philomena."

"Call me Sister Pip, everyone else does." She stared at him for a moment, squeezing his arm before moving her hand. She twisted the rosary hanging from her habit as she spoke. "You look very much like her."

"Who?" he asked, confused.

"Your mother."

Roman went still. "I beg your pardon?" What was the old nun playing at?

"I met her once," Sister Philomena clarified. "Just once"

Roman narrowed his eyes. "And you remembered her? All these years later, and after just one meeting?"

"You sound suspicious, young man," the Sister pointed out. "I don't suppose I blame you, given who you are."

"Now you know who *I* am?" Roman couldn't contain his scoff.

"Of course," Sister Philomena confirmed with a smile. She winked at him. "Everyone knows about the rebel mafia prince."

Roman groaned, momentarily derailed. Would that nickname ever stop following him around? He vowed to find the news press who had first called him that and slaughter every one of its employees.

Sister Philomena laughed loudly. "You don't like the moniker?"

"Not at all," Roman responded. But he was smiling once again.

"I don't blame you," the woman offered. "What should I call you then?"

He considered the elderly nun carefully. She looked innocent enough. But so did some of the worst people in history. His gut had only ever failed him once. And since then, he'd made it a point to fine-tune it to the nth degree. And now, he trusted his instincts implicitly. They were telling him the canny old woman was a friend and not a foe. But the reference to his mother was bothersome. In the end, he

112

inclined his head towards her, saying, "Roman. Just Roman."

She smiled. "Well, Roman. To answer your question, I met your mother when she asked me for aid to escape your father."

His renewed good humor fled in an instant. He didn't even try to censor his language. "What the fuck?"

"Come," Sister Philomena urged. "Walk with me. I know it doesn't look like much from this side, but there's a lovely little garden in the back. I believe your mother liked gardens."

Roman's jaw clenched, and he wanted to demand answers immediately. He thought about calling Salvatore and getting him to follow, but surely Roman could deal with whatever the Sister was going to do. Or say. He idly wondered if he was going to be forced to kill a nun. And whether that would reserve him an extra special place in hell.

He followed her, his thoughts swirling, and was surprised to discover the nun hadn't been exaggerating. The back of the main building had a paved courtyard with towering trees and flowers in full bloom. His throat constricted in recognition—many of them were the exact ones he had tattooed on his chest in memory of his mother.

Sister Philomena sat on a stone bench. "Luciana

came to Monash on a business trip with your father, I believe. This place was already aiding the community, and she came to offer a helping hand whilst in town. She was very beautiful, Roman. She lit up whatever space she was in."

"Yes," Roman said, swallowing hard. "That was her."

Sister Philomena smiled at him. "You do the same."

He grunted but didn't correct her. He knew it wasn't true. He was too much like his father. "Keep going," he urged.

"She spent the day working here in the garden. It gave her peace, I believe. And courage," she added, meeting his eyes. "After a few hours, she confessed her husband was not a good man, and she was looking for a way to leave him. She had just discovered she was pregnant. Becoming a parent has a way of changing a person at their very core. Or so I have observed."

Roman's head swirled. This was certainly not what he had expected when he decided to pay a visit to the shelter. Was the old woman lying to him? If so, for what purpose? And if she was not, well, it meant he was standing in a space where his mother had once been. Where she had once tended to the earth. Gardening had been her one joy—other than her children. And the one thing she could do to escape his father's company. His father had hated dirt—unless he was burying someone in it, of course. He would need to look into the nun, as well as everything she had just said. He would get Luca onto it. His brother had a vested interest in the subject of their mother as well. It was only fair.

"Are you okay? Have I misspoken?" Sister Philomena asked solicitously, her eyes kind.

"I . . ." Roman cleared his throat when his voice cracked. The small sign of weakness annoyed him, and he closed off the part of him that was the little boy yearning for information about his mother. Compartmentalization was one of his strong suits. "I am fine. And you didn't misspeak. I appreciate the information. This is all very unexpected. I wasn't aware anyone in my family had business ventures in Monash. It's one of the reasons why I made it my base of operations."

"And your home," Sister Philomena added, causing Roman to look at her. "It is also your home, is it not?"

Roman nodded but didn't speak.

"Unfortunately, your father returned before I was able to offer more than a sympathetic ear to your mother. She left, and I never saw her again." She shook her head sadly, reaching forward to stroke a petal in vibrant red. "I heard she died in childbirth."

"I heard that too," he replied. The Sister didn't question his tone or response, but he saw the shrewd look she tossed him. *Oh, yes,* he mused. *She is more than she seems.* It would do him no good to wonder what his life would have been like if the woman before him was successful in aiding his mother. So, again, he pushed the useless thoughts away, locking them up.

"I also heard you killed your father," Sister Pip said next.

She said it so easily that it threw Roman for a moment. "I've never been charged with his murder."

The nun snorted, waving his comment away. "Of course, you haven't. It wasn't a question, Roman. Merely a statement." She looked him over again. "I would hope someone who holds no love for the type of man your father was would treat women very differently than he did."

"I would hope so, too," Roman agreed, unsure where the conversation was going.

"Good. That means I can trust you with a certain green-eyed doctor," she stated. "Come now, help me up."

Roman was speechless as he offered the Sister his arm. She used it for leverage, though he was sure she didn't need it. The strength in her frame belied the fact. "I'm not sure what you're talking about," he hedged.

Sister Philomena scoffed. "These eyes might be old, but they see just fine. There's also nothing wrong with my brain. You came here looking for a friend, stating you're responsible for a recent large donation. A donation that Dr. Hawthorne brought to me. Of course, it is Angela you're sniffing after."

His mouth fell open. "I'm not sniffing after her!"

"You're not?" Roman shook his head and Sister Pip continued. "Well, you should be."

Roman choked on his own spit. It was embarrassing. The nun patted him on the back until he got himself under control. He eyed her as if she was a bomb about to blow. "You're scary, you know that?"

She laughed. "So I have been told. Anyway, Angela is in the clinic, talking a young woman through her options for an unexpected pregnancy. She will be out soon."

They walked back to the front of the building in silence. Roman really had nothing more to say. He'd been completely blindsided. Both from the information he received *and* due to the wily woman still gripping his arm.

"If you ever want to talk more about Luciana—or anything, for that matter—the doors of Lighthouse are always open." Sister Philomena patted his arm before letting go. "And here is our Angela now."

Roman looked up, spotting Angela leaving the main building with a younger female. She was dressed casually in jeans, sneakers, and a brown sweater. Her hair was pulled back in a messy bun, and Roman thought she looked amazing. The gentle way she wrapped her arm around the teen, and the way she whispered into her ear spoke volumes of her compassionate nature and kind soul.

"Ah, I see." Sister Pip nodded her head slowly. "You don't need to sniff after her, do you? It's already too late for that."

Roman stiffened. "I have no idea what you're talking about."

"Of course you don't," she agreed readily, before pursing her lips. "Will you do one thing for me?"

"If it is within my power, yes," he told her.

"Angela is not all bark and no bite, by any means. But her harsh bite is worth the pain to get to know her," she said, lowering her voice. "Be careful with her, Roman. She's had to piece herself back together once before. I don't want to see her broken again."

The nun knew about Angela's past. Something even his brother hadn't been able to dig up. "What happened to her?" The look she sent him had him immediately dropping his head. "*Mi scusi.* That was rude. It is none of my business."

"It was rude," the Sister agreed. "I'm not about to share the darkest corners of anyone's life with a perfect stranger, let alone Angela's. That's for her to disclose. *If she decides to make it your business, that is.*" Her face softened, and she smiled at him. "If you get very lucky, she just might."

Before he could reply, Angela noticed his presence. The way her mouth dropped open would have been comical if the glare she sent him wasn't so nasty. She was well and truly pissed. And he thought she looked fucking beautiful. He watched her long, curvy legs eat up the distance between them, and before he could say anything, she ground her pointer finger into his chest.

"What are *you* doing here?" she demanded. "It's not enough that you have me followed by that big dumb ogre, Abel, but you have to come and invade my personal space as well?"

"Angela," Sister Philomena said, stepping between them. Roman was grateful to the nun. "Roman and I were just enjoying a nice chat. It was such a lovely opportunity to thank our *silent* donor personally. You didn't tell me you two were friends."

"We're not," they said simultaneously.

Roman smiled thinly. At least they agreed on one thing. "I was just passing by on my way to work, and thought I would stop in," he offered.

"Bullshit." Angela did her best to mask the curse word with a cough.

"What was that, dear?" Sister Philomena's expression was the very picture of innocence.

Angela smiled at the nun. "Just a tickle in my throat."

"I hope you aren't coming down with something," the Sister said.

"It's nothing," Angela replied before turning to Roman. "Can I speak with you for a moment? In private," she added through gritted teeth.

"Of course." He turned to Sister Philomena, unsure if he was about to tell the truth or one of the biggest lies of his life. "It was a pleasure meeting you. Thank you for the chat."

"Any time," she told him with a warm smile. "Perhaps you will stop in on your way to work another day," she suggested, before tilting her head curiously. "Where might that be?"

Roman pointed to the east. "You can see it from here, actually. The Omertà complex."

Sister Philomena gasped. "That tall monstrosity of a building in the center of the city?"

He laughed. "That would be the one."

She leaned in close, murmuring, "Just between you and me, I always thought the owner of that building must be compensating for something."

Angela gaped at her. "Sister!"

"What? It's the truth. And I took a vow of honesty," Sister Pip reminded her with a wink to Roman. "But I see now that isn't the case."

Roman laughed. "Why, thank you." he bowed to the nun, enjoying the hell out of himself. "Angel didn't tell me how wonderful you are."

"*Angela*," the fired-up beauty emphasized, "didn't tell you anything about the Sister or the Lighthouse."

Sister Philomena patted Angela on the arm. "Well, he knows now." She turned to him. "And he is welcome any time. I'll leave you to it." She patted his shoulder once before walking off.

"What the hell are you doing here?" Angela demanded as soon as the older woman was out of earshot.

"I have a proposition for you," Roman said.

"I'm not interested in anything you have to offer," she told him, crossing her arms over her chest.

Roman watched her breasts plump, wanting to see them naked again. "Not even if it's this place?"

"What?" Angela asked with a shake of her head.

"I understand you're trying to save this place," he began. "The current owner is content to let this place be used as a community resource center as long as he doesn't have to do anything himself. He has a soft spot for the nun. But not soft enough to reach into his own pockets for repairs. All costs fall to Sister Philomena."

"How do you know all that?" Angela wanted to know.

"I know a lot of things. I have my finger on the pulse of a lot of people in this city," he pointed out.

"Well, get your finger off mine," she grumbled. "I don't need or want your help, Roman."

"Really? I'll just take my hundred grand back then, shall I?" he asked with a quirk of his brow.

"Fine," Angela agreed readily. "You go and tell Sister Pip that you want your money back, and I'll head down to the police station, shall I?"

When Angela glared at him, he glared right back. She was something else. Eventually, he sighed. "I have to be honest with you, Angel. I think you have the easier job. I'm pretty sure that nun terrifies me." When she laughed, he felt like the king of the world. It was loud and boisterous, and it made her eyes light up. He grinned at her, sharing her amusement. "Don't laugh. It's the truth."

"Sister Philomena is unique, I'll give you that," she allowed.

"So, how about you save me from the scary nun and agree to my terms." He did his best to keep it casual, wanting the stick that was typically up her ass in his presence to stay out. "You agree to be the personal physician of Omertà Corp, and I'll donate enough money to the Lighthouse Resource Center that Sister Pip could paint the walls in gold leaf if she chose to."

"Wait . . ." Angela held up a hand in a classic stop gesture. "Private physician? You want me to be your doctor?"

The look of absolute horror and disbelief on her face was a little insulting, but Roman sucked it up. "Not just my doctor. The doctor for my corporation—Omertà. That includes dozens of people under my employ. As well as others on a case-by-case basis. You could choose whom you treated—within reason. I won't force you to treat someone if you're uncomfortable. But I *would* need to know I can rely on you."

Angela stared at him in silence for a moment before asking, "What happened to your last doctor?"

"His mistake almost cost Luca his life. Do you really want to know?" Roman questioned in return.

"I don't want to know anything about you," Angela was quick to respond, backpedaling.

Roman chuckled. "Liar," he said seductively. "We both know you loved what I did to you against your kitchen wall. I'm sure you'd like to know what else I can do."

"You're wrong," Angela said stubbornly, a lovely

shade of pink flushing her cheeks. "And it won't happen again. I mean it, Roman." She met his eyes. "My body can't be bought."

He frowned. "I'm offering you payment for your medical knowledge and services. I didn't mention your body—nor do I intend to. I don't need to pay for sex, Angel."

"Good to know," she said with a dip of her head. "But the answer is still a resounding no."

"Think of all the people you could save," Roman urged. "Luca tells me this place is a refuge for old and young alike. You treat hookers and veterans, LGBQT youths, and everyone in between. It's a place to get food, shelter, medical help, and even mental support. Correct?"

"Yes," she confirmed, casting her eyes over the sad-looking building. "Why would you want to be involved in any of that?"

"I don't," Roman assured her quickly. "But *you* do. And *I* need a physician I can trust. It's a good deal."

Her green eyes swung to his. "You trust me?"

He weighed up whether to tell her the truth or not. In the end, he decided it was best. For some reason, lying to her left a bad taste in his mouth. "I do."

"Well, you shouldn't," she snapped.

Roman sighed, feeling frustrated. She was so damn

prickly. It was interesting because, usually, he was the grumpy asshole. He ignored her waspish attitude in favor of coaxing a yes out of her instead. "Come on. You already spent my money. Why don't you spend some more?"

"That was a one-off," she informed him primly. "I don't want your blood money."

Roman rolled his eyes. "And why do you assume my money has blood on it? I own half the businesses in the city. And hundreds more around the world. I don't need to kill people for wealth, Angel."

"Stop calling me Angel," she said. But it held no heat. He was wearing her down. He just knew it. "And if you don't need to, then why do you? Kill people, I mean."

He shrugged. "I do it for pleasure, of course."

"Of course. What a wonderful hobby," Angela replied dryly.

"I've always thought so," he agreed. "Now, what do you say? This place, for a few hours of your time every month."

Angela chewed on her bottom lip for a moment, thinking things over. "Let's say I agree. What am I supposed to do? Watch you kill people as I wait to secure enough money to save people?"

Roman rolled his eyes. She was like a dog with a

bone. "I don't spend all day shooting people. Sometimes I stab them," he pointed out.

Angela snorted. "Charming."

"I am, actually," he confirmed. "Multitudes of women have told me so."

"I'm sure they have. Insipid twits who value power over depth," Angela said scornfully.

"I have depth," he reminded her. He leaned in close enough to smell her hair. It smelled like a tropical island. "I can go very *deep.* Are you saying you've forgotten so soon?"

Her jaw firmed, and she took a step back. "I thought we agreed not to talk about that. It's been, what, two minutes? That doesn't bode well for you keeping your word."

"We agreed you wouldn't prostitute yourself for me. Not that we wouldn't speak of our history," he corrected her. He was willing to bend a little where she was concerned because, despite his better judgment, he liked her. But he wouldn't let her get away with bullshit. "Stop being such a bitch, Angel."

She glared at him for a moment before groaning. She scrubbed her hands over her face before peeking at him through her fingers. "You're right. I'm being a bitch."

"Are you telling me we finally agree on something?"

he asked in mock surprise. "And what a thing to agree on!"

"Yeah, yeah. Enjoy it while you can," Angela grumbled. But she was smiling.

"So, you'll do it?" Roman pressed.

She looked around one last time, her gaze falling on a female teenager sitting on an old bench. Her shoulders slumped a little, but her expression was determined when she faced him once again. "I'll do it."

Roman wanted to jump for joy, but he reminded himself his kill count was much too high for such shenanigans. "Excellent. Stop by Omertà tonight, and I'll give you a tour of the building. I'll have Luca set you up with the necessary access passes."

He received a nod before she stalked away. He watched the sway of her hips and the roundness of her ass, and his mouth curved. His smile widened when he noticed Sister Philomena giving him a thumbs-up from the door of the building. He couldn't help it—he returned the gesture, feeling oddly awesome.

CHAPTER NINE

Angela followed Roman's truly great ass from floor to floor as he gave her a personal tour of the Omertà complex.

It was massive, spanning sixty stories and taking up half a block in the center of the city. It was all windows and steel, making it look like something from *The Matrix*. The bottom forty floors were rented out to companies and individuals ranging from solicitors to bodyguards, as well as Roman's own legit enterprises.

"We offer personal protection services, cyber security, investment advice and opportunities, as well as martial arts training," Roman was saying as they made their way to the fifth floor where the public gym was.

"And these are all legitimate businesses?" Angela

asked, a little wide-eyed. She hadn't realized how big of an operation Roman had.

"For the most part," Roman hedged. "Yes. We've even worked with the local SWAT team in the past. Some of the best defense experts in the industry work and are trained here."

Angela hummed, looking around at the large, well-equipped gym. It was busy, but the atmosphere was good. "And for the other part?" she asked.

Roman shrugged negligently. "Working in security, real estate, and importation comes with certain work perks."

"I'm sure," she replied sarcastically. She knew Roman owned the entire block that Omertà was on, as well as many other coveted parcels of land, including the marina and surrounds. It was necessary, she supposed, if you wanted to ship things illegally to have your own marina.

She felt a pang of guilt for allowing herself to associate with Roman and his men. Perhaps she was making a mistake? But if she could save the Lighthouse, wouldn't it be worth it? She groaned internally. As long as she was careful to keep Roman at arm's length, she would be fine. He hadn't touched her since she had lost her damned mind in her kitchen and allowed him to screw her against the wall. She couldn't so much as chop vegetables now without thinking of the man's spectacular pierced dick.

"Importation, huh? Weapons, drugs, or people?" she questioned before she could stop herself. They had been making their way to the elevator, but Roman stopped so suddenly she nearly slammed into his muscled back.

"I do not now, nor have I ever, peddled human flesh. People are not commodities," he told her, glaring.

For some reason, Angela believed him. "I'm glad to hear you say that," she told him honestly. For many reasons, she added silently. Not the least of which was personal.

He stared at her for a few seconds before holding the elevator door open for her. She braced herself to be in the confined space with him yet again. They had hopped in and out of the elevator twice already.

"The shooting range is on the lower level," he said. "I bypassed that, but you're welcome to check it out sometime. We're open to the public."

"A shooting range, a medical facility, apartments, and gyms. You really do have everything here, don't you?" Angela paused before murmuring, "This is your castle and you're the king."

"This is my *home*, first and foremost," he corrected her. "Leaving my family and starting afresh was difficult. Yes, I wanted to prove to both sides of my family that not only would I survive without them, but I would also thrive. But the thing I wanted most was a home. With my *real* family."

"Luca?" Angela guessed.

"Luca," Roman confirmed. "And Abel and Salvatore. As well as Morrigan and a few others."

"Must be nice," she muttered as they made their way out onto the fiftieth floor. "To have family."

"You're not close to yours?" He punctuated his question by motioning politely for her to make her way into an entrance hall of sorts.

"No." The one word was clipped. She hoped he got the message that it was not a subject she was willing to discuss. Ever.

"From here up are the personal floors. A few common areas, private gym, swimming pool, bars . . ." Roman listed, making no further inquiries about her family. "The apartments for myself, and my family and guests are from fifty-five upwards. This level has the medical suite, as you probably remember."

Angela looked around, recognizing the sofas and the artwork on the wall from the night she was abducted. She peeked inside the doors, finding the clinic. It was empty. "I'm going to want to do a full inventory."

"Be my guest," Roman bade her. "If there's anything you need, let me know. I'll see that you get it."

She made a sound but didn't reply. She was impressed with his set-up but didn't want to say so.

"You have access to every floor except the top floor," Roman went on to say.

Angela looked at him. "Is that your personal floor?"

"No. My living quarters are on the fifty-ninth floor. You're welcome there any time," he invited, heat filling his eyes.

"Hard pass," Angela said swiftly.

"It's hard all right," Roman muttered, adjusting his cock brazenly.

Angela's mouth fell open. The man was about as subtle as a sledgehammer. "Really? How old are you?" she snarked.

"Thirty-four," came the prompt reply.

"That was a rhetorical question," Angela pointed out dryly. Then she thought about it for a moment. "But also . . . I'm five years older than you."

Roman's slow smile was sexy as sin. "Hmm, there's something to be said for an older woman."

"Yes. We're too mature for the likes of younger men like you," Angela responded primly.

Roman chuckled, the sound sending shivers through her system. "No. That's not it."

"Whatever," Angela said, refusing to flirt with the man. She asked instead, "So, what's on the top floor? I figured you for the penthouse type."

"You figured right in a way," he admitted. "The top floor is the dungeon."

Her mind was immediately flooded with visions of Roman dressed in leather and smacking his palm with a riding crop. "You have a sex dungeon?"

Roman choked, turning red. "A sex dungeon? No. I was referring to a literal dungeon. As in, a prison, or a torture chamber."

Angela's cheeks heated. "Oh," was all she said.

Roman gave her an appraising look. "Like I said, older women are appealing."

She rolled her eyes. "Don't hold your breath in that department."

"You're into breath play? Kinky."

Angela smiled sweetly at him. "I'd be more than happy to put a plastic bag over your head. Just tell me when."

Roman laughed but didn't banter back. He showed her down another hall. "This is the private gym for those I consider *mi famiglia*. You're welcome to use it any time."

Angela looked at the expensive equipment, the

weights, and the open floor area with the thick mats. "What makes you think I work out?"

"I've seen you naked, *mia angelo*," Roman reminded her. "I've felt the strength in your thighs. It was an easy deduction."

Angela clenched her legs together, telling herself to ignore the seductive purr of his words. "You think that was strength? You ain't seen nothing yet."

"Ah, a challenge." His light-brown eyes lit up. "I look forward to what the future brings."

She gave herself a mental spanking. Was she really flirting with Vincenzo Romano? He was her enemy. He was the bad guy. But it was funny, he didn't seem so much like the boss of a criminal organization just then. Just a hot as fuck man who had already had his cock inside of her once.

"What are you thinking about?" Roman inquired, his gaze running over her face hotly.

"Paint colors," Angela replied, slightly panicked.

Roman's lips twitched. "Paint?"

"That's right," she confirmed with more confidence. It wasn't as though he could read her mind, after all. "What is this color? It's lovely."

Roman followed her gaze to the wall of the gym. "I believe it's called white. And this one," he pointed to the wall near the weights. "It's called black."

"Ass," she muttered, walking away from him. His amused chuckle followed her.

"Like I said, this is the private gym. But the public one we just left offers self-defense lessons to the public. Salvatore teaches them, along with Morrigan and a few others."

Angela turned to him, surprised. "Really?"

"Yes. Our women's class is on a Monday night if you're interested. No charge, of course."

"Maybe. Thank you," she said.

Roman gasped, stumbling back a step. "Did you just *thank* me?"

"Don't let it go to your head. Besides, I'm already well versed in self-defense, so I probably won't come. Though, I could always use a refresher," she conceded.

"You know martial arts?" Roman asked in surprise. "What kind?"

"Krav Maga," Angela admitted after a moment of hesitation.

His eyes widened in shock, and he gave a low whistle. "Krav Maga is no joke. No wonder you were able to get one over on Abel a few times."

She shrugged, feeling a little embarrassed for some reason. But also prideful. "There was a time when I needed to feel powerful. That I needed to feel like a warrior. Krav Maga seemed liked a good way to achieve that."

"And did you succeed?" Roman wanted to know.

"Sometimes I think so," Angela admitted. She studied herself in the wall of mirrors across from them. She was dressed in jeggings and a simple top, her hair bundled on top of her head. She wore no make-up or jewelry, but thought she looked strong at that moment. Still, she revealed, "Other times I'm not so sure."

"Let's find out."

Her eyes flew to his in the mirror. "Excuse me?"

"Spar with me," he clarified.

Angela watched him remove his suit jacket, unbutton his crisp white shirt and peel it off his muscled shoulders until he stood in just a black under-shirt. He kicked off his black dress shoes before she managed to shake herself out of her stupor. "Roman, I'm not sparring with you."

He raised his dark eyebrows, yanking his socks off. "Afraid you'll lose?"

Only my self-control, she thought, staring at his feet. The man even had sexy feet. It should be illegal. "Roman, I'm not fighting you," she repeated.

He only grinned and lunged at her. Angela darted to the side, dodging him easily. Or so she thought. Roman grabbed onto her blouse and yanked her against his chest. Her back was flush with his front within seconds, and she was breathing hard. She also felt more alive than she had in a long time. "You fight dirty, I see," she remarked. "I wasn't ready."

"Is there such a thing as *not* fighting dirty?" Roman inquired, running his nose up the back of her neck.

Angela shivered, tilting her head without thought. "I don't happen to think so," she replied softly.

"Yet another thing we agree on," Roman murmured.

She felt his lips press against the top of her spine and decided she had to do something before it was too late. She reached up slowly, feigning acquiescence, wrapping her arm around his head and exposing her breast to his now wandering hands. Then she got a good grip on his hair and pulled with all her might. When he roared and dropped his arms, she jumped free. They stood staring at each other for a moment before they both grinned. The thing she liked the most about Krav Maga was that there were no rules. It was essentially MMA fighting but the honorable part of it didn't apply.

"I'd say that's one point each," Roman admitted with a dip of his head.

Angela agreed. He didn't say anything further and made no move to grab her again. Now that the element of surprise was gone, he was waiting for her to make the first move. It wasn't a shock. He was a tactician, a strategist. She recognized it in him the same way she did in herself. She decided to humor him to get the ordeal over with. She rushed him, wrapping her arms around his knees and toppling him to the ground. She straddled his waist while he was still in a state of shock and gouged his eyes with her thumbs. She didn't do it for real but added enough pressure for him to feel it.

"Ow! Fuck!" Roman yelled.

Angela eased up on his eyes, watching them slowly blink open. They really were such a lovely caramel color, she mused. Roman went lax beneath her, his hands dropping to the mats.

"You win," he announced. "I yield. Time to have your wicked way with me. My safe word is stegosaurus."

Angela sputtered out a laugh. "Stegosaurus?"

"It's always been my favorite dinosaur," Roman informed her, looking like the cat that ate the cream.

And no wonder, she thought. She was sitting on him. "That's fascinating. But you won't be needing a safe word." She went to get off, but his hands quickly went to her hips to stop her.

"Do *you* need one?" his voice rumbled in his chest.

Angela stiffened, losing her playfulness. "I'm not into bondage."

Roman immediately loosened his hold, smoothing his hands over her thighs so she no longer felt trapped or threatened. She tried very hard not to melt. She got up, using a knee to his ribs to boost herself up. It was petty, but his pain-filled groan made her smile once again, so it was worth it.

"Not even if you're the one doing the binding?" Roman inquired from his place on the mats.

Angela was immediately assaulted by visions of Roman bound in red silk . . . and nothing else. She shook her head, dislodging such thoughts. She was there to earn money for the resource center. Not to get her rocks off or explore her kinks. "Not even," she eventually replied.

"Pity," he said, rolling swiftly to his feet.

She moved away from him, hoping he read the room right and didn't try to spar with her again.

Roman regarded her for a long moment, his face softening for some inexplicable reason. "Come on," he urged. "I'll show you the security hub. Luca's office is on the same level. He'll have your passes and security codes organized by now."

She nodded, telling herself she wasn't bitterly disappointed when he put his shoes and shirt back on.

CHAPTER TEN

Kicking off her shoes, Angela made her way from her front door to her couch. She bypassed sitting and went straight to face-planting instead.

It had been a long twelve hours, with ten of those having been in surgery on her feet as she tried to repair a heart nicked by a bullet. She wasn't sure if the teenager would make it through the night. And she knew *she* wasn't going to make it much longer if she didn't get some rest herself. So, she had forced herself from his bedside and his praying parents and made her way home.

She told herself she should get changed, maybe wash her face, and have something to eat. But she just didn't have the energy. So, she simply closed her eyes, ignoring the few spots of blood on her socks as she tucked her feet up. Thankfully, she fell into a dreamless sleep . . . until the ringing of her cell phone woke her up.

She bolted upright, her heart pounding as she fished for it between the couch cushions. Thinking it was the hospital, she answered as she stood up and began looking for her keys. "Dr. Hawthorne speaking."

"Angel, I need your help."

Angela stopped her frantic movements, only for her heart to take off for a whole other reason. "Abel? What's wrong? Is it Roman?" She blurted out, cursing herself for sounding so worried. She didn't want him—or anyone else—to know how much she cared. Hell, *she* didn't want to know much she cared.

"It's not Roman," came Abel's quick reply. "I kidnapped someone."

Angela pulled the phone from her ear and scowled down at it. Here she was worried about Roman and his crime family, and Abel had gone and kidnapped someone again. "Goodbye, Abel." She hung up and tossed her cell onto the couch, shaking her head and grumbling to herself.

It rang again almost immediately. She considered not answering it, but she knew that wasn't the best way to deal with Abel and his friends. She sighed, annoyed with herself, even as she picked up the ringing device. The name flashing on the screen wasn't Abel, but *Roman*, and she cursed the way her body came alive just by the sight of his name. Which is why she was rather rude when she answered. "I'm not fucking interested, Roman. Find some other poor, unsuspecting doctor to embroil in your illegal activities."

"Hello to you too, Angel." Roman's smooth voice came through the speaker loud and clear. "You're already embroiled, and you know it," he informed her calmly. "Besides, Abel insists only *you* can help."

"Abel is misguided," Angela snapped back.

"Sometimes," Roman allowed. "But not this time. I agree with him. The woman he saw fit to steal off the streets had a panic attack. She passed out."

"A woman?" Angela practically screeched. "Abel went and kidnapped another woman? What the hell, Roman?!"

"I know. I'll be having words with him, I assure you," Roman promised darkly. "But in the meantime, will you please come and check on her? Abel is worried about her. Which means *I* am worried about her."

Angela had to give the man credit. He looked after his family. An injury to them was an injury to him. But then, that was the mafia for you. "And I'm supposed to care?" Angela finally replied. The sexy chuckle that came through the phone had her gritting her teeth and squeezing her legs together. She suspected the man could make her come with his voice alone. But she wasn't willing to test the theory, so she quickly reprimanded him. "It's not funny, Roman. Kidnapping is not a joke."

"I agree with you. That's not what I found amusing," Roman said. "It's you, Angel, who is so entertaining. Because we both know that you do indeed care. Abel is your new bestie, and you have coffee with Luca and Salvatore at least once a week. You're not fooling anyone."

Angela gasped. "Abel is *not* my bestie!"

The mere thought was ludicrous. So what if she and Abel shared a love of trashy reality TV and gourmet food? It wasn't her fault Roman had ordered his second-in-command to follow her around everywhere. She was merely making the best of the situation, that's all. And so what if she enjoyed a hot coffee and a quick bite with Luca and Sal? They were an adorable couple and easy to talk to. But it didn't mean she cared about any of them. At all. She saw to their medical needs for the money. Full stop.

"Uh-huh. Whatever you say," came Roman's dry reply. "Can you please come? It's been ten minutes, and she hasn't woken up."

Ten minutes was a decent amount of time to be

unconscious from a fainting spell, Angela thought. She chewed her lip for a moment, eyeing the medical bag she had dropped by her front door.

"You came when Abel got delirious from chickenpox," Roman reminded her.

"Of course, I came. I felt guilty for lying about his dick falling off," Angela replied briskly.

Two months earlier, Abel had called her in a panic, much the same as he had done just minutes ago. His beloved dick had sported spots, and his high fever had convinced him it was about to peel off—just as she had predicted. Sure, it was funny. And wonderful payback. But her darn doctor guilt had kicked in and she had rushed over to ensure it wasn't anything more sinister. It meant she had now seen Roman's dick *and* Abel's. And though Abel's cock was longer than Roman's, it did not spark the same amount of lust. She was still seeing Roman's cock with its silver jewelry in her dreams almost nightly. It pissed her off.

"It's not illegal to have chickenpox, though, Roman," she pointed out. "It *is* illegal to kidnap people. When we made our deal, it was for medical emergencies only. No crime shit." But she was already slipping her shoes back on. Her feet protested, and she cast a quick glance at the clock hanging on the wall in her living room. Two hours. She had been asleep for two hours, which apparently was not enough time for her soles to recover.

Deciding she would rather be comfortable than fashionable; she went with the soft purple slippers next to her work shoes instead. Her feet practically sighed when she slipped them on. She then picked up her bag and headed out the door.

"You're already on your way, aren't you, Angel?"

Roman's voice was soft, almost a purr, igniting the desire that was always lying dormant in her system where the crime lord was concerned. But it was the smug tone that had her hanging up without responding. "Damn sexy, know-it-all thug," she grumbled as she made her way down the stairs in her building and to her car.

The trip took all of ten minutes. She lived ridiculously close to the Omertà building—another source of annoyance to her. Because it meant Roman was *always* close. It was knowledge she could have done without. Especially since her sex drive was up and running again. She went through periods of time when sex was more of an inconvenience than anything else. She was busy and tired, and the last thing she wanted was to get naked with someone. She didn't resent the dry spells. On the contrary, she was grateful for them. Sometimes, sex was just more trouble than it was worth.

But then, there were other times when she felt the need to bang her stress out on some willing, random male. They were always random because she had a thing about intimacy. She had no desire to get to know the men she screwed. She considered it therapy—a coping mechanism for a shitty day at work. It had nothing to do with getting to know someone or making a commitment. Not that she'd so much as entertained the idea of sex with anyone in the past three months. At least, not with anyone whose name wasn't *Roman* anyway.

The past two months since agreeing to Roman's proposition had flown by. It had also gone rather smoothly. She really wasn't needed that often, and only for minor things. Nothing like when Luca was injured, which she was grateful for. Still, Roman was true to his word, paying her exorbitantly whenever she provided medical assistance at Omertà.

Ten stitches to one of his employees netted her twenty thousand dollars, and a concussion diagnosis garnered her ten thousand. The money went directly to the Lighthouse and Sister Philomena. Roman and Luca set up a direct deposit system. Angela didn't question it and wasn't privy to the specifics. They had liaised directly with Sister Pip, who assured Angela the money was being received and everything was above board. That was all she cared about.

She used her pass to gain access to the underground parking garage and quickly parked in her reserved spot. It was right next to the elevator. She used the same pass to get her up to the fiftieth floor where the medical suite was. She nodded her head, smiling politely at familiar faces as she passed, marveling at the turn her life had taken since that fateful night three months ago. The shelter was thriving, with new repairs happening daily, and Angela was happier than she had been in a long time. She chose not to look into that fact too deeply.

She entered the clinic, where Roman was waiting for her. Her heart gave a curious thump and her stomach lurched. She chose not to investigate that either.

"Thank you for coming, Angel," Roman greeted her.

"Don't thank me yet, Roman," she warned. "And will you quit calling me Angel?" The complaint was more habit than anything else now. He, along with everyone else at Omertà, had called her Angel for the past few months. No matter what she did or said, they wouldn't be swayed. She rolled with it most of the time. But with Roman, she still put up a token fight.

"But it suits you," he insisted, smiling winningly.

Angela scoffed. "I'm no angel."

"I beg to differ. You saved my brother. You help strangers every day. You donate your time and expertise. You put up with my crazy family." Roman used his fingers to tick off his list.

"Because I'm forced to," she immediately declared.

Roman chuckled and shook his head. "Keep telling yourself that. Just know that when you're ready, I'll be here."

She frowned. "Ready for what?"

"You know what," Roman all but growled.

Angela clenched her jaw, looking away. She was very afraid she *did* know what he was talking about. She also knew she would never be ready for him. She would never be able to accept him or the things he did. Not with her history. He was a bad person. She needed a good person—if only to balance herself out. "Where is the poor woman Abel assaulted?" she asked, ignoring his previous statement.

"Abel didn't touch a hair on her head—other than to toss her over his shoulder and put her in his car," Roman vowed. "She's in room number two."

Angela moved off without further ado, aware of Roman's presence as he followed closely behind. She didn't waste her breath telling him to stay outside. She had learned how invested he was in his people. She found Abel looking a little frantic—an unusual thing for him. He was pacing at the foot of the hospital-grade bed, muttering to himself.

"Abel," she said. He turned to her, and the look of relief on his face did wonderful things for her ego. "Tell me," she ordered, already moving to check on the unconscious woman.

"She won't wake up," Abel said, wringing his hands. "I didn't hurt her. I swear!"

Angela took a moment to reach over and grab Abel's hands in her own. "Hey, I believe you. Okay? Take a deep breath and start at the beginning."

He followed her instructions, giving her hands a squeeze in thanks before dropping them. "I had just dropped off some merchandise at the docks when I heard a scuffle and a woman scream. I ran behind a dumpster and found some bastard trying to mug her." He gestured to the woman. "I pulled him off and beat him to a pulp—which is about when she started screaming at *me* instead of him."

Angela didn't scold him because he looked so damn sheepish. And also because, technically, he had done a good deed by saving the woman. "Do you know her name? Did she hit her head when she fell?"

"Her license says her name is Claire," Abel replied. "And she didn't hit her head. I caught her. When she started screaming like a banshee, I spun around. Some blood from my hands flew off and hit her on the face. She looked horrified. Angel, I've never seen anyone go so white before. Her eyes literally rolled to the back of her head and she keeled over. I jumped and grabbed her before she landed on the concrete though."

"I guess that explains the dried blood on her face," Angela muttered, taking vitals.

The woman's blood pressure was low, but not dangerously so, and her heart rate was within normal limits. Angela shone a light into her eyes, noting normal pupillary responses in both. She then pinched the skin on the back of the woman's hand, counting how long it took for the color to return. She was definitely dehydrated. Placing a pulse oximeter on the woman's right forefinger, she discovered her blood oxygen levels lower than she'd like. She quickly went about removing the woman's shoes, and tucking pillows beneath her knees and feet so they would be above her heart. She then moved to the cabinet to find some smelling salts. It wasn't her preferred method of waking someone up from syncope, but it was effective.

Moving back to the bed, she grabbed a face mask with some oxygen and paused to explain the situation to a hovering Abel and Roman. "Her blood pressure and oxygen levels are low, and she appears to be dehydrated.

I'm going to wake her up before I give her some oxygen and the option for some IV fluids. Fainting is typically short in duration. It's been close to thirty minutes now, so I'm inclined to think something else is causing it." She looked at Abel drolly. "More than just having blood flung at her."

"It was an accident," Abel swiftly defended himself. "How was I supposed to know she'd be so fucking dainty?"

Angela shook her head, but she was smiling. Abel was kind of like a cross between a Labrador and a wolf. He was cute and dopey for the most part, but also dangerous when in his natural environment. It was a combination that she found rather endearing after three solid months of exposure to him. "Most women— and men, for that matter—don't like witnessing violence. You said you beat her attacker to a pulp. Then you threw that pulp on her face."

Abel scowled down at her. "It sounds bad when you say it like that."

"I'm going to wake her up," Angela said. There was no point belaboring the issue. Abel would never get it. "Would you mind stepping back, please? I'd like her to just see me at first." Abel dutifully moved back, standing next to the door with a silent Roman.

She got the salts and held them under her patient's

nose. The woman gasped almost immediately, her eyes fluttering open. "Claire, can you hear me? My name is Dr. Angela Hawthorne. You're safe. Do you understand? You're safe."

She always made it a priority to reassure her patients that they were safe whenever they had been in a violent situation. Claire's eyes proved to be hazel—and very bloodshot. She bolted upright, a look of panic on her face. "Easy now, Claire. You're safe," Angela repeated.

"Where am I? What happened?" Claire asked, looking around frantically. Her eyes landed on Abel and she screamed. Loud.

"Shit!" Abel exclaimed.

"Christ, woman, will you keep it down?" Roman shouted with a wince. "Didn't you hear Angel? You're safe. Nobody is going to hurt you."

Claire's shrill scream broke off, and she stared at Roman with her mouth open. Angela couldn't blame her. Roman was looking particularly dashing in a dark blue suit and light blue button-up shirt. He rarely wore ties, but he had one on this afternoon in a deep burgundy. Either he no longer needed it, or he had only just put it on, because it was hanging loose around his neck. His top two buttons were also undone, completing the look. *And what a look it is,* Angela mused silently.

She shook off the inappropriate thought, giving Claire her entire focus. "Claire, I'm Dr. Angela Hawthorne. You're in a private medical facility. You lost consciousness for quite a while. Has anything like this ever happened to you before?"

Claire looked at Angela straight on. She was very pretty and also appeared very young. Her hazel eyes were bloodshot, with dark smudges beneath them. She had a tiny frame and would likely be much shorter than Angela. Her light-brown hair was short in a pixie cut, and she was wearing scrubs, though not from any of the hospitals Angela knew.

Angela smiled at her, hoping to reassure her. "I'm going to give you a bit of oxygen through this mask, okay? And I'd like to check your blood pressure again while you talk to me." She was glad when Claire licked her lips and nodded her head.

She still didn't speak and Angela didn't rush her. She went about administering some basic first aid with the oxygen, pleased when Claire's blood pressure and oxygen levels rose. "You're dehydrated—which can also cause fainting spells. I'd like to hook you up to some fluids. It will help you feel better."

"I . . ." Claire finally spoke in a raspy voice. "I don't

think I drank anything today at all. Maybe I could just have some water instead of a needle?"

"You don't like needles, huh?" Angela smiled, leaning in closer and winking. "That's a shame. Needles are my specialty. But we'll try it your way. Abel, would you mind getting Claire some water, please?"

When Abel moved to follow Angela's instructions, Claire's eyes fell on him once more. She scooted back on the bed when Abel held out the glass to her, staring at it like it was a snake. Poor Abel looked like he'd just discovered Santa wasn't real. "It's just water," he said gruffly.

Claire eventually reached out a shaky hand, taking the glass. She sipped it slowly, murmuring a small thank you. "You were the one who hit Robert."

"The guy assaulting you?" Abel questioned. "You know him?"

Claire nodded. "He's my boyfriend."

Angela saw the way Abel's fists clenched and heard Roman's soft curse in Italian. Or it could have been Sicilian. He interchanged the two languages often. She shot them both a look, urging them to simmer down, before stepping into Claire's line of sight and blocking the males from view. "Your boyfriend? He's abusive?"

"No," Claire said swiftly. She recoiled, ducking her

head. "Force of habit. I mean, yes. Yes, he is. Which is why I left him. I should have said *ex*-boyfriend."

"You dumped his sorry ass? Good," Abel snarled.

Claire flinched, and Angela cleared her throat. "Perhaps you and Roman could step outside?"

Before Abel could reply, Roman did instead. "Sorry. No dice. We don't know her. You aren't staying in here alone. We stay."

Angela was about to tell Roman what she thought about that when Claire spoke up. "It's okay. They can stay. Because *I'm* leaving." She looked at Abel. "Thank you for saving me. Robert didn't take well to me breaking up with him." She slid off the bed, looking at her socked feet. "Where are my shoes?"

"Claire, I would really like you to stay a little longer. You were unconscious for a long time. Are you hurt anywhere I can't see?" Angela asked quietly.

Claire shook her head. "I'm not hurt. But I haven't been sleeping much," she confessed.

"So, no water, no sleep, and lots of stress? Yep, that would explain your long nap," Angela said lightly before turning serious. "Claire, my medical opinion is that you're on the verge of exhaustion. And you've had a big scare today. I'd advise you to rest here for longer before I take you to the police station."

Claire's eyes widened. "The police? What for?"

"Because you were assaulted," Angela stated simply.

"I'm not pressing charges," Claire said quickly.

"Yeah, no point in that," Abel agreed. "I'll just go kill the guy. I think he was still breathing when I left. But that's easily fixed."

Angela closed her eyes, praying for patience. Poor Claire looked about ready to collapse again. "He doesn't mean it," Angela offered.

"Like hell, I don't," Abel growled.

Angela glared at him, mouthing, *"Shut up."* The last thing the poor woman needed was Abel plotting murder.

"I want to leave. Now," Claire insisted.

Before Angela could try to convince her to stay, Claire edged past the two men, not bothering with her shoes. When she opened the door, she came to a standstill. There were two men blocking her path. Angela frowned at Roman, who merely shrugged.

"She's an unknown. Security is necessary," he offered.

Angela sighed, moving closer to Claire. She had been correct: the younger woman stood about eight inches shorter than her. She was hobbit sized. "Claire, your ex is clearly a risk to you. Let me help."

"No one can help," Claire said, looking defeated. "I

broke up with Robert *six* months ago. He's been stalking me ever since. But he's stepped up his game lately. He got me fired from my vet nursing job today, and my landlord kicked me out last week—thanks to Robert. I'm not safe anywhere."

"You'd be safe here," Angela stated. She closed her mouth with a snap. She hadn't meant to say that but couldn't deny it was true. Thankfully, Roman didn't correct her, though she could feel his gaze boring into her back.

Claire faced her, looking hesitant. "Where is *here* exactly?"

"The Omertà complex in Civic," Angela replied. "You said your landlord kicked you out. Where are you staying?"

"I've been staying on a friend's couch," Claire said, looking embarrassed. "I paid her. But now that I have no job . . ."

"You're not going anywhere," Abel declared. "I'll hunt down Robert and tell you when it's safe to leave."

Angela wanted to throttle him. She could appreciate the sentiment—men who hit women were low on her list of people to save—but she didn't think Claire needed to be subjected to Abel's bloodthirsty ways. "Do you want to stay here?" she asked. When Claire looked at Abel and Roman apprehensively, Angela said, "Don't worry about them. If you want to walk out of here, you can."

"No. She can't," Abel snarled.

She shot him a dark look. "Was I talking to you, Abel?" When no reply was forthcoming, she raised an imperious brow. "Well? Was I?"

"No," Abel ground out, hands fisted at his sides once more.

"That's right. I was talking to Claire." She turned back to the wide-eyed woman. "Ignore them." She gestured to the two armed men at the door and the other two in the room. "They all know you can walk out of here with me if you want to."

"Uh, no she can't," Roman spoke up.

Angela ignored him. "I know you don't know me. And I know this is the last place you thought you would be when you woke up today. I've been there, trust me," she added. "But you can take some time to rest. To heal. To formulate a plan. Then you can go back into the big bad world."

Claire looked like she wanted to cry, but she sucked it up like a boss. "Would I truly be safe here?" she whispered.

Angela placed a comforting hand on her thin shoulder. "Claire, you would be safer here, with these men, than any other place on the planet."

Claire let out a shaky breath. "Okay. I'll stay."

Angela squeezed her shoulder gently. "Good choice. Now, come on. I'll do another medical check and then I'll let Roman here set you up with a room—or six."

The small chuckle that escaped Claire's lips had Angela's tense muscles relaxing in her back. As well as her stomach. She hadn't been aware of how anxious she was until that moment. She wanted the young woman to be safe. If she had demanded to go, Angela would have kept her word and led her straight down to her car. Then she would have taken her to Sister Pip at Lighthouse. But Roman's building was much safer.

It surprised her how much of an easy admission that was. And how much she believed it.

CHAPTER ELEVEN

It took four hours for Claire to get settled into a guest suite on the fifty-fifth floor. Angela knew that all the residential quarters were from floor fifty-five to fifty-nine. Claire wouldn't have access to nearly all the floors like Angela did, but Robert getting in would be all but impossible.

"Thank you for doing this," Angela said gratefully to Roman as they walked down the hallway in the direction of the elevator.

"I didn't exactly get a choice," Roman pointed out. "But you—and she—are welcome."

Angela blushed. She *had* kind of steamrollered over him. "I guess I should apologize. I'm so used to making decisions in the operating room and having my instructions followed. But I know this is your home. I should have asked first."

Roman hummed. "It's fine. In fact, if you hadn't convinced her to stay, I would have." He shrugged. "She seems like a nice girl in a shitty situation. And it's not like I don't have the space."

"She's twenty-one," Angela said, Claire having told her earlier. "Hardly a girl."

"That's one year younger than Luca. And he's practically still a kid," Roman stated.

Angela's lips twitched. "A kid? He's sleeping with one of your best friends," she said, enjoying his disgruntled look.

Roman shuddered theatrically. "Don't remind me."

Angela laughed. "Luca seems happy to have Claire around for a while anyway." He had stayed with Claire in her new suite of rooms when the rest of them had all left. Salvatore was still there too, of course. But Luca's presence had put Claire at ease even more than Angela's had. "I'll talk to Sister Pip about finding Claire more permanent housing tomorrow."

"Don't rush on my account. She's such a little thing. It's not like she'll be in the way. Besides, Abel will need some time to deal with that Robert character." Roman's face twisted into a sneer.

"I don't want to know about it," Angela told him. "Plausible deniability."

"Look at you, getting the hang of the crime business," Roman teased, grinning.

Angela didn't respond, but she was smiling on the inside. When she had first agreed to be Roman's private doctor, she tried to keep ignoring him. But it was extremely difficult when he made it his mission to be around whenever she was. Even if it had nothing to do with him, he was still there. He could be chatting with his guards, working on his tablet, talking on his phone. She had even seen him reading a book a few times. He had kept his word, not talking about the time he had impaled her with his lovely cock. But that didn't stop Angela from feeling the sexual tension between them. It was thick enough to cut with a knife.

She shook those thoughts off, as always. "Well, I'm heading home," Angela said, pressing the button on the elevator.

"Do you want me to arrange for a driver for you?" Roman offered. "I know you had a long shift last night, and you've been here for hours now." He waved the guard walking behind them over. "Lenny can do it."

Her lips thinned as she took in the other man. He didn't look pleased with the prospect of playing cab driver. "That's not necessary. I'm fine," she promised.

"I'm not working tonight at all. Plenty of time for plenty of rest."

Roman was about to argue—she could tell by the look on his face. But his cell rang. He looked at it, his face shutting down. It was amazing how he could do that. Go from an open, charming man to a cold, blank canvas. "I have to take this," he said.

"Of course. Call me if Claire needs anything."

Roman nodded and walked off in the opposite direction, already answering the call. She watched him, wondering what it was about. And promptly felt annoyed for wondering. Roman and his calls were none of her business.

She stepped into the elevator, lost in her thoughts. She hoped Claire had a chance to recover, in more ways than one. Her plight hit rather close to home; Angela knew she would do anything she could to help keep her safe. When the back of her neck itched, she looked up, realizing with a jolt that Lenny had stepped into the elevator behind her. She could see his reflection in the shiny door. His expression was sour. She glanced at the descending digits: forty. The elevator suddenly felt like it was moving at a snail's pace.

"You're taking too many liberties," the man said abruptly.

"Excuse me?" Angela turned around, not liking him at her back.

"You heard me," he grunted, an annoyed look on his face. "The way you spoke to Roman earlier. Who do you think you are? You're not *famiglia*. You have no say here, bitch. Yet you were ordering him around like it's your right."

Angela's eyes narrowed. Lenny had been one of the guards outside the medical suite. He clearly didn't like her vocabulary choice. She raised her chin and planted her feet. "I didn't hear Roman complaining. And that's Dr. Bitch to you."

Lenny snorted in derision. "Of course, he didn't complain. Everyone knows he wants to get in your pants. He's a patient guy. He can put up with that mouth of yours until it's wrapped around his dick."

Angela saw they were just passing floor twenty. She hoped she could keep him talking until the elevator doors opened but could tell that wouldn't be the case when he stepped forward, invading her personal space. Instead of moving back, she held her ground. The act of defiance seemed to piss him off even more. She had no idea what his issue was. Roman didn't need anyone, least of all this sorry excuse for a man, to stand up for him.

"You really think an outsider like you can tell

Roman whom he can and can't have in his home? You disrespectful cunt," Lenny snarled. "I think it's time someone brought you down to size."

He grabbed her arm, and she allowed it so she could get close enough to inflict some damage in the confined space. Only five floors to go. "Back off."

"Or what?" Lenny sneered.

"Or I'll drop you," Angela promised. And she meant it. This was the first time she'd had any trouble with one of Roman's employees. She had meant what she said to Claire; Omertà was one of the safest places to be in Monash. But perhaps she had spoken too soon about *all* of the people in it. She didn't doubt Abel or Salvatore or even Roman. But this guy—Lenny—was looking at her like he was about to choose violence.

When he squeezed her arm to the point of pain, Angela brought her knee up with all of her strength, smashing his balls. Lenny's scream was quickly cut off when she jabbed him in the throat. He fell to the ground, and she stepped over him. Not bothering to do or say anything further. She was shaking a little and wanted to get the hell out.

Later, she vowed, she would call Roman and tell him he had a schmuck working for him. That is, if he didn't already know.

CHAPTER TWELVE

Roman fisted his cock, working it roughly from base to tip. He groaned from the pleasure-pain of it. It wasn't the same as having Angel's pussy wrapped around him, but it would get the job done.

He was locked in the private bathroom of his personal office. After taking the call from a prospective new associate, he had hastened to his office on the fifty-second floor. It was where he conducted his shadier business dealings. It afforded more privacy than his more accessible office on floor thirty.

And that was important when he was masturbating to thoughts of Angel telling people she believed his home was one of the safest places in the world. That she believed *he* was one of the safest places in the world. It should have been laughable. And had anyone else said it, he would have refuted it. But because it was Angel, he'd had a semi for the past four hours.

Hence why he was now Lone Rangering it in his bathroom.

Over the last two months, he had seen Angel a handful of times when she visited for various medical reasons. He'd seen her that many times again when she hung out with Luca or Sal. Or even Abel once or twice. She had thawed a little towards him, and he could see them making progress toward a civil relationship. It wasn't a friendship, but she didn't try to bite his head off every time she saw him anymore, either. He made it a point to be near her whenever she was around. Call it exposure therapy. Because he was convinced she was the one person who could fill his dark days with light.

He had an inkling the moment he held a gun to her head that she was special. And it became clear *why* over the last few months. It was because she was his. She didn't know it yet. Hell, she was actively fighting against their mutual attraction. But he had faith that one day she wouldn't. Until then, he would do what he needed to do to prove he was worthy of her. He couldn't change who he was; it was too deeply ingrained. But he could change some of his behaviors. There was a difference.

The only time he stayed away from her was when he ended up with chickenpox as well. He was so insulated as a child that he never got the virus, just like Abel. It took him two weeks to get over it. And, to his horror, Abel wasn't the only one who ended up with spots on his dick. Ordering his second-in-command to inspect his cock piercings to make sure they weren't infected hadn't been the proudest moment of his life. He had no desire for the holes to close up because he sure as hell wouldn't do it again. And given he knew what Angel's orgasm face was like, he was determined to put the metal bars to good use in the future.

In the end, Abel steadfastly refused, and he was forced to get Salvatore to look instead. It was just as much of a nightmare, with Roman agreeing to buy Sal and Luca a private island for their wedding gift in exchange for playing nursemaid. Thankfully, it wasn't infected, and his magic cross remained in place. There was just a giant blister covering it. It had hurt and itched so badly that he was worried he was going to scratch his dick off. But there was no way he was going to allow Angel to see it in that state. His peen had a reputation to uphold. So, he had slathered it in calamine lotion for a week and wondered why his dick looked so good in pink.

Speaking of his dick, it was tingling at the base and

steadily leaking precum at the tip. He squeezed it tighter, increasing the friction to the skin sliding beneath his slick hand. He jerked on it faster, the filthy sound echoing off the Italian glass tiles. He spread his legs as wide as his slacks would allow, reaching down to play with his sac. He groaned, his head falling forward to watch his hand move up and down. He'd always had a thing for watching, and his bedroom had huge mirrors installed as a result.

Pushing away from the counter, he watched his hand move in the mirror, the tip of his cock becoming red and the silver bars glinting in the low light. He pictured Angel on her knees in front of him with her pretty tits out and her mouth wide open. His dick kicked in his hand, cum spurting out onto the floor where his fantasy Angel was. He envisioned painting her with his seed, her hands rubbing it into her breasts as her greedy mouth drank him in and begged for more.

His orgasm went on, and he continued to stroke himself roughly, drawing out the pleasure. His chest rose and fell in time with his fast breaths and his forehead was dotted with sweat. He squeezed one last time, just beneath his piercing, wringing out the final drop of cum, which he smoothed over his crown. His legs were a little shaky and his dick felt over-sensitized, but overall, he felt damn good.

"If you're done jacking off, Sal and I need to talk to you." Luca's voice came through the locked door loud and clear.

"Fucking hell!" He couldn't even enjoy a private jerk session without someone wanting something.

He looked around for a hand towel or a tissue, coming up empty. Probably because he had used them up the last time he flogged himself to images of Angel. He yanked a drawer open, yelling when it came out all the way and landed on his foot. Luckily, he still had his shoes on.

"Are you okay in there?" Salvatore shouted, banging once on the door. "Did you rip your dick off? What did my mother always tell us? Your cock is not a toy."

"Fuck off!" Roman yelled back. He could hear the pair of assholes laughing as he finally found a pack of wet wipes and cleaned the cum off his hands and cock. He quickly zipped and buttoned up, moving closer to the sink now that he wasn't at risk of breaking his neck from his pants. He scrubbed his hands and then splashed cold water on his face. He was feeling flushed.

He made quick work of the mess on the floor before unlocking the door and flinging it wide. "What do you fuckers want?" was how Roman greeted two of his most favorite people in the world.

"Enjoy yourself?" Sal asked, grinning like an idiot.

"As a matter of fact, I did. You see, I do this thing where . . ." Roman broke off with an evil grin when both men blocked their ears and started singing loudly. He thought it was a little hypocritical of Salvatore, given all the porn they had watched together as teens. Discovering he liked men, or rather, Luca, had been a late-in-life surprise.

"Ugh! I don't want to hear what yanks your crank," Luca groused, looking disgusted.

"We already know," Sal pointed out. "Himself."

Roman shoved his friend. Hard. "Get fucked."

"I have been. Just this morning. Good and proper," Sal replied, looking satisfied.

Now it was Roman's turn to pretend ignorance. He didn't want the details of Luca's sex life. But he was glad his brother was able to have one. He guessed he owed Sal for that. Walking to the galley-style kitchenette on the far wall, he grabbed a bottle of water from the mini refrigerator. "If you're all quite done judging me, tell me why you're here. It's getting late."

It was just after five in the evening, and he wanted to go home. "Is it Claire?"

"She's fine," Luca said. "Really sweet, as a matter of fact. I'm glad she's here. She's had a rough time. You're going to help her, aren't you?"

Roman drank half the water, regarding his brother for a moment. "Are you okay with her being here?"

Luca frowned. "Why wouldn't I be?"

"I don't want her presence to bring up bad memories," Roman clarified gently.

Luca smiled and shook his head. He walked over and hugged Roman. He was an affectionate guy with those he loved. "You're sweet, Roman. But it's fine. I'd rather have her here than not. I'm going to look into that Robert douchebag. He sounds dangerous."

"I'm not sweet," Roman immediately refuted.

"You keep telling yourself that," Luca advised. "Because nobody else here believes it."

Roman didn't argue further. It would do no good. Luca was the stubbornest of them. And that was saying a lot. As long as she didn't cause trouble for his family or his businesses, Roman didn't care that Claire was staying. It wouldn't be the first person in trouble he had housed. And if Abel decided to ignore everyone and clip the ex, it wouldn't be anything new either.

"We're here about Lenny and Dane," Sal said, looking grim.

Lenny and Dane were two of his crew. Or, maybe more accurately, *cugine*. They were young and full of gusto, and wanting to be made. Roman was convinced they had it in them. "What about them?"

"They've been bragging about going to Bertha's," Luca replied, walking back over to Sal.

"And?" Bertha's was a popular brothel, just on the outskirts of the city. Roman used the establishment frequently for business meetings. Many of his colleagues and clients liked to mix business with pleasure, and Bonnie, the madam, was a discreet woman. She had been a lover of his many years ago, and when she told him of her aspirations to own her own brothel —one that was run *by* women and *for* the women who worked there—he was happy to become a silent partner and give her the start-up costs.

"They've been bragging about getting down and dirty. Beating on the women when it's not a BDSM thing," Salvatore informed him.

"What?!" Roman yelled, reaching for his cell. "Bonnie hasn't said anything."

"She hasn't called us either," Luca confirmed, gesturing at Sal. "But Lenny and Dane are being pretty vocal about it."

"And descriptive," Sal added with a frown. "There's a chance they could be talking themselves up, but just in case..."

"Absolutely. You know I don't condone that shit," Roman growled, thumbing through his contacts.

"We know," Luca and Sal answered simultaneously.

Roman called Bonnie's direct number, wasting no time in asking her if there was any truth to the allegations. She confirmed that there was. In fact, she was in the hospital with one of her girls now.

"I was planning to call you, Roman," Bonnie said from the cell. "But things have been hectic. I wanted to get Crystal sorted out first. I'm sorry."

"Of course you did. You've done nothing wrong. I am the one who is sorry. Rest assured, the men will be dealt with." He spoke with her for another few minutes before hanging up. He immediately made his way to the door. "Sal, contact Abel. Tell him I want him in the security room. I'm going to find where Lenny and Dane are."

"Done," Sal said, already on his cell.

Luca and Salvatore accompanied him in the elevator, and when the doors opened a few floors down, Abel was waiting for them. "What have those idiots done now?" he questioned.

Sal filled Abel in as they filed into the main security room. "Teague, I need you to find Lenny and Dane. Now."

Teague snapped to it, pressing buttons and pulling up video feeds. "I know where Lenny is. I figured you'd want me to keep an eye on him. Who told you?"

Roman frowned at him. "What do you mean?"

"You want Lenny because of what he did to Dr. Hawthorne, right?" Teague asked, looking confused.

The blood in Roman's veins turn to ice. "What are you talking about?"

Teague looked around at all of them. "He pulled some shit with her in the elevator. I saw it on the security feed about an hour ago. She handled herself just fine, but I knew you'd want to deal with him."

"Show me the footage," Roman demanded. "Now!"

He couldn't hear what was being said, but he saw Lenny grab Angel hard enough to make her wince in pain. She proved herself to be the badass she was once again, but Roman was not appeased. At all. "Get me Lenny right fucking now!" he fumed. "And Dane. Take them to the pit and round up the crew. It's example time."

He stalked from the room, rage making it hard for him to see straight. He went directly to the top floor, staring out at the city as his people filed into the open space known as the pit. They murmured quietly, but no one approached him. Only when he heard Lenny demanding to know what was going on did he turn around.

He watched Abel drag Lenny by the arm and toss him into the center of the room. Sal did the same for Dane. Luca was not with them. This wasn't his scene.

"You done fucked up," Abel told the two men, glaring at Lenny with malice.

"Huh?" Lenny gaped around the room, jumping to his feet. His eyes landed on Roman. "Boss! What's the deal?"

"The deal is that you've been touching things you shouldn't be," Roman growled, prowling closer.

"No, boss. I ain't touched nothin'. I'd never steal from you," Dane said, looking like he was about to piss his pants.

"I didn't say anything about stealing. Bertha's," Roman stated. He would start there, otherwise he was likely to put a cap in Lenny's ass in a fit of anger.

Dane's eyes widened, and he looked at Lenny. He lowered his gaze, his face turning pale. It said a lot about how he felt, and the shame-faced reaction had just saved his life. It wouldn't be enough to save him from receiving everything he doled out on Bertha's girls. Nor the banishment from his crew. But it would protect him from a dirt nap. Lenny, on the other hand, *smirked*. Roman lost his shit a little, backhanding the little fucker without a word.

Lenny went flying, landing on his back. Blood sprayed from his nose, and he spat out more of the red stuff when he sat up. "The fuck?" He gaped up at Roman.

"The women at Bertha's are under my protection," Roman snarled, his hand tingling.

"Bu-but they're whores," Lenny stuttered.

"And? What's your point?" Roman demanded, towering over the man.

"That's what they get paid for," Lenny answered, like a complete fuckwit.

Abel kicked him in the back, sending him sprawling once more. "You stupid fuck. You could have walked away from this. But not anymore."

Roman agreed. Lenny was already a walking dead man. His fate had been sealed the moment he touched Angel.

"What? You can't be serious? Over a cunt?" Lenny yelled, aghast.

"Not just any cunt," Salvatore intoned. "You also touched Dr. Hawthorne."

That caused murmuring to break out in the peanut gallery, plus several curses in multiple languages, and some spitting on the ground. Angel was well-liked and respected by many.

"I didn't. I would never," Dane promised frantically. He wasn't as stupid as he looked.

"You didn't," Roman agreed. "But that doesn't absolve you of your other sins." He whistled, and several men stepped forward. Roman nodded towards three of them at random. "The boys here are going to teach you a lesson in manners. After today, you'll know how to treat a woman right. And you'll never step foot in Omertà again."

Roman watched impassively as the three men beat Dane with their fists and feet. The man's pleas and eventual sobs fell on deaf ears. Lenny watched in growing horror, his predicament finally dawning on him. Roman only called a halt to the lesson when Dane passed out. Unconscious men couldn't feel pain. Then he turned to Lenny. "Did you like the show? Your ending won't be so happy, I'm afraid."

"Happy . . .?" Lenny repeated, watching as Dane was dragged away. The blood trail left in his wake was a stark message to everyone in the room.

"Tell me what you said to Angel that made her feel the need to break your balls," Roman demanded, loosening the cuffs on his shirt.

Lenny swallowed audibly. "Nothing. She overreacted."

At least he didn't try to lie about Angel beaning him in the nuts and throat, Roman thought silently.

"Is that right? She doesn't seem the type to overreact," Salvatore commented, circling Lenny.

"As someone who has been on the receiving end of her ire, I can attest that she chooses violence when she feels threatened," Abel said. He moved in closer, locking Lenny inside the three of them. He leaned in close to Lenny's face. "How did you threaten her?"

"I did it for you, boss. She disrespected you. She *always* disrespects you. I was just standing up for you." Lenny did his best to justify his actions.

"You did it for me? Because you're so loyal to me," Roman stated flatly.

Lenny nodded frantically. "Right."

"Then you'll have no problem doing me a favor," Roman pointed out. He pulled out one of his guns from his ankle holster. It was a small Diamondback DB9, but it was effective. "Shoot yourself in the head and save me the trouble."

Lenny's eyes widened, and he looked at the gun Roman held out. "What?"

"You heard me. Go ahead. Take it," Roman urged.

Lenny looked at him like he was crazy, making no move to accept the weapon. "I'd take the easy way out if I were you," Salvatore suggested. "The other way will be much messier."

"And much more painful," Abel added, cracking his knuckles.

"You're really going to kill me over some bitch? Is she that good of a lay?" Lenny added stupidly.

Roman lost it for a moment. The charming veneer

he donned on a daily basis so he could be civil, and a functioning member of society, sloughed away. He gripped Lenny by the hair and brought his knee up, smashing the man's nose against his kneecap. Lenny screamed, blood sprayed, and Roman pushed him away before kicking him in the ribs over and over. He paused to catch his breath, watching Lenny writhe on the ground.

Lenny groaned but managed to speak. Every word dug him into a deeper hole. "I've worked for you for three years! You'd kill me over a few words with a woman. She's—"

"MINE!" Roman yelled. "She's MINE! And *nobody* touches what is mine."

"Yours? But . . ." Lenny looked around, clearly seeking help, but none was forthcoming. In fact, the rest of Roman's employees had a hard time meeting the doomed man's eyes. "I didn't know. I swear I didn't know, boss. Since when? Fuck, *no one* knows. It ain't just me. But I'm sorry. I'm sorry, okay? I'll apologize. I'll make it right," he all but begged, gripping his broken ribs.

There was no making it right. Roman turned his back on the pathetic man, addressing the room. "Is this true? No one knows the doctor belongs to me? Do I have any other oblivious, idiotic people working for me?"

Nobody spoke. Nobody moved. "Let me be clear: Angela is mine. *My* woman. She is mine to protect. Mine to worship. And mine to fuck. Nobody touches her. Ever. Do I make myself clear?" He received silent, emphatic nods before he turned back to the man curled up on his side. "Now get up. You're embarrassing yourself."

Twenty minutes later, Roman dismissed his crew, save for a couple who volunteered to take Lenny's mutilated remains down to the incinerator. He'd had the huge burner installed when the building was first built. It was in the basement, with direct elevator access from the penthouse.

"I'm going to see Angel," Roman said, stalking to the door. He was still riled, so when Abel got in his way, he snarled at him. "Move!"

"I have no issue with you going to check on Angel, Roman. But maybe wash the blood off first, huh?" Abel suggested mildly, familiar with Roman's moods.

Roman looked down at his bruised knuckles and the blood splattered on his pale blue shirt. His *capo* had a point.

CHAPTER THIRTEEN

"Roman? What are you doing here?" Angel greeted him when she opened her front door. "Is it Claire? Does she need—"

He placed a stilling hand on Angela's shoulder when she started to walk around him. "She's fine, as far as I'm aware. She's a guest until she chooses not to be. That's not why I'm here. Are you okay?"

Angela looked confused. "Why wouldn't I be?" she asked, looking him over for the first time. Her mouth parted, and he heard her breath catch. "What are you wearing?"

Roman looked down at the old jeans and the gray long-sleeved Henley he was wearing. He shrugged, unsure why her reaction seemed almost . . . explicit. He did his best to use The Force on his dick, willing it to stay down. This wasn't about him. It was about Angel. "They're called jeans. And I'm here because of Lenny."

"Who is Lenny?" she asked, practically staring a hole through the denim at his crotch. "And since when do you wear jeans?"

"Lenny is the man who had the poor sense to put his hands on you," Roman told her. "And I wear jeans all the time. Just not when I have business dealings— which is most days during business hours." He stepped inside, closing the door behind him and crowding her a little. "But if I'd known a bit of denim would put that look on your face, I would have bought stock in Levi's weeks ago."

Her apple-green eyes flashed to his, and she licked her lips. He moved closer again, the tips of her breasts now brushing against his chest. Unfortunately, she snapped herself out of whatever daze she was in. "No," she said, her palm flattening against his chest. "We're not doing this."

"Not doing what?" he asked lowly.

"We're not having sex again," Angela replied, taking a single step back.

"We could," Roman pointed out. She had created some space between them. But not much.

Angela shook her head, taking another step back. "We're not."

Roman shoved his hands into his pockets to stop himself from reaching for her. "Ever heard of friends with benefits?"

"I don't do friends with benefits," Angel replied quickly.

"Why not?" he couldn't help asking. He wanted to know how she ticked.

"Because I don't have any friends." The words came out in a rush. She groaned in apparent embarrassment, covering her face. "Forget I said that."

The words hit him in the center of his chest, his lust backing off a bit. He reached out, toying with one of the thick waves of her hair, which was loose. It was rarely out. "You do have friends, Angel."

She rolled her eyes. "Your criminal family. Great."

He dropped his hand with a frown. "They are great," Roman stated quietly.

Angela was all kinds of frazzled from Roman's unexpected visit. And he was looking so damn good in his casual wear. She had never seen him in jeans before. It was probably a good thing because she may have cracked and agreed to more orgasms before now if she had. But being sexually bamboozled was hardly a good excuse for being rude. And the censure in Roman's eyes made her feel ashamed.

"Yes. They really are. I'm sorry." She was quick to apologize.

He sighed, moving further into the room and placing his wallet and keys on her kitchen island. "Have you considered that it's about time to embrace who you really are?"

The comment brought her up short. "What do you mean?"

"Each time you react like that and make those snarky, insulting little comments, you bury your true self deeper. Because they're not you. Not a true reflection of you, anyway," he declared. "You're not a cruel person. In fact, you could just be one of the kindest people I've ever met."

Angela turned away from him because his words hit her right in the feels. "The last time I was the real me, a lot of people died," she admitted after a long moment, her voice no more than a whisper.

"What a coincidence," Roman murmured, coming up behind her so close she could feel the heat from his body. "The last time *I* was the real me, a man died. Just an hour ago."

She spun around, finding his expression hard. "Lenny."

Roman nodded once. "That's right."

"Why?" She needed to know.

"Because he touched you," Roman replied simply.

Angela sighed, shaking her head. "You can't kill everyone who touches me, Roman."

He raised a single eyebrow. "Why not?"

"Because . . ." Her mind went blank because, truth was, knowing there was someone out there who wanted to slay dragons for her was a miracle. "You just can't."

Roman reached for her, pulling the sleeve of her shirt up. His eyes landed on the bruise from Lenny's fingers. "He hurt you."

Angela looked down at the discolored skin. It was very minor. "Hardly. It's just a bruise."

"No one hurts you," Roman all but growled.

Against her better judgment, Angela caved and let herself melt. She bowed her head, and it came to rest on his chest due to their close proximity. "Where were you twenty years ago when I needed a knight to save me?"

She didn't want Roman to know about her past, but the words slipped out before she could stop them. She was tired. She was also emotionally drained.

"I'm sorry I wasn't there," Roman said, stroking her head. "But I'm here now. And I'm not going anywhere."

She wanted to tell him to go—that she didn't want that. But it would have been a lie. A big one. So, she simply said nothing, allowing Roman to pull her in closer so she was flush against his chest, and he was hugging her. She snuggled in before she could stop herself. "Someone who killed a man today has no right being so snuggly," she told him grumpily.

Roman chuckled. "I think you're the first person to ever call me snuggly."

"Don't worry, I won't tell anyone," Angela assured him, her words coming out slightly muffled against his solid warmth.

"I appreciate that," he said, his hand trailing down the length of her hair to her waist. "And if it makes you feel any better, it wasn't just because of you. The bastard was also taking advantage of some women under my employ."

Angela pulled back far enough to see his face. "What do you mean?"

"Have you heard of Bertha's?"

She frowned. "You mean the brothel on the south side of the city?"

"That's the one," Roman confirmed. "I'm a silent owner. Lenny and another man, Dane, took certain liberties with the workers. They were scum. The world won't miss Lenny. And I feel confident that Dane has learned the error of his ways."

"So, you're telling me you weren't just avenging me, but also other women as well?" She sought clarification.

"I don't condone violence against women," Roman told her. He paused and thought about it for a moment. "Unless they're nasty bitches and deserve it. Then I don't discriminate."

"Women can be evil, too," Angela agreed softly.

"Indeed they can."

Roman kept up the slow strokes of her hair and back, and Angela started getting sleepy. She knew she was leaning more heavily on him, but he had no issue taking on her weight. And hers was considerable. She was no wafer. *It's nice to be held,* she thought, tracing her finger over the seam in his shirt at the shoulder.

"What are you thinking about?" Roman asked softly, as if he didn't want to break whatever spell they were under.

"That it might be nice to come home to someone," Angela answered honestly.

"Someone?" Roman's voice was guarded.

Angela stepped back so she could see his expression. She shrugged, sending her thick hair spilling over her shoulder. "I've been alone for a long time, ever since I was eighteen. I've always liked it, but lately I've been thinking it might be nice to have some company. Your place is always busy. There are always people around, and always someone to say hello to." She cast him a droll look. "And please, don't remind me that most of those people are there to do your bidding and carry out your nefarious orders."

"Nefarious?" Roman's lips twisted in a grin. "You think I'm nefarious?"

Angela shot him a dirty look. "Don't try to be cute with me, Roman. You are nefarious, and you know it."

Roman threw his head back and laughed. His eyes lit up, the corners crinkling. When he was done, he met her gaze. "You make me happy. Did you know that?" Angela's eyes widened, and her mouth fell open. Roman grinned. "You look adorably shocked, Angel." He reached over to close her mouth with a gentle finger beneath her chin. "Careful there, Doc. You don't want anything to fall in."

Like your cock, Angela thought. She slapped her hands over her mouth, praying she hadn't accidentally said that out loud. She sometimes did. It was a bad habit when she was tired and overworked. When he didn't react, she breathed out a sigh of relief. "I make you happy? Really?" she finally said, addressing his statement.

"You do. Why are you so surprised?" Roman asked curiously.

Because I don't want it to be true, she thought. Because it would be an honest and vulnerable reality, and the nicest thing anyone had ever said to her. So, she did what she always did when she was feeling exposed. She lashed out, ruining the peace and comfort of the moment. "Don't pretend to be a nice guy, Roman. We both know you're not."

His face shut down, losing all its softness. "You're right. I'm not."

"Roman . . . wait." Angela grabbed his hand, stopping him from moving when he went to grab his keys. She sighed, hating her self-destructive behavior. "I'm sorry. I don't know why I feel the need to constantly tear you down. But I have a feeling it's a *me* problem. Not a *you* problem."

Roman regarded her for a moment before he spoke. "I know why. And I can easily tell you, Angel. But I believe it will lose something in translation."

She was sure he was right. Angela cursed her runaway mouth. Yes, it was a defense mechanism, pure and simple. But that didn't make it okay. Roman had been nothing but nice to her since that first night. Sure, he'd held a gun to her head. And he'd since admitted to killing people. But he was also respectful, protective, and loyal. *And he is a good cuddler,* she added.

As Roman walked away from her, she was afforded a wonderful view of his spectacular ass. She tilted her head, watching the way the faded denim cupped his strong cheeks lovingly. The plain gray Henley was tight, showing off his broad shoulders and muscled arms. But it wasn't one size too small, like she believed all of Abel's to be. The thought made her snicker.

"Something funny?" Roman asked, leaning against her kitchen counter.

She shook her head, biting her lip when her gaze strayed to her kitchen wall. The same wall the sexy Roman had screwed her spectacularly against. Her pussy clenched, and she fought the urge to press her legs together. She didn't need him to know just how potent she found him. He was dangerous enough to her as it was. "I was just thinking about Abel," she finally revealed.

Roman's scowl was instantaneous, as well as fierce. "You're thinking about Abel when I'm standing in front of you proposing sex?"

"Stop saying sex," Angela ordered—rather weakly. "And you're not proposing that. We were in the middle of a kind of fight, thanks to my mouth."

He smirked at her, crossing his arms and making his biceps bulge. "*Mio angelo*, whenever you're in my presence, I'm proposing sex. Never forget that. But I was referring specifically to the friends with benefits offer. And that wasn't a fight. Though, it could be if you're talking about Abel and sex in the one sentence."

Her stomach fluttered from his admission, but she ignored it. "I wasn't thinking about him like that," she assured Roman. "Gross."

Roman stood up straight, looking suddenly cheerful. "You think Abel is gross?"

"I think Abel is extremely good-looking with a body built for sin," Angela corrected him honestly. "But he does nothing for me. It's another reason why I don't do friends with benefits. I can't sleep with my friends. It's weird."

Roman hummed, prowling toward her with all the grace and lethality of a jungle cat. "And do you consider *us* friends, Angel?"

"I . . ." She closed her mouth because there was no way she was going to win. She would be damning herself with her own logic, no matter what she said.

"Just as I thought. Do you know what that means, Angel?" Roman all but purred.

"Stop saying my name like that." Angela did her best to snap, but her voice came out too breathless.

"Like what?" Roman asked innocently. He leaned in close, running his nose along her neck—something he did with alarming frequency. He inhaled deeply, nuzzling behind her ear, sending shivers throughout her entire body. "Angel . . ." he whispered again, before nipping her earlobe.

"Damnit, Roman," Angela groaned, her knees literally going weak.

Roman caught her against his chest. His eyes mapped her face tenderly, but the heat in their chestnut depths was unmistakable. "You are so very beautiful," he told her.

Angela wasn't proud of the whimper that came out of her mouth, but she couldn't help it. The man was deadly. And not because he was a killer. She pushed up onto her toes, aligning their mouths before kissing him with all the pent-up frustration of the past few months. She moaned when his grip tightened on her hips, pulling her against the hardness straining the front of his jeans. She wrapped a leg around his waist, doing her best to increase the erotic contact.

It was a bad idea. It was wrong. She knew it. But she couldn't bring herself to stop. The way he kissed her like he wanted to devour her made her feel wanted. It made her feel *whole*. And though she had worked hard over the years with a shitload of therapy, the feeling of completeness—of being whole—had remained elusive.

Why now, with this particular man, did she finally feel safe? It didn't make any sense. But she decided to go with it. Just for a little while longer. She had no doubt the real world and her insecurities would intrude soon enough. *Better make the most of it while I can,* she told herself.

They kissed and kissed, their tongues dancing and their hands wandering. When Roman retreated, she was the one to chase his mouth with her own. It was his rough chuckle that caused her to open her eyes. He'd said she was beautiful. But he was wrong. *He* was the beautiful one. His honey-brown irises shone with fervor, the small lines beside them creased thanks to his smile. A smile which was wide and uninhibited.

His dark-brown hair was a mess, one thick portion flopped carelessly over his forehead. He had a solo dimple in his right cheek, and she wanted to lick it. Hell, she wanted to lick him all over. So, she reached for the button on his jeans, only to be brought up short by his calloused hand over her own.

"Nope," he reprimanded her. He took her hand, tugging her closer to the couch. "Tonight is just for you. Let me adore you."

Roman managed to lower her gently onto the sofa

before his words penetrated her lust-filled brain. "Wait . . . what?" Angela tried to scramble away, but he grabbed her by her wrist, hauling her back. "No. We have crazy, high-spirited sex or nothing at all," she told him.

Roman *tsked* at her. "I know what you're all about, Dr. Hawthorne. You want us to slake our lusts and call it a day. Because simple fucking allows you to keep your distance."

She raised her chin. "So what if it does? There's nothing wrong with fucking. In fact, we seemed to be quite good at it."

"Indeed. I agree with you. And I'm all for fucking," he promised with a rumble. "But that isn't what this is about tonight."

"It's about that or nothing at all," Angela told him, staying strong.

Roman laughed low. "Is that right?"

She licked her suddenly dry lips. "That's right."

Roman picked up her hand, kissing the back of it before nibbling along her knuckles. He met her eyes. "What if I want to worship you? What if I want to humble myself before you? What if I want to treat you like the queen you are, on my knees before you? What if I want to give you so much pleasure that it begins to feel like pain?"

Angela's breath stalled in her lungs. "I . . . don't want that," she stuttered.

"Your mouth is saying one thing, Angel. But your body is saying another." Roman reached out and stroked her beaded nipple through her shirt. "You do so much for others, Angel. Let me give you something back."

Angela didn't say yes—she couldn't—but she also didn't say no. Taking the tacit agreement for what it was, Roman quickly stripped her of her clothes. Within seconds, she was naked in front of him whilst he remained fully dressed. After a moment's hesitation, he unbuttoned his jeans and lowered his zipper, allowing his erection to spring free. "Better safe than sorry," he told her. "I don't want my fly to damage my favorite appendage."

Angela didn't want that either. She accepted his next kiss, relishing the weight of him as he came down on top of her. The feeling of his denim-clad thighs against her bare ones was erotic as hell.

He made his way to her breasts, kneading and squeezing. He plumped them together, a rough growl leaving his throat. "One day, I'm going to watch my dick fuck these pretty tits of yours, Angel."

"Oh god," Angela cried out, wetness flooding her core from his wicked words. He bent his head, taking her nipple into his mouth and sucking hard. When her hands started to shake, she gripped his hair.

Roman played with her nipples long enough for her to squirm and start humping his stomach like a dog. Anything to get more friction and to find release. His mouth finally journeyed south, his tongue tracing around her belly button, and she felt the way her soft stomach quivered from his attentions. She wasn't self-conscious about her body. As a doctor, she had seen so many bodies of all shapes and sizes and had come to understand that the human body was just a vessel. Its purpose was to carry you through life. A functioning body was a privilege not given to all, so she was damn sure going to enjoy hers.

And enjoying it, she certainly was, especially when Roman was between her parted legs in the next moment, leaving a trail of open kisses. When his mouth met her heated core, she arched sharply, feeling her back crack from the movement. He flattened his tongue and licked her from bottom to top several times before using two fingers to open her hole so he could stab his tongue into her and lick her out. Her keening cry of surprise and pleasure seemed to fuel his appetite because he began eating her like a starving man.

Angela gripped the couch, panting. Typically, she disassociated from such an intimate act. She usually let her mind drift while her body stayed present, soaking up the pleasure. But she found herself unable to do that this time. All she could think about was the man between her thighs.

Looking down, she took in his dark hair messed up from her wandering hands and satisfaction spiraled through her. *She* had done that. The possessive feeling was new and sent a warning alarm to her head. But it was easily ignored, thanks to the way Roman was devouring her. One hand gripped her thigh, opening her wide and holding her steady against the sofa when she practically tried to put him in a choke hold from what his tongue was now doing to her clit. And that's when he switched things up. His fingers abandoned her wet hole, tugging and pressing down on the most vulnerable part of her body, while he fucked her with his tongue.

She finally let her mind go, her hips undulating and working with Roman to find a rhythm that would bring her the most pleasure. It didn't take long. Apparently, letting go was the key, and she shouted as her orgasm rolled through her. "Ugh, ugh, ugh!" she moaned over and over again, writhing as much as his restraining hands would allow.

To her shock, he wasn't satisfied with wringing just one orgasm from her. As soon as her body stopped spasming from the first wave of pleasure, he went to town again, drawing a startled cry from her. "What are you doing?" she gasped out.

Roman's eyes, darkened in passion, met her own. He licked his lips, groaning from her flavor. "Isn't it obvious?"

"No more," she said, pushing him away weakly. "I can't."

"You can. And you will," Roman told her with a growl. He reached up, gripping her breasts again with two hands, massaging and plucking at her distended nipples, making her gasp and moan and writhe.

His face was flushed as he moved over her, his exposed dick falling against her wet, sensitive clit. He was so hard and felt huge, and she couldn't stop herself from rocking against him. His piercing added to the experience, eliciting sparks of pleasure each time it glided over her clit. "Roman!" she yelled, her fingers digging into his shoulders, and he growled in approval, lowering his head to her right breast. He sucked her nipple in roughly, tweaking the other with his thumb and forefinger.

Her legs wrapped around his hips, and she knew she was going to make a mess out of his pants because she was just so wet. But she couldn't bring herself to care. Not when another orgasm was barreling down on her. She curled her legs inward, trapping his ass between her crossed ankles, forcing his weight and his cock onto her center more. She rocked and ground herself against him as hard as she could.

"That's it, *mio angelo*. Fuck yourself against me. Take what you need from me," Roman encouraged her, his voice raspy against the shell of her ear.

He kissed her neck before biting down—hard enough to leave a mark, she was sure. Also hard enough to have pleasure flooding her pussy for a second time in as many minutes. She cried out, grabbing handfuls of his ass as she came. Roman stopped chewing on her neck long enough to cover her mouth with his own, kissing her savagely and swallowing her sounds of pleasure.

Her hands and legs fell away from his body, having no strength to keep holding on. Before she could remind her brain to get back online, her body was already switching off.

The last thing she felt before sleep claimed her was the softest of kisses on her forehead.

CHAPTER FOURTEEN

The following morning, Roman found himself in a great mood. He whistled as he shuffled papers around on his desk, not really seeing what was printed on them. And also not really caring.

He was in his private office, having difficulty focusing, unable to wipe the smile off his face. Worshipping Angel the way she deserved was going to be his new mission in life. She had been a work of art beneath him, open and raw and uninhibited. He loved how she wasn't afraid to take what she wanted—what she *needed*.

He had been surprised when she allowed herself to fall asleep with him still there. And completely naked, too. It just showed how badly she needed rest—and also how much of a release she'd had. He held her for a while, until his dick had seen fit to deflate. He was tempted to rub one out, but it felt skeevy. So he waited out his throbbing erection until he could safely tuck it back into his pants. Then he covered her with the throw from the back of the sofa, cleaned up in the bathroom, and gently but quickly wiped Angel down with a warm washcloth. He kept it brief. Not because he had a problem cleaning her up—in fact, he found he enjoyed taking care of her in any way—but because he didn't want to take liberties with her body while she was sleeping.

He had debated carrying her to her bed but decided to leave her where she was in the end. She needed rest and her navy-blue sofa was comfortable. He had left not long after, tempted to stay, but knowing she wouldn't want that. Not yet.

"One day," he murmured, running his finger over the edge of a letter opener.

When his phone rang, he practically lunged at it, fumbling to see who the caller was. He felt like a tool, but that was minor when he saw Angel's name flashing on the screen. He answered with a smile. "Angel, good morning."

"Roman . . ." she began, clearing her throat uncomfortably.

Roman's good mood plummeted. She didn't sound

like she'd had an earth-shattering experience just hours ago. She sounded aloof. Distant. It had him moving his coffee mug away so he didn't shatter it in a fit of rage. "Why do I get the feeling you regret last night?"

"I don't. I mean, I do. I just . . ." She sighed, and he pictured her rubbing her temples. "I wanted to make some things clear."

"Oh?" he inquired mildly, doing his best not to hold his breath. The power she held over him was mind blowing. The realization caused him to hate her a little.

"No more orgasms. No more sex," Angel said flatly. "We are not lovers, Roman."

He picked up the letter opener again, tempted to stab himself in the back. It would save Angel some time. He kept his voice calm as he responded. "We're not?"

"No. We're not. That means no more seduction. No more pity orgasms. And no more nice-nice. I'm your medical professional, an employee like all your others. Nothing more."

He leaned back in his chair. Angel was much more than that. And he feared she always would be. But he let it go. For now. It was becoming much harder to do every time she pulled her hot and cold act. He reminded himself that she was broken. Broken in ways he knew nothing about. He could afford to be patient. So, he didn't argue with her when he next spoke. "Fine. No more sex stuff. Does that mean we can officially be friends?"

"Friends?" she asked, sounding shocked. "What? No!"

Roman twirled the letter opener expertly. "Why not? You said you don't do friends with benefits. There are no benefits between us. Ergo, we can be friends now."

"*Ergo?!*"

Roman pulled his cell from his ear. Her voice was becoming rather shrill. "Ergo. It means consequently, therefore, hence . . . shall I go on?"

"No," Angela ground out. "And the answer is still no as well."

"You're friends with Luca, Sal, and Abel. We cleared that up last night," he reminded her.

Angela huffed. "Well, I don't need any more friends."

He was pleased she didn't deny the trio at least. "You're an introvert," Roman noted. "I can respect that."

"Good. Great. So, you agree? No more sex," Angel said in a rush.

Roman shrugged and lied through his teeth. "I agree."

"And we're not friends either, right? We keep this professional."

He didn't want to be her friend. Or not *just* her friend, anyway. He wanted much more. Seeing her softer side and her vulnerability the previous evening made him want to hold her when she was sad, soothe her when she was sick, laugh with her when she was happy. He wanted to be her everything. But he wanted the same from her. He may be a man who did bad things, but he knew his worth. If his feelings weren't reciprocated, he would grow to resent her—and himself. And that was a ticking time bomb.

"We keep this professional until you're ready for more," Roman told her.

"More? That won't—"

"Don't!" he snapped, losing his cool a little. His patience had its limits. "Don't say it. We both know that's setting you up for failure."

Angela's angry gasp was clear. "Why, you arrogant—"

"Be very careful, Angel," Roman warned, no longer feeling amused. "I'm not some dog to be tugged around on a leash."

She was silent for a moment before a heavy sigh came across the line. "I don't think you're a dog, Roman. I just . . . I can't . . ."

He knew what she was referring to—*him*. She couldn't be with him. And he knew why. It wasn't because she didn't want him. It was clear she did. It was about her past. A past she fought off daily. A past he still knew nothing about. Even Luca, who made a habit out of hacking into NASA, hadn't been able to find any dirt on Angela Hawthorne. There was a two-year gap, where she went away to a prestigious boarding school in another state when she was sixteen, but nothing dark or sinister showed in official and unofficial records. However, Roman knew it was there. He saw it every time he looked at her. She had admitted as much last night when she said there was death in her past.

"I know," he replied. "And until you *can,* no more orgasms." He waited a beat before adding, "All of you, or none of me." Then he hung up, stabbing his desk with the letter opener.

"Was that the doctor? Did you really just say that? What the fuck, Roman?"

Roman looked up to find Morrigan and Abel in his doorway. He groaned internally. The pair of bickering ingrates were the last thing he wanted to deal with. "Have you ever heard of knocking?" he asked in return, ignoring her question.

Morrigan glared at him and crossed her arms over

her chest. "I've never had to knock before. That doctor..."

"What about her?" Roman interrupted with a snap. When his cousin remained silent, he said, "Well?"

Morrigan shook her head. "I thought the whole Lenny thing was more about Bertha's. That maybe you were laying things on a bit thick as a lesson to others. But you weren't, were you?"

"Since when has Roman ever exaggerated?" Abel replied for Roman, taking a seat on the couch and looking at the fruit bowl.

"Are you in love with her?" Morrigan asked, ignoring Abel completely.

Roman held Morrigan's intense gaze but remained silent. It wasn't as if he could deny it. But he also wasn't ready to admit it out loud.

"You are!" Morrigan pointed an accusing finger at him. "For fuck's sake, Roman!"

Roman cocked an eyebrow, watching as she began to pace. "I don't know why you're so pissed."

"Because she's a bitch," Morrigan snarled.

"And you're not?" Abel questioned.

"I'm going to cut a smile into your throat," Morrigan threatened, palming a knife from out of nowhere.

Abel didn't flinch. He just kept picking at the fruit

bowl, trying to find the best apple. Roman stood up and moved around the front of his desk. He leaned back against it, crossing his ankles and watching Morrigan pace some more. "What's with you? Abel has a point, Morrigan. I'd think Angel was someone you could appreciate."

Morrigan paused, pointing her blade at him for emphasis as she spoke. "I don't appreciate her dragging you around by your balls. You need to keep your head in the game, Roman. Not up some female's skirt."

His jaw clenched, and he straightened up slowly as his temper ignited. "Careful, Maria." He used her given name unintentionally, but it showed just how angry he was. "You'd do well to remember who you're talking to."

"I'm sorry." Morrigan was quick to apologize. "Sorry," she repeated, putting her knife away.

Roman regarded her for a moment, wondering why she was so opposed to Angela. "Have you ever known me to be led around by my dick?" he wanted to know.

"Not until now." Morrigan snarked. She winced, holding up a hand. "Sorry. I'm sorry. That just slipped out."

Roman snorted, relaxing back against his desk once more. It was hard to stay mad at someone who was just being themselves. Morrigan was woefully and socially inappropriate. She just didn't give a shit about insulting most people. Thankfully, he was on the list of people she *did* give a shit about. So, he knew that apology was genuine.

"Why don't you get to know her?" Abel suggested, shining a green apple against his shirt.

"Why the fuck would I want to do that?" Morrigan demanded, looking disgusted.

"Because your cousin is in love with her," Abel pointed out mildly.

When Roman didn't deny it, Morrigan clipped, "Fuck." She scowled at her feet for a moment before looking back up. "Fine. I'll see what all the fuss is about."

Roman's lips twitched. Morrigan looked like she had just agreed to go to slaughter or something. "No maiming," he saw fit to remind her. Even though he wasn't feeling warm and fuzzy towards Angel thanks to the phone call, he wouldn't have her hurt.

Morrigan looked outraged. "But . . ."

"No," he said firmly. "Do not touch her. You remember Lenny, don't you? The fucker who thought it was okay to lay hands on her?"

"Fine!" Morrigan snapped. She spun and flounced to the door. "Take away all my fun, why don't you," she said. Then she slammed the door on her way out.

"She is mental," Abel noted from his spot on the couch.

Roman agreed. "I know it."

"Thank God she's on our side." Abel studied his freshly polished apple for a moment before taking a bite. "I do feel sorry for the man she ends up with, though."

Roman found the comment interesting. Just a week before, Abel would have been insinuating that *he* was the man who would one day tame Morrigan. "How is Claire doing?" he asked his friend casually.

Abel shrugged, munching his apple. "She's doing good, I guess. She hasn't come out of her room yet. She's so timid. Like a little mouse."

"And you don't like mice?" Roman questioned.

"I like them just fine," Abel replied. "Until they start chewing through your electrical wires and all your shit stops working."

"You think your shit is going to stop working?" Roman pressed. If Abel was being philosophical, he was already in deep.

Abel frowned at him in confusion. "What are you talking about? My shit never stops working. You know that."

Roman did know that. "What are we going to do about her? Has Luca found anything on her ex? I can have one of the guys from the bodyguard team assigned to her."

Salvatore was the manager of Sentry Personal Security, one of Roman's high-earning businesses. It wasn't filled with your typical bodyguards. But his team of mercenaries and ex-military personnel always got the job done.

"Luca is my next stop," Abel said. "And no to Sentry for now. There's not much point when she's hiding in one of the guest rooms. She hasn't said much else about what's happened to her. Just that her ex has been following her and making her life hell. I'll take her to get her stuff when she's ready to venture out."

Roman didn't like the thought of her out on her own for various reasons. One of them being her safety. But the larger one being the possibility of her going to the cops and ratting on Abel for beating up Robert. Yes, the guy had been attacking her. But the psychology behind domestic assault victims and their abusers was complicated. Roman knew that personally. "Do you think she's a flight risk? Will she talk?"

Abel grunted, finishing off his apple. "No more than Angel," he answered quietly.

Roman raised his brows, rocking back on his feet. "Interesting."

Abel's blue eyes flashed to his. "I didn't mean it like that, and you know it."

"Like what?" Roman prodded.

Abel rolled his eyes in annoyance and got to his feet. "I'm not claiming Claire. I haven't fallen for her like that."

Roman latched onto the bit of wiggle room Abel's response allowed. "Like what?"

"Like she's going to be the mother of my future babies," Abel teased with a grin.

Roman thought about Angel round with child, and his heart did a roll in his chest. He had never, not once in his life, given any thought to having children. He'd never had any desire for them. His mother had been a wonderful woman and an even better *matri*. But his father had been a terrible role model and was responsible for shaping Roman into the man he had become.

Abel whistled low, drawing Roman's attention. "Damn, man. You should see the look on your face. You have it bad."

Roman couldn't deny it. He just hoped, one day, Angel would have it bad as well. Otherwise, he was going to be a nightmare to live with.

CHAPTER FIFTEEN

A ngela screamed in frustration, tossing her make-up into the sink. Trying to cover the bruise left by Roman's very talented mouth was useless.

She was filled with regret. "So much regret. *All* the regret," she told her reflection.

The pleasure had been just as he promised. So good it transcended from pleasure to pain—in the best way possible. It wasn't the orgasms that had her mourning the previous night. It was the way she had melted against him afterwards. The way she had fallen asleep against his chest as he stayed fully clothed, running a soothing hand up and down her back. He'd left some-time in the night, tucking her in warmly with one of her fuzzy blankets. She slept soundly until her alarm had gone off for work just an hour before.

She'd spent five minutes attempting to camouflage the half-hickey, half-bite on her neck before she spotted the happy smile on her face in the mirror, along with the dreamy, glazed look in her eyes. And that was something she couldn't accept. So, she called Roman immediately, setting stronger boundaries for their relationship. His easy acceptance proved she had done the right thing. She couldn't afford to fall for the likes of Roman. Which meant no more altruistic head jobs from the man. His ready agreement to the rules annoyed her a little, but it was for the best. What wasn't for the best was a sex bruise that couldn't be covered.

Sighing, she moved to her closet, hunting for something that would cover it. It wasn't winter, but it was a cool enough fall day that a turtleneck sweater wouldn't be questioned. She pulled the soft blue fabric over her head quickly, casting a critical eye over herself in the mirror. The mark was covered, but it still tingled, reminding her of how it came about.

"Damnit!" she groused. She scowled at her reflection, telling herself to get the satisfied look off her face, and grabbed her things. She had one hour to spend at Lighthouse before her twelve-hour shift at the hospital.

Within twenty minutes, she was there, and she

was pleased to see the construction crew working away on the roof. Roman's money was being put to good use. She walked inside, looking for Sister Pip, but noticed a familiar face instead. Morrigan. Angela hadn't had much to do with the woman. She knew who she was—she worked for Roman and was a relative of some kind—but that was about it. She had never spoken to her.

"Morrigan?" Angela called out as she hurried over. "It *is* Morrigan, isn't it?"

"Yep," the other woman replied, looking her over critically.

Angela waited for her to say something else, but when the silence stretched out, becoming awkward as hell, she cleared her throat. "Can I help you with something?"

"Nope. I've seen this place from the outside often enough. But I've never been inside. It's bigger than I expected," she said, looking around.

Angela frowned. "What do you mean?"

Morrigan's dark eyes met Angela's. "I saw lots of things from the outside thanks to me following you around like I did for the past couple of months."

That gave Angela pause. "Wait . . . you've been following me around?"

"Duh. Do you think Abel's tiny little brain could

stay focused endlessly?" She scoffed. "Not likely. I had the nights, and he took the days."

Angela clenched her jaw, feeling annoyed and frustrated. She hadn't even noticed the other woman. Not once. "I didn't see you."

"That was kind of the point," Morrigan informed her drolly.

"I saw Abel plenty of times," Angela pointed out.

Morrigan waved the comment away. "Pfft. That's because he's a loser. I'm much better at my job."

Angela fought back the urge to defend Abel, asking instead, "And what job is that, exactly?"

"Assassin."

It was stated so boldly that Angela knew it was the truth. She looked around, making sure they were still alone. "Shh. Please lower your voice."

"Why? I'm not ashamed of who I am. Are you?" Morrigan challenged.

"Ashamed of you? Absolutely," Angela said quickly.

"That's not what I meant. But . . . good one," Morrigan allowed, her mouth curving up a little.

"I'm glad you approve of my humor," Angela said dryly. "Why are you here? Is someone hurt?"

"There's always someone hurt, Doc. You should know that better than most," Morrigan muttered, looking Angela over from head to foot once more. "But if you must know, I'm here to check on Roman's investment."

Angela had a feeling there was a double meaning there, but she didn't have the patience to figure it out. "The place is coming along nicely, don't you think?"

Morrigan screwed up her nose, looking around the old building in distaste. "If you say so. It looks like a pit to me."

"This *pit* is saving lives, I promise you." Sister Philomena's voice sounded amused as well as gently chastising.

Angela turned around, smiling when she saw the nun. "Sister, good morning."

Sister Pip took Angela's outstretched hand with a warm smile, squeezing it.

"Good morning, Angela," the nun greeted her happily. "Thank you for stopping by. I know how busy you are."

"It's no problem. I'm always happy to help," Angela replied sincerely.

Morrigan coughed, saying, "Ass-kisser."

Angela frowned at her. "Really?"

Morrigan simply shrugged. "You're not fooling me. Nobody is *that* altruistic."

"I am," Sister Philomena interjected, looking amused rather than insulted. Morrigan grunted, causing the nun's smile to grow. "Are you another friend of Angela's? I've been meeting a lot recently."

"I'm really not," Morrigan said, looking a little offended. She turned to Angela. "Anyway, why don't you join me for a drink later?"

Angela was sure she heard wrong. "A drink?" The other woman nodded. "Why would I want to do that?"

"So we can get to know each other better." The *duh* was implied by Morrigan's tone.

Angela shook her head. "And I repeat: why would I want to do that?"

Morrigan stared at her with eyes that held the promise of death before she grinned, slugging Angela in the shoulder. "You know what? You might just be all right." She gave Sister Pip a jaunty salute before turning and walking away. "Let's make it next week. I have things to do today. Later," she yelled over her shoulder.

Angela stared at her retreating back in confusion. "What just happened?"

Sister Pip patted her arm. "I believe she is trying to make friends with you."

"I'm sorry to disagree with you, Sister, but you're wrong. That woman is the last person on the planet I could be friends with."

"Didn't you once say that about Abel?" the older

woman reminded her slyly. "She seemed lovely to me. Very honest. It's a good virtue."

Angela made a non-committal sound, not wanting to argue with a nun. "Anyway, I only have forty-five minutes left. What can I do?"

"I was halfway through making up new first aid kits to hand out on the streets this evening."

Angela nodded. "I'll help. Do you need any more supplies?"

It was one of the things Angela had instigated when she began volunteering at the refuge. She had access to a bunch of out-of-date medical supplies. But really, do bandages and tape really expire? The amount of waste at the hospital was enough to give her hives. She understood it in theory, but in a world where there was such a huge divide between the haves and the have nots, it just wasn't practical. Or ethical. So, she had gone to the hospital board and arranged for certain expired products to be donated to various shelters across the city. Then she had personally gone to dozens of them and shown the organizers and volunteers how to make small, but useful, first aid kits.

"Roman already arranged for everything. Enough to see us through for the next few months," Sister Philomena disclosed.

Angela stumbled a little and did her best to cover it

up by walking faster. "Roman?"

"That's right. He has visited a few times now. Such a polite, handsome boy."

"Boy?" Angela looked at Sister Pip askance.

"When you're as old as me, dear, everyone is a boy." Sister Pip nudged her with her shoulder.

Angela laughed, touching the nun gently on the arm. "You're not that old, Sister."

Sister Philomena huffed. "Almost ninety. I'm more than double Roman's age. And yours."

Angela didn't like to think about Father Time creeping up on the elderly woman. Since the passing of her grandmother, she didn't have any maternal figures in her life. Sister Pip was the only one.

"I didn't hear you correct me about him being handsome?"

Angela returned her attention to the other woman. "What's that?"

"Roman, my dear. He's very good-looking. Sexy even," she added with a twinkle in her eye.

"You're a nun," Angela reminded her.

"And? I have eyes, don't I? They may be old, but they still work." Sister Philomena paused, pursing her lips. "For example, I see today you're wearing a turtleneck sweater."

Angela sputtered, dropping one of the bandages she

had just picked up from the stack in the center of the table in the storage room. "What does that have to do with anything?"

"Ask me how many times I've seen you wear a high-collared top since I've known you."

It sounded very much like a dare, and Angela wanted nothing to do with it. "No. I don't think I will," she replied primly.

Sister Philomena laughed. "Because you know the answer is zero."

It *was* zero, Angela admitted silently. The canny old nun was correct. She didn't wear the sweater often, even though the color was gorgeous, and it was super soft. She couldn't stand anything around her neck for long. She found it restrictive and, at times, triggering. So she chose not to wear certain items of clothing. "It was time for a change," she finally responded.

"It suits you. The change," Sister Philomena clarified. She patted Angela on the cheek. "You're a good girl, Angela."

She thought about Roman sticking his tongue inside of her until she screamed his name last night. *Good girls don't come like that*, her conscience whispered. But she kept the thought to herself, knowing she had done her best to stop the madness with Roman before it went too far.

CHAPTER SIXTEEN

Angela's shift went quickly for a change, and she was pleased to make it to the end of the day without any major casualties. Being the hospital with the biggest trauma center in the city meant mass casualties were a common occurrence, and it was rare for her to make it through a shift without anyone dying.

"And isn't that just fucking depressing," she muttered out loud.

"What was that, Dr. Hawthorne?"

Angela smiled self-consciously at the male nurse behind the desk. "Sorry, Finn. I was talking to myself."

Finley grinned back. "All good. I do it all the time." He winked, his dimples flashing appealingly. "It's the only way I get an intelligent conversation around here."

Angela laughed. "Good point. I guess you can't blame us then."

"Not at all," Finn agreed. "You have a good night."

"Thanks, Finn. You too," Angela said, handing him the last of the files she was carrying.

Finn had been working at the hospital for almost as long as Angela. He was a friendly, happy guy who was very nice to look at. But what Angela liked best about him was that he was a damn good nurse. He was competent as well as kind, and knew his way around an emergency. She could always count on him, and she breathed a little easier whenever they were on shift together.

Saying goodbye to the nurses and the night janitors, she made her way to the hospital exit. They were the backbone of the hospital, and she always made sure they knew how much she valued them. Not all doctors gave the same level of shits she did, though. Especially some of her fellow surgeons. Which was why she didn't really hang out with any of them socially. She'd seen and heard enough of the elite growing up—it wasn't something she wanted to be a part of anymore. And luckily for her, she was a grown-ass woman and could choose whom she gave the time of day to.

"Angela, a word?"

Angela sighed a little, slowing down so Dr. Brian

Cosgrove could catch up with her. She smiled politely when he joined her, and they kept walking across the outdoor parking lot. "Hi, Brian. How are you?"

"I'm well, thank you. Sorry to trouble you at the end of your shift. Big day?" he asked courteously.

"It's fine. Actually, today wasn't too bad. Nobody died," she replied.

His eyebrows rose in shock, and he grinned. "Wow. A glowing testament indeed."

Angela snickered. "Right?" Her shoulders relaxed a little. Brian was an okay guy and a very talented surgeon. She'd had a drink or two with him in the past and knew he had once been interested in her romantically. Thankfully, he had taken it gracefully when she'd told him she didn't date. And certainly not colleagues. That was a recipe for disaster.

"I was wondering if I could pick your brains about . . ." he began, only to cut off. "Hey, you have some fluff on you. Allow me . . ."

Before she could react, Brian reached up, brushing her sweater high up on her neck. The motion tugged the material down, revealing the sex bite to his shocked gaze.

"What happened?" he demanded, stepping in closer.

Angela moved back, well out of his reach. She

reached up, making sure her turtleneck was back in place. "It's nothing."

"Is that a bite mark?" Brian persisted with a frown.

"It's nothing, Brian," she told him in a no-nonsense tone.

"Ah, I see." His dark blue eyes lit up and a raunchy grin curved the corners of his mouth. "I didn't realize you were seeing anyone."

"Not that it's your business, but I'm not." She did her best to smile to soften her words. She really didn't want to discuss her hickey, Roman, or the fact that her clit was still sensitive after last night's one-sided sexcapades.

"Sorry. I didn't mean to imply . . ." He paused, looking sheepish, then repeated, "Sorry."

Angela smiled a little, telling herself not to be so touchy. Brian was a very good doctor—one she had been working with for over five years now. "No, *I'm* sorry. I didn't mean to bite your head off. It's been a long day." She winked at him, trying to lighten the mood. "Even though nobody died."

He laughed a little. "I know how you feel. My heart valve surgery ended up going for eight hours."

"Complications?" Angela queried as they continued to walk. She paused when she made it to her car, noting his black Mercedes was right next to hers.

"Yes. A few," Brian admitted, placing his briefcase on the ground next to his car's front wheel. "Which is why I wanted to talk with you, if you don't mind."

"I don't mind at all," Angela assured him.

They stood by their cars for twenty minutes discussing arrhythmias and genetic bleeding disorders and how open-heart surgery was not a good time for them to be discovered. They were just saying goodbye when a familiar voice spoke from the darkness.

"Angel."

She squinted in the direction of Salvatore's voice. The handsome man had a boyish smile on his face as he made his way to her, but Angela was not amused. "Sal. What are you doing here?" She asked nicely enough, but gave him the stink eye behind Brian's back.

"I was just in the area. Jogging," Salvatore explained, gesturing to his workout wear. "You know I often jog by the hospital."

Angela's smile was strained. "Of course. You jog by here most days, don't you?"

"Sure do," Salvatore confirmed happily.

The smile on his face was wide, and the glint in his eyes was mischievous. Angela wasn't fooled. He was there to watch her. Roman wasn't having her followed twenty-four seven anymore, but a select few, including Abel, Sal, and apparently Morrigan, still randomly checked in with her. As if she could forget about any of them, or the deal she had made with Roman.

Both men were looking at her, and she realized one —or both—must have asked her a question. "I'm sorry. What?"

Salvatore moved a little closer. "Everything okay?" he asked.

"Of course. Sorry, I'm being rude." She laughed a little, gesturing between the two men. "Salvatore, this is a colleague of mine, Dr. Brian Cosgrove. Brian, this is Salvatore. He's a friend."

The two men shook hands, holding on longer than was typically polite. She saw Salvatore squeeze and Brian wince before he quickly let go and stepped back. She frowned. She was surprised by the power display because Sal was very laid back and secure. She knew he could be lethal if the occasion called for it but wasn't aggressive without cause. And right now, he was looking at Brian like he wanted to punch him in the face.

"Nice to meet you," Sal told Brian, staring him down. He turned to her, wrapping an arm around her waist and kissing her on the temple. "I better keep moving. Let's do dinner again soon, okay?"

Angela smiled with genuine warmth this time. Luca was very physically affectionate, and she soaked it up like a sponge. Sal was a little less so, but his hugs felt just as good. *Not as good as Roman's,* her brain saw fit to supply. She gave herself a mental slap, agreeing to dinner with Sal before he jogged off.

"He calls you Angel?" Brian asked as soon as Salvatore was out of earshot.

She laughed lightly, doing her best to dismiss her colleague's clear curiosity. "A nickname. It's no big deal."

"But you hate nicknames," Brian pointed out with a frown.

She arched a brow. "Do I?"

"Well, I mean, you've never offered any alternative to Angela before. But if you prefer Angel . . ."

"No!" Angela cut Brian off, wincing because she had spoken rather loudly. "No," she repeated more quietly. "I don't prefer it. Angela is fine. Thank you." She didn't know why, but the thought of Brian calling her Angel just didn't sit right. She wasn't sure when it became okay for Sal or Luca—or even Roman—to call her Angel . . . she just knew it didn't piss her off like it used to.

Brian shifted uncomfortably, and Angela tilted her head in his direction. "Problem?"

"No problem," Brian swiftly assured her. "It's

just . . . he's not the one who gave you that hickey, is he?"

Her mouth fell open. "I beg your pardon?"

"Sorry. None of my business. I know. It's just, I know when a man is trouble, Angela. And that man has it written all over him."

She swallowed down her automatic defense of Salvatore and aimed for flippant. Brian was getting far too personal for her liking. "You can relax. That man is gay." *Or at least bi*, she amended silently.

"He may not be interested in you romantically, but that doesn't mean he can't cause problems for you. How do you know him?" Brian pressed.

Angela was beginning to get pissed. What the hell was Brian's problem? "I'm not sure why you're being so persistent. He's a friend, Brian. That's all there is to it. Not that it's any of your business," she added, allowing her displeasure to seep into her voice.

Brian held up his hands. "I'm sorry. I don't mean to be rude. It's just . . . he works for Vincenzo Romano."

Angela stilled, narrowing her eyes at her colleague. "Does he? And so what if he does?"

Brian scoffed a little, looking at her like she was an idiot. "Come on, Angela. You must know who Vincenzo Romano is. The man is the biggest criminal in the city."

"A criminal? Why isn't he in jail, then?" Angela

cursed herself silently. *Why am I defending Roman and his crew? Why I am challenging Brian?* She needed to shut up, say goodnight, and get her butt home.

"You know he is, Angela. And the reason why he isn't in jail is because he has cops in his back pocket," Brian answered with some bite.

"Is that right? And how do *you* know that?" Angela questioned, crossing her arms over her chest.

Brian was looking frustrated, running his hand through his perfectly styled hair and messing it up. "People talk," he explained. He placed his hands on both of her shoulders, turning her fully to face him. Softening his voice, he said, "I'm just saying be careful, Angela. They are not the type of people you want to get involved with."

She carefully stepped back, dislodging his hands. She wanted to rub her shoulders where he had touched her. The sensation of his hands on her was not a pleasant one. "I'm not involved with anyone," she assured him. "But thank you for the advice."

He stared at her for a moment longer before he smiled and nodded. "Sure. Whatever you say. Just trying to be a good friend."

Angela frowned. They weren't friends. They were colleagues who, before this encounter, had been on friendly terms. But she was seriously reconsidering even that. Something about the other doctor rubbed her the wrong way. Still, she decided to give him the benefit of the doubt. Smiling, she said, "Thanks, Brian. I appreciate it. But honestly, you have nothing to worry about. Salvatore and his partner are coffee buddies of mine. There's nothing sinister going on. They're good people—despite who you say Salvatore works for."

Brian smiled back, shrugging his shoulders. "Sure. Well, I better get going. You have yourself a good night now."

"You too. See you tomorrow." Angela got in her car, locking her doors quickly. It was a move she found silly, even though she had been abducted from this exact location just months ago. What was Brian going to do? *Nothing* was the answer to that—and she knew it. But the fact that he knew who Salvatore was on sight, and was also aware of Roman's reputation, bothered her.

Shaking it off, she pulled out, taking the exit in the opposite direction from where Brian's car was headed. As she paused to give way, she found Sal waiting for her by some bushes. She considered ignoring him, but it made her feel petty. She didn't unlock her doors, but she did press the button to lower the passenger-side window. "What the hell, Sal? You guys are still following me? I thought we were past this?"

Salvatore squatted down, resting his forearms on

the window frame. "We check in on you sometimes, Angel. It's no big deal. We do the same for everyone in our crew."

"I'm not a part of your crew," she was quick to point out.

Salvatore rolled his eyes. "Fine. You're an employee. It's a courtesy. It's also for safety. Who was that guy? I don't like him."

"He's a fellow surgeon. And what's not to like? You only just met the guy." She didn't know why she was defending Brian, given he had caused her own hackles to rise.

"My instincts are legendary, babe. And they are screaming about that guy," Sal informed her.

"Oh? Screaming what exactly?" Angela tapped her fingers against the steering wheel in agitation. Should she mention Brian knew who Roman was? And knew Sal worked for him?

"They're screaming that he's a douche," Sal told her point blank.

Angela side-eyed him. "He's a surgeon. Most of us are douches."

"You're not," Sal said, smiling winningly. "How about you give me a lift home?"

She glared at him accusingly. "I thought you were jogging."

Salvatore wiped nonexistent sweat from his forehead. "Phew. What a workout. I'm so tired."

"Uh-huh," Angela said dryly, shaking her head. He was almost as incorrigible as Abel. Still, she unlocked her doors for the crazy man.

"What? You don't think I'm fit enough?" he asked as he plonked his solid mass onto her front seat. He flexed his arm, making his right bicep bulge. "Check out my guns."

She eyed his muscles with appreciation. There was no denying the man was fit. *And hot*, she added. But that was not the point. "Your *guns* could use a little work," she told him, finally pulling out into traffic.

Salvatore just grinned. "Yeah, right. I don't get any complaints from Luca."

"He's a lucky guy," Angela agreed sincerely.

"No," Sal said decisively. "*I'm* the lucky one."

Angela sighed, melting from the love easily detectable in his voice. "Don't be sweet. I'm still annoyed with you."

"I can't help it. Sweet is my default," he told her happily.

"Right. And what's Roman's default?" she asked without meaning to.

"Rage," Sal supplied quickly. "Especially when he's worried about those he cares about. Which is why I'm going to advise you to stay away from that other doctor."

Angela flashed her passenger an annoyed look. "I work with that other doctor. It's a little hard to stay away from him. Besides, Brian is harmless. *And* Roman has no say in whom I talk to. Besides, he doesn't care about me like that. We cleared that up just this morning."

"Still in Egypt, I see," Sal said obscurely.

Angela frowned. "What?"

"Denial, it's a river there," he clarified.

Angela scowled at him, pulling into a reserved car space out the front of the Omertà complex. It was a quick drive, especially so late at night. "Get out."

Salvatore laughed a little before obediently opening the door and exiting her car. He leaned his head back in the still-open window before she could drive off. "Seriously, Angel. Be careful, yeah?"

"I always am," she told him. Then she pressed the window button, forcing him to step back or risk decapitation. "It's why I'm thirty-nine years old and only just discovering what having friends is like," she added when she was once more alone.

She wondered what it said about her that all her new friends were criminals. And why she was suddenly okay with that.

CHAPTER SEVENTEEN

"**M**r. Romano, your four o'clock is here."

"Thank you, Marcia," Roman replied, pressing his intercom.

Before he could do anything else, his office door suddenly opened. He was about to kick his next appointment out on his ass for simply barging in, but it was just Abel. "What do you want? I have a meeting."

"I know you do. With a potential new associate," Abel responded, walking over to the desk. "It's why I'm here."

Roman glared at his friend. "I told you I don't need a bodyguard for business meetings."

"And most of the time, we allow you to handle them on your own. But not when it's a new player wanting to take over Raz's old territory," Abel explained patiently.

"We? Who the hell is *we*?" As if he didn't know. His inner circle was filled with mother hens.

Abel shrugged. "Me, Sal, Morrigan. And Luca, of course. Would you like me to notify your brother that you want to handle this solo?" He got his phone out of his pants pocket and began to type.

Roman reached out and snatched the cell from Abel's hands. "Don't you dare." His brother was the worst of them.

"So, you agree to me staying? Excellent. I knew you'd see it my way." Abel smiled charmingly and took his phone back.

"Why don't I ever just shoot you?" Roman asked Abel, glaring at him over steepled fingers.

"Because you love me," Abel replied instantly. "Now, how do you want me to be? Rage monster protector? Or calm voice of reason?"

Roman rolled his eyes, knowing there was no way Abel was going to leave. "Calm, please. There's no point making enemies when we can make business."

He was a businessman at heart. He loved all the inner workings of buying and selling and making a struggling business profitable. Which was why he had been so open when Mr. Hennessy contacted him about taking over Raz's shit. Thankfully, the war with The Razors had blown over with nothing sticking to him or his men. It helped that the police hated Raz almost as much as Roman had.

In the past three and a half months, Roman had done the bare minimum to ensure no new big players took over Raz's territory. His reputation had been enough. *Which is flattering,* he thought with a smirk. But it was poor business to leave so much space and so many buildings empty. He was intrigued to hear what Mr. Hennessy had to say.

When a knock sounded on the door, Roman looked at the time. "He's prompt," he noted.

Abel nodded silently, taking up a position next to Roman's desk. When a rough-looking man entered a moment later, Roman stood up. A second man followed a step behind, and Roman greeted the strangers. "Mr. Hennessy, it's a pleasure to meet you."

"Dominic," the man corrected easily enough. "But I go by Midas if you don't mind. And I'm hoping that the pleasure is all mine." He gestured to the other man. "This is Crow, he's my second."

Roman nodded in greeting, taking both men's measures. They hadn't dressed up for the meeting, but that didn't bother Roman. He didn't base a man's worth on what he wore any more than he judged family on the blood that ran through one's veins. There were far more important things.

They were dressed almost identically in leather pants, boots, and t-shirts. Their club cuts were over their shirts. Roman wasn't sure where they had stashed their helmets, but they weren't carrying them. "Drink?" he offered, gesturing to the bar in the left corner.

Midas shook his head. "No, thank you. Perhaps after our meeting."

Roman's opinion of the newcomer rose. He never mixed alcohol with business either. "A few preliminaries, and then we can get down to business. Are you armed?"

"I'm not, no, as per our agreement. But my friend here"—Midas motioned at Crow—"could not be convinced, unfortunately. He's packing." Midas paused, thinking about it for a moment before adding, "A lot."

Roman found himself more amused than pissed and relaxed back into his seat. "Your bodyguard?" he queried.

Midas rolled his eyes. "He seems to think so."

Roman watched the pair carefully, seeing affection as well as annoyance on Midas's face. The two men were clearly more than colleagues. They were friends, perhaps even family. But that was motorcycle clubs for you. Roman gestured to Abel. "This is Abel. He seems to believe the same thing as your man here."

"I hope you don't mind that Crow is here," Midas

said quickly. "He's my VP and will be heavily involved in the business. I thought it was a good idea to bring him along."

The sound Roman made was neutral. "Abel is just here to look pretty."

"Hey!" Abel yelled, glaring at Roman.

The laughter that came from Midas and Crow was heartening. Perhaps the meeting would go well after all. "I will warn you, though. Abel is also heavily armed. As long as you don't do anything stupid, we'll all get along just fine."

Crow looked Abel over from head to toe. "He could try to take me on."

Abel immediately lost his playfulness, fists clenching as he glared daggers at the man. "Bring it," he clipped.

Roman didn't say anything, watching the dynamic between Midas and his subordinate.

"There will be no *bringing*," Midas snarled, spinning around and getting up in Crow's grill. "Damnit, Crow, stand down. If I wanted a loose cannon, I would have brought Torque with me."

Crow bared his teeth. "You never let me have any fun."

"We're trying to establish a working relationship; fun can come later," Midas said sternly. He faced

Roman once more. "Sorry. I swear, being the prez of a motorcycle club is more like running a preschool most of the time."

Roman shared a commiserating look with the other man from across his desk. "I know exactly what you mean."

"Hey!" Abel and Crow said simultaneously, glaring at their respective bosses.

Roman smiled when Midas looked pained. "I think we're going to get along just fine. Take a seat."

Midas dipped his head, settling into one of the two chairs on the other side of the desk. Crow remained standing. "I certainly hope so. I've heard good things about you."

"Tell me more about *you*," Roman invited. "Why is the president of a motorcycle club interested in the old territory of a gangbanger like Raz?"

"We knew the guy," Midas said, resting his elbows on his knees. "I appreciated the way you dealt with him and his crew."

"I pulled them apart piece by piece," Roman pointed out.

Midas's gaze remained steady. "Like I said, I appreciate it."

"Bad blood?" Roman guessed. Luca had given him

some background information on The Midas Touch MC, but there was no mention of Raz.

"Something like that," Midas hedged.

Roman let it go for the time being. "It's quite a large territory. Why should I just hand it over?"

"I'm not looking for a handout. I was hoping we could work something out that was mutually beneficial. As I'm sure you know, my club is based a couple of towns over, a good four-hour drive from here. We have a lot of successful operations in Dalton, but I've been looking to expand for a while. Razor territory is a good business opportunity," Midas explained.

Roman regarded the man in front of him for a moment. He was saying all the right things, but Roman didn't buy it. Not completely. "How about you tell me the truth."

Midas frowned, and Crow shifted subtly on his feet. "That is the truth," he insisted.

"Sure," Roman agreed before adding, "but not all of it. I didn't get to where I am by being naïve, Midas. I'm good at reading people. This is personal for you. Why?"

Midas shared a look with Crow before he sighed, leaning back further in his seat. "Raz's brother is the president of a rival club. A real fucker. Knowing I have possession of his baby bro's territory will really chap his ass."

"So, this is vengeance? That's never a good idea for business," Roman said with a frown.

Midas shrugged his heavy shoulders. "Sure, part of it is about sticking it to the prick. But it has other side benefits too. Like taking the heat off you. Blaze and Raz weren't best buddies or anything, but Blaze isn't the sort to let this kind of thing go. He'll come for you."

"Then I'll deal with him the same way I dealt with his brother." Roman wasn't worried.

"I'm sure you would," Midas agreed. "But why bother if you don't have to? Let us deal with him. Besides, if you thought Raz was a cunt, you haven't seen anything yet. Blaze is the biggest fuck-knuckle I've ever met."

Abel snickered. "Fuck-knuckle."

Roman snorted in amusement as well. "Are you planning to move your club into the city?" he questioned next.

Midas shook his head. "No. At least not permanently. Our clubhouse is in Dalton. It was a labor of love to get it built. I have no intention of leaving our home. But expansion is good. I know Raz ran The Morgue—a good club, by all accounts. I'm confident my brothers could make it great."

"You run drugs?" Roman asked. There was a lot to arrange, but he was already leaning towards agreeing with Midas. He had some excellent points. And sticking it to an enemy was one Roman could appreciate. He also didn't seem like a bad sort, and Roman prided himself on his judgment of character. Roman had a lot of MC members working for him at Omertà. He appreciated their sense of loyalty.

Midas frowned, shaking his head. "Nah, man. Not into drugs. Weapons mostly, but we diversify a little. I'd be happy to tell you more about it if we end up striking a deal."

Roman nodded his head, banging his fist on the table once. "I'm not a fan of drugs, personally. Especially in my city. There's enough of that shit around, so if you'd said yes, my answer would have been no."

"We're not dealers. Or peddlers," Midas guaranteed.

"I believe you," Roman assured him.

Midas took a deep breath, looking relieved. "So, do we have a deal?"

Roman looked at Abel. His friend nodded his head almost imperceptibly. But it was enough for Roman to know that Abel agreed; Midas was an okay guy. "I already own clubs, as well as most of the property at the marina. I have no interest in the warehouse district. If you and your club *do* have an interest . . ." He paused, inclining his head at Midas. "I'd be okay with that. For a small percentage as a silent partner."

"How small?" Midas asked, his gray eyes narrowing sharply.

Roman's grin was slow in forming. It was negotiation time. This was the fun part. "Forty percent."

"Forty? The fuck?!" Crow exclaimed.

Midas snorted, patting Crow on the arm. "Relax, man. He's fucking with us." He looked Roman in the eyes, offering, "Five."

"Five? You're dreaming," Roman told him.

By the time they argued back and forth, hammering out all the finer details, Roman was well satisfied he had made a good choice. He would get twelve percent of the profits from all future business endeavors The Midas Touch MC set up in Raz's old haunts. And they would spread the word that it now belonged to them. Roman and his crew had nothing to do with it. It was a good deal, considering he had only wanted ten percent. And if Blaze, Raz's blood brother, was anything like Midas seemed to think he was, Roman had dodged another bullet. It was a win-win.

"They seem like okay dudes," Abel said as soon as they were alone.

"They do," Roman agreed. "Still, I'll have Luca do a deep dive into the club. Especially Midas. If something pops up, we still have time to pull the plug on the deal before we make it all legal next month."

Abel poured himself a scotch, passing one over to Roman as well. "How is everything else?"

"Fine," Roman replied. He hadn't spoken to Angela since the phone call. But he had stopped by Lighthouse to talk with Sister Philomena again. Luca had confirmed that Roman's father and their mother had been in town when the nun said. Roman had questions, to be sure. But he also just wanted to talk with someone who had known his mother, even if it was a short acquaintance.

"I gotta say, man," Abel paused to polish off his drink in one swallow. "I applaud you for your restraint. I thought you'd be more impatient."

Roman cocked his head, nursing his drink. "When have I ever been impatient in business dealings?"

"Not that." Abel slashed his hand through the air. "About Morrigan and Angela. I thought you'd be chomping at the bit to spy on them."

Roman's focus narrowed to a pinpoint. "What the hell are you talking about?"

"They have a playdate scheduled," Abel revealed. "I figured you knew."

"A playdate?" Roman was stupefied.

"That's what Morrigan called it, anyway.

Remember how you told her to get to know Angel better? Well, she took it to heart. She invited Angel over for some girl time. I believe alcohol will be involved," Abel said with a wince.

Roman was absolutely horrified. "Please, tell me you're joking."

Abel grimaced. "You didn't know, huh?"

"No! I didn't fucking know!" Roman snapped, slamming his glass onto his desk. He stood, striding out of his office and to the elevator, praying Morrigan hadn't killed the woman of his dreams already.

CHAPTER EIGHTEEN

Angela sat across from Morrigan at the bar on one of the private levels in the Omertà building. She was more than a little apprehensive. She didn't know if she was being dramatic or not, but the other woman seemed a little . . . unhinged.

"What's your poison?"

"Poison?" Angela questioned with a squeak. Was the crazy woman going to poison her right then and there? But she looked across the mahogany wood to find Morrigan holding up a bottle of Jack in one hand and a bottle of gin in the other. "I, ah, don't drink," she replied.

Morrigan's dark eyes narrowed on her. "You don't drink?"

"Nope," Angela replied with more confidence.

"At all?" Morrigan pressed. Angela shook her head. "Why the hell not?"

She watched Morrigan pour a healthy glass of whiskey—mixed with air. "I don't drink because alcohol lies."

Morrigan tossed back the Jack in one gulp. She didn't even blink, let alone wince. "What do you mean?"

She poured herself another glass as Angela watched in fascination. The other woman was smaller in stature than her. It would be interesting to see how well she could hold her liquor. "It lies to you. *You're so awesome, Angela. You can dance, Angela. Trust me, Angela, that's a great idea!*" Angela said in a high-pitched voice. "And all the while, you're doing the running man in the middle of the dancefloor with your skirt tucked into your panties and your bra on your head."

Morrigan's next sip coincided with Angela's explanation, and she choked, snorting whiskey and coughing up a lung. Angela rushed around the bar, smacking her on the back, praying the assassin wasn't about to aspirate. As Morrigan bent over and wheezed, Angela thought, *Oh god, I've killed Roman's favorite killer!*

Morrigan eventually settled, and she stood up, looking Angela in the eye. "I can promise you there will be no dancing. So . . . what do you say?"

Angela eyed the bottles of liquid for a moment before sighing. "Fine. Scotch. Neat."

Morrigan grinned at her. "Well, would you look at that?" She switched out the Jack for Lagavulin. "We have something in common."

The amount she poured was triple what a standard drink would be, but Angela didn't correct the other woman. She would simply sip it and sit on it for the remainder of their talk.

Morrigan passed her the glass, resting her elbows on the bar. "Real talk time: I don't like you."

Angela blinked rapidly, unsure how she was supposed to respond. In the end, she simply went with, "Okay."

Morrigan snorted, pointing at her with her glass. "See, this is one of the reasons. You're not nice."

Angela's mouth dropped open. "*I'm* not nice? Don't you kill people for a living? Besides, why should I care if you like me or not? Your opinion of me is none of my business as far as I'm concerned."

"Ah, but you see, I don't go around pretending to be nice. I am what I am, and I'm cool with that. But you . . ." Morrigan sneered at her. "You swap who you are when you don't like a given situation. That's sneaky. And cold. And very *uncool*."

"I do no such thing!" Angela exclaimed, glaring at the beautiful, deadly woman.

"You really do. You have a great bedside manner, Doc. I've watched you. You treat your patients well. You're kind and respectful to strangers. You clearly give a shit about the world because you work to make it a better place at the Lighthouse," Morrigan said. "But then you go and treat Roman like shit. But only on even days. On odd days, you're friendly to him. It pisses me off, Angela. You're not good for him."

Angela hunched her shoulders, trying her best to escape Morrigan's words. She wished she could unhear them, but they were already taking up prime real estate in her brain. Morrigan had hit the nail on the head, and Angela felt like she'd been spanked. "Well, luckily for you—and apparently, for Roman—there's nothing between us," she responded.

Morrigan's expression turned incredulous. "And you accused alcohol of being a liar! You can lie to yourself all you want, Angela, but don't lie to me. You don't *want* there to be anything between you and Roman. There's a difference."

"You're right," Angela confessed. "Unfortunately, I'm not at a point where I can do anything about it."

Morrigan grunted, tossing back her drink. "Are you at least working on it?"

"Why do you care?" Angela wanted to know. "You just told me you don't like me and I'm no good for Roman. So, what do you care if I'm doing shadow work or not?"

"Maybe I'd *like* to like you. Did you ever think of that?" Morrigan put forward.

"No. I didn't," Angela answered honestly. She paused, making some circles with her thick-bottomed glass on the bar. She peered at Morrigan a little shyly. "Is it true?"

Morrigan grumbled under her breath, hoisting herself onto the bar and swinging her legs. "Maybe. I'd do just about anything for Roman. If you're important to him, you're important to me. It would be good if that were more than just an obligation, though. It would be nice if it were real."

Angela cleared her throat, thinking, *fuck it*, before knocking her drink back in one swallow. It burned like a bitch, but the expensive scotch was damned smooth. "It would be nice," she replied quietly.

"Good. Great," Morrigan agreed irritably. "Do you have a problem with my life choices?"

"Um, do you mean being a contract killer?" Angela asked. Morrigan nodded once, and Angela shrugged. "No. I mean, I probably should. But in the spirit of honesty and because it's an odd day . . ." She grinned, pleased to see Morrigan's lips twitch. "No. Your life choices don't bother me."

They were silent for a moment as Morrigan poured them more alcohol. She handed the glass over and held hers up. Angela clanked hers against Morrigan's as the other said, "So . . . if you have no issue with what I do morally, why do you have such a problem with Roman?"

Angela sighed, taking a sip of liquid courage before she answered as openly as her trauma would allow. "I have a bad history with his type."

Morrigan frowned, tilting her head to the side. "His type?"

"A criminal overlord," Angela supplied.

Morrigan surprised her by bursting into laughter. "Overlord? Roman would love that so much." She grinned, still chuckling. "More than being called a rebel or prince."

Angela groaned. "Please don't tell him I said that."

Morrigan cackled. "No promises." She eyed Angela over the rim of her glass. "Care to elaborate more about knowing his type? Because Luca looked into your history and didn't find any shit to affect your shine. Now, don't look so offended, Doc," she said briskly. "Of course we were going to check you out. Rich girl from the good side of town, professional parents, big house in a gated community, and a free ride at college in medicine. Nothing at all to suggest you've had any dealings with criminal organizations in the past."

"Yeah, well, things aren't always as they seem," Angela muttered, guzzling her drink. She shoved the memories of her parents back into the locked box they were trying to escape from.

"On that, we can both agree," Morrigan concurred. "Take Roman, for example. He's the best man I know. Even though I've seen him beat a guy to death with his bare hands."

It wasn't the first time Angela had been told that about Roman. She could definitely see a pattern emerging amongst his tribe. "You really mean that, don't you?" Angela asked curiously.

"I really do. And if you take the time, maybe stop being a miserable, snarky shrew to him on even days, then maybe you might find he'll be the same thing for you."

Angela rubbed the almost-faded bruise on her neck. The collar of her shirt concealed it enough now that it was almost gone. Roman had been correct when he said her body wanted one thing and her mind another. But what he didn't know was her heart was becoming more and more aligned with her body, and that was where her main resistance was coming from. She knew it was true; Roman was, in fact, a good man. And more than that—he was the man for her.

The knowledge absolutely terrified her.

"Well, Dr. Angel," Morrigan said, breaking the comfortable silence that had formed between them. "Now that I don't feel like slitting your throat anymore, how about another drink?"

Angela looked down, shocked to discover she had polished off the entire glass of her second scotch. She ignored the throat-slitting remark, holding up her glass. "Why the hell not?"

———

"So, Doc. Tell me why you don't do commitments," Morrigan bade her about two hours later.

"Because people always let you down," Angela replied quickly, letting out a small burp. She was shocked to find herself having a great time with Morrigan. They were both on the same side of the bar now, with Angela having moved her stool so she had easier access to the alcohol.

Morrigan nodded, pouring them another glass of scotch. Some spilled over the edges, but neither woman cared. "I hear that, sister. People are fuckers."

Angela nodded, feeling her head spin a little. "People are fuckers," she agreed.

"I mean. They say they're going to be there. And you come to like it—rely on it even," Morrigan said, her eyes narrowed dangerously. "But then, do you know what they do?"

Angela wasn't sure if it was a rhetorical question or not, but she answered anyway. "They fuck you. And not in the fun way."

"Exactly!" Liquid sloshed out of Morrigan's glass when she swung it around before taking a healthy swallow. "You get used to them being there, then you wake up one morning, and the next thing you know, they're gone."

Angela nodded somberly. "Just like the center of a donut."

"Yes!" Morrigan shouted, holding out her fist for a bump. "Gone, just like the center of a donut." She paused for a moment, her gaze distant, before she remarked, "What's with that? What's with the hole?"

"I have no idea. It's such a waste," Angela replied.

"It really is. Donuts are delicious. Why would someone deliberately poke a hole in the middle of such deliciousness? And then throw it away? Like trash?" Morrigan questioned, her eyes turning misty.

Angela's throat constricted with emotion. She knew what it was like to feel like trash. "Those poor donuts."

"We should rescue them," Morrigan declared, leaning in close.

Angela perked up. She sat up straighter, slipping from the stool and finding herself on the floor. She made no attempt to get back up. "Rescue the donuts?"

Morrigan stood up before crossing her feet and sinking to the floor next to Angela. She nodded vigorously. "Yes. We should rescue the donuts. We could do it. I'm sure we could. I have weapons. Like, soooo many weapons."

"You're awesome," Angela told her new friend. "Weapons are awesome."

"So awesome!" Morrigan agreed.

"You know, I keep a gun in my kitchen drawer." Angela puffed up her chest proudly. "Pretty badass, huh?"

"Totally," Morrigan agreed. "I bet you'd be good at slicing people up too."

"Oh, abso-fucking-lutely. I can slice and dice the bestest," Angela promised.

"I just sliced a guy last night," Morrigan revealed, listing to the left a little. "He was a real swine's butt-hole. Smacked my ass as I was walking past. So I cut his palm up. He won't be slapping any more asses for a while." She smiled, whispering, "I predict twenty stitches."

Angela offered her a high-five. Both women missed. "Sometimes, men need to be punished," Angela agreed wholeheartedly. "There was this one guy, Anthony, he tried to launch a sneak attack in the back door."

Morrigan gasped. "He didn't!"

Angela nodded seriously. "He did."

Morrigan screwed up her face in disgust. "Not cool."

"Right? I mean, we all know that kind of tomfoolery takes planning." Angela tossed her glass back, wondering why the Lagavulin suddenly tasted so diluted.

"And patience," Morrigan added.

"And lube," Angela stated.

"*Lots* of lube," Morrigan agreed, her almost-black eyes wide in her pretty face.

CHAPTER NINETEEN

R oman couldn't believe his ears. He had run as
fast as he could, praying he wasn't too late to
stop Morrigan doing something stupid to
Angela.

He figured there would be blood. Or at least some
bruising. But what he found concerned him even more.
The pair of them were on the floor, drunk off their
pretty little asses. Not only that, they were talking
about . . . *Sweet baby Jesus!* Roman thought. He turned to
Abel, who had followed him. "Are they talking
about . . .?"

Abel nodded gravely. "Going into the Batcave? I
believe so."

Roman's eyes widened in panic. "Jesus fucking
Christ! They've bonded."

Abel swallowed noisily, looking a little pale. "What have you done?"

"Me?" Roman glared at him, shoving his shoulder. "You were the one who told Morrigan to get to know Angel."

"But you agreed!" Abel shot back, shoving him in return.

Roman regained his balance easily, but remorse weighed heavily on his heart. He and Abel stood silently in the doorway, watching as the two women, each dangerous in their own right, bonded over . . . *Batcaves.*

"Oh, and FYI," Angela was saying. "Spit is not lube."

"Totally," Morrigan concurred.

Abel looked at Roman accusingly, and Roman hunched his shoulders a little. "What?" he snapped. "I know spit isn't lube." *Unless I'm rubbing one out on myself,* he added.

"Whatever, man," Abel said. "Just stop whatever this is. This is terrifying."

Because Roman concurred, and because Angela was talking about past lovers and it made him feel all murdery, he stepped further into the room and cleared his throat. The women ignored him completely. He coughed loudly, only to be ignored for a second time. He looked at Abel in the doorway, who shrugged, and Roman flipped him off for being useless.

"So, you and Roman, huh?"

Morrigan said it with a teasing wink. At least, Roman assumed it was supposed to be a wink. Both her eyelids had come down, but one not quite as much.

Angela shook her finger at Morrigan as if she was a naughty child. "Ah ah ah. I already told you there is no me and Roman."

Morrigan huffed. "But if there was . . .?

Angela hummed, rocking side to side for a moment. "Let's just say I'd let him put his golden key into my backdoor lock whenever he wanted."

The two drunk women cackled, falling onto their backs and rolling around the floor. Roman worried he was going to faint because there was no way that much blood should be able to move that fast from his brain to his cock, and for him to still be okay. In fact, he thought he may never be okay again. Angela had said that. She'd really said it.

"Do you know what would be funny? If Roman was right behind you," Morrigan said, finally making eye contact with him and acknowledging his presence.

Angela snorted inelegantly. "Yeah right. That would be a nightmare. The man already has a big enough head thanks to his big enough dick."

Morrigan blanched. "Ugh. That's my cousin. I don't

need to know the size of his junk. And I'm sorry, but he really is right behind you."

Angela snickered drunkenly, punching Morrigan on the biceps. "Good one. You're so funny."

Roman cleared his throat loudly one last time. Angela looked up at him from her position on her back on the floor. Her face was flushed, and her eyes were a little glassy. Her lips immediately moved into a pout, and he instantly pictured them wrapped around the head of his dick. He wanted to paint her lips with his precum before sliding down her throat. His cock throbbed painfully.

Angela made a disgusted sound as she peered up at him. "Why are you so pretty?" she demanded.

Roman couldn't help but stand a little taller. "You think I'm pretty?" This time, the rude, disgusted sound came from Morrigan. He shot her a dirty look before inquiring, "What exactly is going on here?" She looked innocent enough in her drunken state, but he wasn't fooled. Morrigan didn't have an innocent bone in her body.

"I'm just getting to know your doctor. Like you suggested," she reminded him in answer.

"By getting her drunk?" he demanded. "This is not what I meant, and you know it."

"Hey!" Angela yelled. "I'm right here. And I'm not drunk," she denied, attempting a straight face.

"Ha! You really are . . . Running Man." Morrigan cackled evilly.

Roman had no idea what she was talking about.

Angela gasped. "I am not!"

Morrigan shouted right back, "Are too!"

When Angela responded in kind yet again, and the pair of women continued to shout back and forth at each other, Roman pinched the bridge of his nose. They were giving him a headache. And anxiety. "Ladies, enough."

"I'm no lady," Morrigan asserted. But she did sit upright finally.

Angela didn't move—other than her mouth. Which was being very loud. Apparently, she had forgotten what an inside voice was. "And I'm no lady, either," she was saying. "I'm a donut-hole saving machine!"

Morrigan cheered, and when they begin to sing "We Are The Champions" by Queen, Roman had finally had enough. "That's it, Angel. You're cut off."

Angela blew a raspberry at him. "You're not the boss of me."

"Actually, he kind of is. He pays you," Morrigan reminded her.

"Pfft. Semantics," Angela muttered, waving her hand around wildly.

Roman had to jump back swiftly to avoid being hit in the nuts by her uncoordinated hand. He wasn't going to argue with her, so he simply reached down and picked her up, holding her close to his chest.

"What the hell do you think you're doing?" she shrieked, grabbing onto his shoulders.

"I'm taking you to bed," he responded with a grunt. She was damn strong.

"Nope," Angela said, beginning to struggle. "I'm out of here."

He put his face close to hers. "If you think I am going to let you drive home in this state, think again. You have two choices: I can set you up in a guest suite, or I can take you to my room and tie you to my bed like I've been longing to do."

The rapid rising and falling of her generous breasts caught his attention, derailing his lecture. His hands flexed on the handfuls of Angela he already had. He personally liked option number two.

"Stop looking at my breasts," Angela ordered him. But it sounded a little weak to him.

"I can't seem to help it," he admitted.

"Well . . ." Morrigan said, pushing herself to her feet. "You seem to have things well in hand, cousin. I'll leave you to it." She stopped and spoke to Angela on her way past. "Doc, don't give up the booty on the first date."

Angela nodded earnestly. "I won't. I'm not that kind of girl."

Roman snorted because she had indeed given her body over to him within twenty-four hours of meeting him. Hell, he didn't even need to take her out on a date first. "Goodnight, Morrigan," was all he said. "Abel? Help Morrigan to her room, will you?" He didn't bother to look at the bickering pair as they left. Morrigan didn't live at Omertà full-time, but she still had her own suite of rooms.

"This is a nice tie," Angela murmured, picking up his tie and rubbing it along her face.

Roman didn't know whether to be turned-on or horrified. "It's silk."

"Hmm, I like silk," she said, slurring a little and moving the tie down her neck.

Roman gritted his teeth, telling himself that she was drunk and didn't know what she was doing. His dick didn't know the difference, though. And it was hard enough to pound nails. He headed towards the elevator and his private floor. Level fifty-nine had been renovated to be one huge apartment. It spanned seventeen hundred square feet and had four bedrooms, five bathrooms, an office, and three common areas. He had an entire wing where his bedroom and office were, and he spent most of his time there. But one of the bedrooms, on the opposite side of the apartment, had its own living space and bathroom. That's where he intended to put Angela.

"Look how good we look together."

Roman's eyes flew to hers in the mirrored elevator doors. She was staring at them, looking dreamy, wistful, and also a little scared. But he agreed with her; she looked fucking amazing in his arms. "I knew you would be trouble the moment I laid eyes on you," he told her, kissing the top of her head.

"I knew the same," she whispered, resting her head on his shoulder. "It's not the type of trouble I need or want."

Remembering what he had just overhead, he questioned, "Are you sure about that? You seem to be pretty cozy with my crew."

"Your crew isn't you," Angela said.

She nuzzled against the crook of his shoulder as the elevator doors opened and he walked directly into his apartment. He was sure she wasn't aware of what she was doing, but his heart turned over in his chest, nonetheless. She was soft and warm and relaxed, and she felt like she was made to be in his arms. It sounded trite, and he would have scoffed had anyone else said the same thing. But he couldn't help embracing the truth of it.

As he walked to the guest suite, Angela raised her head a little. "I don't feel so good."

He looked down to find her very pale. "Shit!" he exclaimed. "Don't throw up on me."

She took some deep breaths as he moved faster, opening the suite door, bypassing the living area, and depositing her on the bed. She hiccuped, covering her mouth with her hand. He left her for a moment, returning with a water bottle. She was right where he'd left her, with an arm thrown over her head to block out the light.

"Angel, drink some water," he insisted.

"I like water," Angela allowed, sitting up and guzzling half the bottle. "I also like your face. And your body. I especially like your cock and how it has its own little crown."

Roman choked on his own spit, pressing his palm down hard on his erection. She was making it very diffi-cult for him to remember that he was a gentleman. Even so, he was very tempted to question her about her past. It bugged him that nobody could find anything, and he wasn't sure she would ever be at a point where she would volunteer the information. His chances were high, though, if he were to ask now.

He settled her against the pillows, taking her shoes off and covering her with the comforter. She let him tend to her, and he realized that three months ago it was something she would never have allowed. Hell, it was likely something she wouldn't let anyone else do, even now. The implied trust meant he couldn't break it. Whatever haunted her may be stopping her from being with him, but it wasn't putting his family at risk. He decided he wouldn't question her when her faculties were diminished.

But there was one thing he couldn't help but ask before he left. "Do you want me, Angel?"

"Yes," she admitted without hesitation. "More than I've ever wanted anyone in my life. Which is exactly why I can't have you. It makes you dangerous. More dangerous than any gun or knife." She blinked sleepily, rolling onto her side and hugging the pillow. "Not to mention who you are. I know your type. I know what the pursuit of power can do. It changes a person, makes them selfish and careless. It causes them to betray."

"I would never betray you, baby," Roman promised, his throat thick. But Angela either didn't hear him or didn't care because she kept right on talking and breaking his heart.

"I've been betrayed by those I trusted the most." She looked up at him through teary eyes. "It hurts so damn bad. Yes, I have fun with Luca and Salvatore, and Abel—the big oaf—is a good friend. But if they stopped being my friends, it would hurt, but I'd recover. I'd be fine. You, Roman, if I allow myself to like you, if I allow myself to want you, there'd be no turning back. And when it doesn't work . . . because it won't—very little in my life ever does—it would break me. It would break me in ways I don't think I could recover from. I don't understand it, but I know I don't like it. So, you and I will never happen."

She reached out a hand and Roman took it. "Do you understand what I'm saying?" Angela asked him.

Oh, Roman understood, all right. He understood all too well. "I understand," he replied, kissing her palm. It was in that moment he decided he loved her and was able to admit it to himself. He loved her, and he was doomed because of it.

"Get some sleep, Angel," he urged her.

Angela frowned, her bottom lip poking out in a pout. "I bet you say that to all the women, don't you? And they just fall at your feet."

Roman smiled because jealousy looked good on her. "To be honest, I rarely have to say anything to have women falling at my feet. Usually, a look is enough."

"Brainless bitches," Angela said with a sneer, her lids lowering once more.

"Quite so," Roman agreed, looking at her with amusement and affection. "Nothing like you at all."

"Right. Because I'm not brainless," Angela declared. She blinked at him, frowning a little. "Heeeey . . . you have a chunk of vomit on your shirt. Was that me, do you think? Or was that you?"

He looked down, finding a piece of something unidentifiable on his shoulder, surrounded by dampness. "I'm thinking that was you."

"Huh," Angela commented. "Must have been that hiccup." She paused, her creamy flesh turning green before his eyes. "I hate to tell you, but I don't think this will be a hiccup."

Before he could move, the only woman he knew he could ever love, barfed all over his Italian leather shoes.

CHAPTER TWENTY

"Hi, Angela. I was just wondering if you were still coming over tonight?"

"Tonight? Did we have plans?" she asked Luca, who was on the other end of her cell phone. She really hoped they didn't. It had been a nightmare shift and her head was pounding—as well as her face. She had taken a hard kick to the eye from a junkie hopped up on the latest street drug and had a rapidly forming shiner.

"It's Friday. You said Sal's stitches were due out today," Luca reminded her.

Angela grimaced, leaning her back against the headrest in her car. She was in the exact same spot she had been six months prior when she'd been trussed up like a Thanksgiving turkey and tossed in the trunk of a stranger's car. The first few times she'd gone to work, it was difficult to park in her reserved space. But she pushed through the residual fear, and it hadn't bothered her since. It probably also had something to do with the fact that people like Luca and Abel called her so frequently these days. She was well and truly desensitized.

"Angela? Are you still there?" Luca asked.

"I'm here," she replied, not opening her eyes.

"You sound beat," Luca said sympathetically. "Forget I mentioned it. Salvatore has no problem pulling his own stitches out."

Her lids flew open. "Pulling?! Luca, you bite your tongue," she scolded.

The very thought of Salvatore wrenching out her neat stitches, made her break out in hives. Yes, he was ex-military and had enough medical skills to sew himself up, meaning he could easily remove his own stitches. But after getting to know him, she knew he would be just as likely to use his teeth.

Like a savage.

"I'll be there in ten minutes," she stated.

Luca giggled. "Seriously, Angela, you don't have to come. It's not an emergency. You do enough for us."

"And I get paid exorbitantly, don't I?" she retorted.

Roman was still directing funds to the resource

center. Although, the asshole had paid a few hundred dollars less one time to cover the cost of new shoes. The memory of the night she had gotten drunk with Morrigan was still fresh in her mind, even three months later. Well, kind of fresh, she amended. Most of her conversation with her drinking buddy was hazy. But she vividly remembered blowing chunks all over Roman and his beautiful, plush cream carpet. "I'm on my way," she said to Luca. "I haven't even left the hospital yet."

She made it to Omertà within ten minutes, taking the elevator directly to Luca and Sal's apartment. It was on the floor below Roman's and was a warm and fun space. She had spent many nights there eating, playing cards, and laughing. She knocked on the door, counting off the throbbing beats in her head.

Luca opened the door with a wide smile. "Thanks for com—" He broke off with a gasp. "Oh, honey, what happened to your poor face?"

Angela smiled at her younger friend. "It's nothing. A work mishap. Now, where is this man of yours?"

"He's in the kitchen with Roman," Luca replied with a frown.

Angela had just walked inside, and was heading in the direction of the kitchen, but she paused. "Roman is here?"

Luca nodded. "It's Friday." Luca smiled, but it looked strained and worried. "Remember? We kind of just talked about the day of the week on the phone."

Angela would have slapped her forehead if it didn't already hurt so much. Friday night was family dinner night. Each week, the location changed from Luca's to Roman's, but the brothers always got together to share a meal every week. Often, Abel and Morrigan and a few others would join them if they were free. Angela had been invited many times, but she always declined. It may have been a casual meal at home, but it was one reserved for family.

"I'm sorry. I totally forgot about family dinner night," she said.

"It's fine. You know you're welcome," Luca insisted. He wrapped an arm around her waist, resting his head against hers. They were about the same height. "Sit down. You really don't look so good."

Angela sighed, giving Luca some of her weight. She was just about to agree when she heard a commotion. Looking up, she saw Roman charging towards her.

"What the fuck happened?" he demanded.

Angela stood up straight again, making a passable attempt at a smile. "I took a boot to the face."

"Someone kicked you?" Salvatore asked as he entered the room. He looked pissed.

Angela stood still as Roman reached out with his hand. His touch was gentle as he turned her face this way and that, but his face was murderous. As if the bruise was somehow a personal insult to him. "It was a patient. It happens sometimes." She pulled herself free, mostly because all she really wanted to do was lean into his touch.

Roman crossed his arms over his chest. "Explain," he ordered.

Angela started to roll her eyes, but the movement hurt too damn much. "Roman, it's no big deal. It's a bruise. I've had worse. Trust me."

"You're not helping the situation," Luca mock-whispered from beside her.

Angela frowned at him, unsure what he meant. She looked at Roman again who appeared to be doing some kind of deep breathing exercise. "Are you okay?"

"Am *I* okay?" He looked at her incredulously. "Woman, you slay me."

"Oookay," she said slowly. She jerked her thumb at the door. "I'm just going to go . . ."

"Don't," Roman said. He grabbed her hand, holding it in his. "Tell me what happened."

She hesitated, not wanting to get into it. Plus, she had Salvatore's stitches to deal with. "A patient hopped up on the latest street drug had to be held down and sedated. Unfortunately, I was at the bottom of the bed and got a boot to my face for my efforts." She pressed on the puffy skin under her eyes, hissing because it hurt like a bitch.

"Don't do that," Roman ordered, pulling her hand away.

Angela scowled at him. "Don't tell me what to do."

Roman closed his mouth with an audible snap. He looked up at the ceiling, planting his hands on his hips. His lips were moving, but she couldn't make out what he was saying. She thought it was in Italian and tried very hard not to find it sexy as hell. "What are you doing?" she asked.

"Praying," Roman replied, shooting her a frustrated look. "You could test the patience of a saint."

"Me? I'm not the mobster," Angela reminded him.

Roman scowled at her. "I am *not* a mobster."

"Fine then, a Don," she corrected. "I don't know why you're arguing semantics with me." The words were said without any real heat. The last few months had mellowed out their relationship some. She wasn't as antagonistic, and he no longer pressured her in any way.

"I'm not a Don, either. I renounced my family. I've told you this before," Roman reminded her.

Actually, she knew very little about his mafia background. He didn't talk about it, and she had never asked. She could admit to being curious though. "A criminal is a criminal."

Roman took an aggressive step forward, glaring down at her from his impressive six-foot-two height. "Why are you still alive again?" he questioned. "I've killed men for far more minor insults."

"Wait, can you repeat that, please? I didn't have my phone on record." She made a show of sifting around in her bag.

Roman's mouth fell open, and he looked at her like she was insane. "You drive me crazy. You know that, right?"

Angela shrugged. She took a small step back, even though it made her look like she was backing down. They were far too close, and she could feel the heat radiating off his muscular body like a furnace. "It was a short drive, I'm sure."

"Will you two fuck already?" Salvatore asked, looking frustrated. "I swear, this foreplay is killing me."

Angela shot him a filthy look. "Do you really want to piss me off when I'm about to be close to you with a pair of scissors?" Sal closed his mouth, muttered a quick farewell, and all but ran down the hallway in the opposite direction. "Coward," she muttered. But it was with affection.

Luca snickered into his hand, giving Angela a kiss on the cheek as he walked past. "I'll check on him. His stitches aren't going anywhere. Take a bit of time for yourself first."

Angela smiled gratefully, nodding silently.

"He's right about one thing. We should fuck. Again."

Angela's head whipped around just in time to see Roman's delectable mouth morph into a sexy smirk. He really was a magnificent specimen of a man, she thought. And she knew what that mouth of his could do to her breasts—and her clit. She had to clear her throat twice before she was able to reply. "No fucking."

His eyes traced her mouth for a moment before taking a lazy ogle of her breasts and the juncture of her thighs. "Your loss," he eventually retorted.

She couldn't help but agree.

"Angel?" Roman waited to speak until her gaze met his once more. "I hope you know the *no fucking* rule applies to other men. If I find out you're sleeping with anyone else, I won't be pleased."

Angela gaped at him. *The audacity!* Had she really just thought he had backed off with the pressure and their relationship had been smooth? "You have no say over my love life, Roman. Pull your head in."

Roman merely shook his head, looking unruffled.

But there was a coldness to him that had Angela shivering. "You've been warned."

She stood there for a moment, unsure how to react. Because she believed him. She just didn't know why he cared who she slept with. "I don't understand you," she admitted softly, feeling unaccountably exposed.

Roman lost his stiffness, his shoulders relaxing. "I know you don't," he responded just as quietly. He tucked a strand of her hair behind her ear, brushing his knuckles against her injured cheek. "But one day you will. And when that day comes, I'll be here. Now, come on," he continued before she could speak. "Let me see to that bruise."

She was feeling so mixed up that she followed him into the kitchen before she even noticed. "Wait. I'm a doctor. I know how to treat a bruise, Roman."

"Then why haven't you?" he asked archly, rifling through Luca's freezer.

"Because . . ." It was the best she could do. Her last shift was catching up to her, and her head was throbbing. She needed five aspirins and her bed in the worst way.

"Despite what you may think, *because* isn't an excuse. Sit down," Roman ordered.

Angela stood where she was, glaring at him. She hated being ordered around.

Roman sighed and shook his head. *"Angelo,* you really are a hard-ass, you know?"

Angela sighed as well, rubbing her temple. "I know I am," she admitted. "I can't seem to help it."

"Well, luckily for you, I happen to like buns of steel," he teased, winking at her.

Angela laughed. She knew he had a good sense of humor, but she rarely allowed herself to enjoy it. "Good to know," she told him with a smile.

This time, when he gestured her over to one of the seats at the table in the attached dining room, she moved with no further arguments. "I can do this myself," she said, only to flinch when the pack of frozen peas met her sore flesh.

"Chiedo scusa," Roman murmured. He kept the cold peas steady against her cheek, easing up on the pressure a little.

Angela did her best to relax, her tenseness easing as the ice did its job and began to numb her skin. She noticed the way his eyes kept flicking to her face to judge her comfort levels, and her brain relaxed enough to admit, "I really love it when you speak Italian."

Roman looked surprised. "You do?"

Angela nodded, sternly telling herself not to blush.

"I'm glad. I was raised speaking Italian and Sicilian —which are two very different languages," he informed her. "Never make the mistake of calling them the same."

Angela laughed a little. "I swear I won't." Roman pulled up a chair and sat down in front of her, his knees brushing hers as he continued to cup her face gently. "You're really good at this."

"I've treated my fair share of shiners," he said. Then he paused as if debating whether to continue. Finally, he disclosed, "My mother."

The pain in those two simple words hit close to home. She realized that no matter what kind of man he was now, he had once been a little boy who had clearly loved his mother. "I'm sorry."

"I am too," Roman murmured.

"Is that why you killed your father?" The question was out before she could stop herself. When he just stared at her silently, she forged ahead. "I knew who you were—and what your reputation was—when you told me your name the very first time we met. I'm a surgical physician of the biggest hospital in the city. I see things. I hear things."

"I'm sure you do," he agreed easily. "But that's a dangerous question to ask."

"I'm not afraid of you," she told him. She said it quietly but genuinely.

"I know," Roman responded. "You never have been.

Not even when I held a gun to your head. Why is that?" he asked, tilting his head.

Angela licked her suddenly dry lips, noting the way Roman's eyes tracked the movement. "I don't know," she murmured.

"Hmm . . ." He lowered the now-warm pack of peas. "*I* know."

"You think so?" she questioned, commanding herself to sit back.

Roman leaned forward into her personal space, picking up her hand and kissing her knuckles gallantly. "Shall I tell you why, my sweet Angel?"

She managed a shaky nod, her pulse going wild.

"It's because you don't fear death. Because you know there are far worse things in life than an eternal slumber," Roman told her. "You've seen them." He waited for her to nod before continuing. "You've *felt* them."

Angela swallowed with difficulty, telling herself not to admit anything. Not to show any weakness. But she was being lulled by his soft voice, somehow holding a sweet, new Italian accent, and his usually honey-brown eyes had darkened. "I have." It felt like a confession.

"Tell me who harmed you, *mio angelo*," he bade her. He cupped her chin in his hand, meeting her eyes. "Tell me, and I will see to it that they discover the true meaning of the word *pain*."

She sighed, leaning into his palm where it now cupped her uninjured cheek. "That is the most romantic thing anyone has ever said to me," she admitted honestly. "What does that say about me?"

"It says you are a queen," Roman said softly. He inched forward, his breath fanning across her lips. "I could seduce you so easily."

Angela felt the truth of that statement in every pore of her being. "I know," she acknowledged. She didn't move, yet managed to whisper, "But please don't."

He remained where he was for another heartbeat, his thumb brushing across her bottom lip before he finally sat back. Angela didn't know whether to be relieved or devastated.

Roman shifted in his seat for a moment before he spoke. "To answer your earlier question—no. That wasn't why I killed my father. But it was a part of it."

The abrupt shift caused Angela to sit up straighter. This was usually the part where she would curse herself for falling for Roman's charms and making herself vulnerable. But she just didn't have it in her at that moment. So, for once, she let herself go. She allowed herself the freedom to be something other than the careful doctor she had molded herself into.

She allowed herself to be *Angel*—a name, and perhaps a person, she now loved.

"Do you want to know the whole reason?" Roman inquired, a solo eyebrow arched high.

She considered saying no. It would have been the smart thing to say. Just say *no* and walk away. But she had never been one for taking the easy road. So, instead, she said, "Yes. I want to know."

CHAPTER TWENTY-ONE

"My parents were part of a business transaction," Roman began.

"They were promised to each other to bring two rival *mafioso* families closer together. It worked for a time. But discord between my two sets of grandparents was inevitable. The Romano family and the Lombardo family have been at war for generations. Nothing so simple as joining the bloodline was going to work. My parents both tried—I do believe that. Mother was very beautiful and father was quite handsome. He could be charming when he wanted to be. But then, so can a snake."

Angela was listening avidly, and there was a part of him that was pleased she wanted to know more about him. But he was also scared it would change how she

DARCY HALIFAX

saw him. He had respected her boundaries over the past three months, since the night she puked all over him. But it wasn't easy. His affection and his need for her had only grown with time. Not diminished. Seeing her lovely face mottled in red and blue made him want to kill something. He wondered idly if he should pay the junkie a visit, but quickly dismissed the idea because he knew Angel would not approve. So, he forged ahead with his tale.

"I was the only child for a long time. My mother doted on me. I was her whole world. And she was mine. I'm not ashamed to admit I was a momma's boy. I even *planted* a flower garden in her memory." He tugged his shirt down to reveal his colorful tattoo.

Angel briefly hesitated, then reached out, running her finger along a bright-purple petal. "Your mother liked gardening?" Roman nodded. "It's beautiful artwork. I've been meaning to ask you about it since that time . . ." Angela cleared her throat, dropping her hand and leaning back in her seat.

Roman knew the time she was referring to. The only time she had seen him without a shirt on. Because thinking about that day gave him a hard-on, and now really wasn't the best time for that, he allowed Angel to get away with the reference without him trying to seduce her again. "I used her favorite flowers and colors. She loved color. She often had colors on her skin. I didn't know what it meant at first. Seeing her bruises became the norm, and I'm ashamed to admit it took a long time for me to question them. She always had an excuse—she was clumsy, she fell . . . But she wasn't clumsy. She was a graceful woman."

"She was protecting your father?" Angela guessed, her expression compassionate.

"She was protecting *me*," Roman corrected her. "By that stage, she held no love for the man. But for me?" He smiled, remembering his mother's face and the way her eyes seemed to sparkle whenever she looked at him. "I was her whole world. She didn't want me to question my father. Which is exactly what I did when I learned the truth at eight years old. My father didn't even deny it. Just told me that some women needed a firm hand and there were consequences for the wrong behavior. The latter I already knew, of course. My mother did her best to protect me from the *famiglia* when I was young, but being the only son made it impossible. I had already been exposed to the shadier side of the business, and violence was as common to me as eating breakfast."

"I'm sorry," Angela murmured.

He shrugged. The violent side of the business had never bothered him, even as a boy. But what had, was realizing his father treated his mother like shit. "My relationship with my father changed after that—as my mother knew it would. It was why she kept the truth from me as long as she did. She got pregnant again when I was eleven. I was ecstatic. And for a while, everything changed. My parents were happy, and there were no more bruises, no more yelling. But then, when my mother was six months pregnant, she became ill and bedbound. Or so I thought."

"So you thought?" Angela repeated. She shook her head, her brow creasing. "She wasn't sick?"

"No," Roman said harshly. "She was being kept prisoner by my father. He used the baby and me to ensure her compliance. She stayed in her room for the next three months, withering before my eyes."

"I don't understand," Angela admitted. "Why? What happened?"

"I didn't understand either. Not for a long time," Roman added. "My father had discovered mother was having an affair." When Angela swore, he knew she grasped the implications. "The baby wasn't his. He wanted to kill my mother immediately but devised a better plan. One that would satisfy his thirst for revenge and inflict the most damage as possible."

He leaned forward, his elbows resting on his knees. "I didn't know any of this at the time, of course. I was blind and stupid," he confessed bitterly.

"You were eleven years old. You were a child!" Angela pointed out passionately.

Roman couldn't help but smile. She looked so fierce —and in her defense of *him*, no less. "I was not an ordinary child, Angel. I had been groomed from the cradle to take the reins of the two biggest organized crime families in America, Italy, and Sicily. I should have known. My naïvety and ignorance cost my mother her life."

"I don't believe that for a second," Angela declared. She softened after a moment, asking, "What happened?"

"I'll spare you all the gory details," he replied. He didn't want to relive them any more than he wanted those images to invade Angel's mind. "Eventually, my father killed my mother's lover Ian front of her. He cut the baby from her belly, then he killed her as well. He told me she died in childbirth and that the baby—my brother—had also died."

He met her horrified gaze levelly, telling her honestly, "I spent the next six years hardening my heart to everything and everyone. I became a cruel, spoiled child of a monster. My father was most pleased," he added sardonically. "I became a mirror image of him and everything he ever wanted in an heir."

Angela reached out, taking his hand in her own without hesitation. "You somehow learned the truth?"

Roman nodded once sharply. "I did. I overhead a conversation between him and my uncle talking about Luca and the life he was living. Turns out, he *didn't* have my brother killed. He had sold him to the highest bidder."

Angela dropped his hand as if it was on fire. "Human trafficking?" she whispered brokenly.

Angela went so white that Roman feared she was about to pass out. He cursed, moving forward to grip her shoulders. "Angel, are you okay? I'm sorry. I shouldn't be telling you all of this."

"No. It's okay. I'm okay. I just wasn't expecting . . ." She swallowed audibly and gave herself a shake. "Continue."

He hesitated. "Angel . . ."

"Please. I want to know," she assured him, taking a deep breath and letting it out. "Hiding from harsh truths never saved anyone."

"I agree with you there. All right." He nodded and sat back in his seat. "Yes, my father trafficked a mere baby. I confronted him. He tried to lie at first, but I soon beat the truth out of him. Right before I killed his hateful ass, I saw the way he looked at me. He wasn't afraid. He didn't beg for his life. He laughed. I had become the monster. And he was proud."

Roman looked away, too afraid to see what expression Angela wore. "I've never hated anyone as much as I did in that moment. And it wasn't my piece of shit father," he told her.

"You hated yourself because you thought he was right," Angela guessed.

His head whipped back around, finding a sympathetic look on her face. It was somehow worse than the look of disgust or fear he thought would have been there. "Because I *knew* he was right," he immediately corrected her. "I *am* a monster, Angel. Make no mistake about that."

They were both silent for a long while, lost in their own thoughts. *I'm going to have to cancel family dinner night*, he thought. He knew he wouldn't be good company. The suppressed pain and rage he constantly lived with had risen to the surface, renewed. "*Mi scusi,*" he eventually murmured, rising from his seat. He needed to go. But he paused when Angela spoke.

"Roman, why did you tell me all that?"

He met her bright-green eyes squarely. "Because you asked."

"You could have lied," she said, her gaze mapping his face.

What she was searching for, he didn't know. He reached down, tracing her bruise carefully, feeling a little sick. "I will never lie to you," he vowed. "Maybe you should remember that whenever you ask me something in the future." Then he strode away.

Angela called his name one last time. "I've looked into the eyes of many monsters, Roman. Yours are not one of them."

Her words were spoken adamantly, but Roman didn't say anything. And he didn't look back. Because he knew, for once, that Angela was wrong.

CHAPTER TWENTY-TWO

"Who's running the drugs?" Roman demanded of Abel two days later.

He had taken an uncharacteristic day off after his talk with Angela. As predicted, he'd been unfit for company and spent the morning pounding a punching bag in the gym until it fell off. He then went for a drive and was surprised when he found himself at the Lighthouse Resource Center. Sister Philomena took one look at him—and his busted-up hands—and told him she'd heard digging in the dirt was good for the soul. She handed him a trowel and left him to it. He dug in the garden in the courtyard for four hours.

His friends gave him space, not questioning him. Luca did, of course. But he didn't pressure Roman when he said he didn't want to talk about it. His younger brother had simply hugged him silently, a balm to the inferno of his inner turmoil.

But today was a new day, and Roman had woken up feeling back to his usual self. He was ready for Abel's report, wanting to know what the fuck was going on with the drugs on the street, and why Angel was getting kicked in the face as a result.

"We are," Abel replied to Roman's question.

"What?!" Roman barked, rising from his chair.

"Well, not us exactly," Abel quickly amended. "Beltane has the current monopoly on the drug market in the city. But he's cooking them up in one of *our* buildings."

Roman grunted and remained standing. Beltane was the head of a small cartel working out of the docks. Roman didn't know him very well, but Luca had done a deep background check and nothing other than a rich drug history had popped up. When the man had come to him asking to rent some of his warehouses along the water, Roman agreed with very few questions.

He liked to think he was very involved with all aspects of his business—both legal and illegal—but he didn't have his finger in every pie. He delegated. He trusted the people under his employ. But perhaps it was time to do an internal audit. A drug kitchen on his property was no longer his speed. Especially one that was cooking dirty drugs.

"Let's go have a chat with him," Roman commanded, grabbing his suit jacket.

Abel followed, and Roman wasn't surprised when Salvatore met them in the parking garage. Roman slid behind the wheel. He rarely used a driver, preferring to be in control of where he was going and when. They were followed by two more SUVs filled with his people, just in case Beltane proved to be an asshole.

It was closing in on ten in the morning when they pulled up in front of the warehouse. It didn't have a view of the water, being set back from the docks by a row of boat sheds. Roman was pleased to see it was in good condition.

"Beltane looks to be keeping it clean at least," Salvatore said, as if reading Roman's thoughts.

Roman grunted, striding to the side door. "Too bad he isn't doing the same with his merchandise."

Beltane opened the door himself. He was a tall man with hazel eyes and an interesting mixed heritage. His skin was dark, yet his hair was very fair, and he was built like a tank. "Roman." Beltane held out his hand. "What a surprise. It's good to see you."

Roman took the offered hand, shaking it briefly. "I hope you still think so after our talk."

Beltane's friendly smile faltered, but he still politely welcomed Roman, Abel, and Salvatore. "I'm sure I will. Come on in."

Roman looked around, finding the inside had an impressive set-up. There were tables and boxes and drugs everywhere—lots of drugs. But it was all neat and tidy, with nothing on the floor. Nothing seemed amiss at first glance, but Angel had a black eye and a swollen cheekbone, so Roman got straight to the point. "I'm evicting you. Shut down your operation. I want you out in a week."

Beltane laughed, obviously thinking Roman was joking. "Good one. Why are you really here?" he asked with a smile.

Roman stared at him. "I just told you why."

Beltane looked from Roman to the other two men in confusion. "I don't understand. Has something happened?"

"Your drugs have happened, that's what," Roman replied. "I want them off my streets. *Yesterday*," he added harshly.

"Off . . .?" Beltane's eyes bugged out. "You can't be serious! Do you know how much revenue this pulls in? I'm sorry Roman, I am. But I can't do it."

Roman ran his tongue over his top teeth, impatience and anger rising. "There's no point being the richest man in the graveyard, Beltane."

"Are you threatening me?" Beltane demanded, his hands fisting at his sides.

"He's not. No," Salvatore said, stepping between them. "He's simply stating a fact."

Beltane shook his head, taking a step back and shoving his hands through his hair. "Since when do you have a problem with drugs?"

Since the creamy perfection of my stubborn beloved's face was marred with dark bruises, he thought. "Since now."

Beltane flung his arms out wide, clearly aggravated. "We've always had a good business relationship, Roman. I don't want to jeopardize that. But this is my world, man."

"Find a new world," Roman stated implacably.

Beltane looked at him askance. "Like what? You want me to take up knitting or something?"

Roman considered the logistics for a moment. Beltane was a decent guy. "I could use another team to help with the weapons going international," he offered.

"Guns?" Beltane shook his head. "I don't know guns, Roman. I know drugs."

"You obviously don't know them very well if you're cutting them with dirty shit," Abel pointed out scathingly. He, too, had taken exception to Angela's bruised face.

"What are you talking about?" Beltane asked.

"Are you saying you don't know?" Roman looked him over carefully. The man was a picture of curiosity, rather than guilt. "There's been an influx of overdoses and people going into drug-induced rages. There's a new drug on the streets—or a dirty one."

Beltane looked genuinely shocked. "That's not me, Roman, I swear it. The stuff we produce is pure. You know our crops are well outside the city. This, here, is just where the packaging occurs. It's a pill press. Nothing more."

Roman scanned the room , noting the two lines of workers operating the presses like a well-oiled machine. Beltane looked to be running a tight ship. But Angel had been booted in the face by some guy hopped up on *something*. And she'd said it wasn't the first case. The drugs were a problem, he had no doubt. "Looks like you've got someone undercutting you, Beltane."

Beltane looked pissed but still asked, "I take it your source is trustworthy? I've heard nothing about it. And my finger is on the pulse of every drug distributor in the city."

"Not *every* pulse, it would seem," Roman corrected. "And yes, I trust this person implicitly."

"Well, fuck," Beltane muttered. His shoulders bunched, and he clenched and unclenched his fists several times before meeting Roman's eyes. "I'll sort it out. You have my word."

Roman thought about it for a long moment, weighing up what he knew about the drug runner in front of him versus his desire for some violence on Angel's behalf. He would much prefer not to have to kill everybody in the warehouse, and Beltane was a good businessman. So, he held out his hand, the other man taking it quickly. "Good enough. I'll give you a month. If the streets aren't cleaned up, you'll have to find a new landlord. And a new set of teeth. Understood?"

Beltane nodded. "I understand. I've got this. I'm pissed, too."

"Then we're cool, you and I," Roman stated. "Contact Abel if you need anything."

"I will. Thank you for bringing this to my attention," Beltane said, walking them to the door.

Roman, Abel, and Salvatore had just stepped outside when they heard a commotion coming from the building next to them. It was another of Roman's, but he wasn't sure who the renters were. "What's that noise?" he asked.

Beltane rolled his eyes. "The neighbors. Fucking rowdy bunch."

"Fight ring?" Abel guessed, looking in the direction of the old steel factory. It sounded like a large crowd was getting pumped up.

"Kind of," Beltane replied. "Dog fights."

"What?" Roman whipped his head around. "Did you just say dog fights?"

There were a few things he refused to dabble in. One was sex trafficking, and the other was the torture of helpless animals. When he was fourteen years old, just two years after losing his mother, his father shot his beloved dog in front of him. The act scarred him for life, in deeper ways than just being an heir to a crime family had. He abhorred animal cruelty.

"This shit is going on under my nose? In *my* place?" Roman snarled, his nostrils flaring. First there was the Lenny and Dane situation. Then the dirty drugs. Now dog fights? What the hell was happening to his crew and his things? "How did I miss this? And how did I miss all the other shit going on?"

"Well, you *have* been paying more attention recently," Abel piped up from beside him.

"I *always* pay attention," Roman snapped.

Abel didn't so much as blink in the face of Roman's anger. "I'm not saying you've been lax. You've always cared about your assets and your people. It's why your crew is so loyal. But you've been different since you met Angela. Now you care . . . well, *more*."

It was true. He was good at compartmentalizing. He had to be. Anything that didn't touch his family personally or affect his businesses negatively wasn't high on his radar. But since meeting Angel, he had discovered many things now bothered him when they never did before. Exhibit A was Beltane. Once upon a time, he wouldn't have cared less if a bunch of idiots overdosed or lost their shit. But now that he saw the impact it had on someone he cared about, he was all about making it golden.

Roman looked at his best friends seriously. "Am I becoming a pussy?"

Salvatore stared back at him like he was daft. "Are you being serious? Finding someone to care about doesn't make you soft," he said, reading Roman's fear correctly. "Did I lose my edge when I fell in love with Luca?"

"Yes," Roman and Abel answered simultaneously.

"I did not! Assholes!" Salvatore snarled at them before turning to Roman once more. "I've known you since we were children. You've always been the best of us, Roman. But since meeting Angela, you've become better. I'm damn proud of you."

Sal's words hit Roman right in the feels. He didn't

respond because he couldn't without fear his voice would crack.

Abel slapped Roman on the back. "What he said." He nodded his head at Salvatore. "Bad boys for life. Now, what are we going to do about the poor, abused fighting dogs?"

Roman switched gears gratefully. "We're going to make someone very sorry for hurting animals on my property."

"Excellent." Abel rubbed his hands together. "And here I thought it was going to be boring. I mean, we didn't even beat Beltane up."

"Uh, thank you?" came Beltane's voice from right behind them.

Roman snorted, amused. He turned to the other man, having completely forgotten his presence for a moment. He hoped Beltane was smart enough not to mention the sweet little interlude with his family to anyone. "Head back inside. Get started on your problem. We'll sort this out. You won't have to worry about noisy neighbors anymore."

Beltane gave him a salute, turning around and walking back inside without saying anything further.

"He's not so bad," Sal commented as the three of them began walking in the direction of the other building. He made a few hand signals to the two parked cars, which had men filing out. He saw the look on Roman's face, interpreting it correctly. "They're just backup. They're not going to take away your fun."

"Good," Roman grunted. One look from security through the peephole had them ushered in without ceremony. Roman could already tell it was a shit operation. What kind of self-respecting criminal allowed a dozen people to walk into something illegal without at least checking for weapons?

Roman had just instructed his men to fan out when a skinny guy with a shaved head and some truly terrible tattoos on his face rushed over. "I'm Louis. Welcome to my establishment. I—" He broke off, his bloodshot eyes going wide. "You're Vincenzo Romano. Hey, man. Good to meet you. I've heard good things." He thrust out a hand.

Roman looked down at it, not moving.

The man looked around nervously. "Ah, you here for the fight? Got some good ones tonight. Real vicious bastards."

"I wasn't aware dog fighting was going on here," Roman commented casually. "I also don't recall leasing out my property to you, Louis."

Louis picked at one of the scabs covering his arms. He laughed nervously. "I sublet. Me and my boy, Calvin, have an understanding."

"Calvin Canty?" Roman asked, receiving a *yeah* in response. He turned to Salvatore, who nodded his head, already typing on his cell. Roman was familiar with Calvin. And Calvin was about to be in deep shit. Subletting was not a thing when it came to Roman's properties.

"What's with the box?"

Roman turned when he heard Abel question Louis. There was a cardboard box in the middle of the crowd. There looked to be about fifty people in a rough circle, all waiting to watch two innocent animals tear each other apart. Roman also made out a bookie and a rudimentary bar with brew on tap. "The box?" he prompted when Louis didn't say anything.

"Huh?" He peered to where Roman was now pointing. "Oh, that's the appetizer. Kittens. We always let the dogs loose on some kittens first. You know, get their blood pumping. They rip up some fluffballs and they're raring to go." Louis rubbed his hands together, laughing. "Makes for a better show."

"A better show," Roman repeated, his lips barely moving.

The other man was oblivious to Roman's silent rage. "Yep. And a better show means better money." He nudged Roman with his elbow. "Not that you need more of that. I hear you're loaded."

"Oh, I'm loaded all right," Roman agreed. "And so is this." He pulled out his gun, shooting Louis in the foot with no further preliminaries. "Watch him," he ordered Salvatore, ignoring the pansy-ass shrieks coming from the bleeding man. "Abel, with me."

He and Abel walked into circle, disregarding the people who were already scattering from the gun shot. "The party's over," he yelled. "This dog fighting ring is officially closed."

"What the fuck?!"

"Go to hell!"

"Boo!"

Roman listened to the voices yelling at him, taking note of the people who scampered away like rodents and those who stayed to shout obscenities. He gripped his gun tighter, wanting to shoot every last one of the fuckers. But he didn't have enough bullets.

"I suggest you all leave. Now," Abel shouted.

"Who the fuck are you?" a stupid person yelled back from the crowd.

"Your worst nightmare," Abel told the hero. He pulled not one, but two guns from the holster beneath his jacket. He aimed them directly at the man, who backed away so fast he fell onto his ass and crawled the rest of the way around the corner like a crab. Abel grinned at Roman. "Badass. I always wanted to say that."

Roman left Abel to his badassery, peering into the box. It was damp and flimsy, and already falling apart. It would have provided no protection from animals trained to kill. He found two kittens. Both were very fluffy, but that's where the similarities ended. One was white with gray tips on its ears, feet and nose. The other was jet black. They were tiny and shaking so badly that the box was moving.

Roman reached in and scooped them up, tucking them close to his chest. "Easy there," he told the now hissing babies. "You're safe. Nobody is going to hurt you."

He continued to croon to them until their shaking stopped, trusting Sal, Abel and the others to watch his back. Only when the pair of brothers—he discovered after a quick look—had settled and fallen into an exhausted sleep, did he look around to take stock.

Louis was still crying on the ground, clutching his bleeding foot. There were a handful of other men left, but all were eyeing them warily. "I suggest you all fuck off," Roman said to them as he passed them on his way over to Louis. "Now. You won't get another chance."

When the five men ran to the door, Louis shouted. "Don't leave me here! Come back!"

Roman ignored his words, glaring down at him. "Where are the dogs?"

"Wha-what?" Louis stuttered.

"The dogs!" Roman yelled. The kittens mewled, and he forcibly calmed himself. He didn't want to scare the clearly traumatized babies. "The dogs," he repeated quietly. "Where are the dogs you were going to make savage each other?"

"Why?" Louis asked, sweat streaming down his face.

Roman sighed. Louis really was a dumb fuck.

"I got this," Sal promised Roman. "Don't lose your shit. You'll scare the kittens." He squatted down in front of Louis, gesturing to his wound. "Didn't that hole in your foot teach you anything? Roman asked you a question. Where are the dogs? The *why* is none of your business."

Louis licked his dry lips, saying, "They're in the crates in the back room."

"I'm on it," Abel said, striding into the darkened corner of the large room in the direction of one of the only internal doors.

"Here's what's going to happen," Roman began, as he squatted down next to Louis. "You're going to leave Monash and never come back. You're going to give my friend here a list of all the dogs in your little fight club and where he can find them. You're also going to tell him who else is involved because I can already tell you're not the mastermind behind this little enterprise. You don't have the smarts."

"Fuck you," Louis spat.

"Not even on your best day," Roman told him hastily. "If you do all that, I might just let you live. If you don't . . ." He shrugged. "Well, I have a feeling there are a couple of hungry dogs who need feeding."

Louis tensed, looking in the direction of where Abel disappeared. "You wouldn't. I don't believe you."

Roman smiled, watching as a puddle appeared beneath Louis. "Oh, you believe me, all right. Names!" he snapped, stomping on Louis's foot. The man screamed loud enough to pierce eardrums.

It took fifteen minutes, but by the time Louis had passed out from blood loss, they had a list of assholes Roman would be sending his crew after. He watched dispassionately as blood continued to flow from Louis's wound. It had been kind of pumping rather than flowing since Roman had stomped on it. "Do you think I busted an artery?" he asked Sal.

Sal shrugged, eating a packet of chips he found at the bar. "Dunno. Maybe. Do feet have arteries?"

"I'll ask Angel," Roman said. He looked to where Abel was sitting on the ground about twenty feet away with two scarred-up, scared dogs. He was surprised by how docile they were, given their circumstances. Abel was handling them well—he had always been good with animals. And Roman knew he wouldn't drop his guard and get his hand bitten off. The dogs' behavior was going to be unpredictable for a long while yet.

"Let's head out," he ordered, looking down at the two kittens wrapped in his jacket. The only time he had put them down was to take his jacket off and wrap them up. Their little purrs were music to his ears. "Leave Louis. If he wakes up in time to head to the hospital, good luck to him."

"I don't think that's a realistic expectation," Sal drawled. Roman watched him kick Louis. The man didn't move. "He's dead."

"Huh, will you look at that? I guess feet *do* have arteries," Roman commented. As Sal and Abel followed him out, a thought hit him. "That's a new record. I've never killed anyone by shooting them in the foot before. Not *just* the foot."

"I know I haven't," Abel said.

"Can't say I have either," Salvatore said, balling up his empty crisp packet.

"That means it's my record," Roman declared with satisfaction. "Write it down." They had an ongoing spreadsheet. Something they'd been adding to since they were teenagers.

"What do we do now?" Abel asked when they were back at the car in front of the warehouse. He gently stroked the two doggy heads. "We have four victims on our hands. But not the same type of victims that we usually do."

"Isn't our guest an animal person?" Salvatore asked.

Abel perked up. "Claire? Yeah, she is. A vet nurse or something."

"Let's ask her to start earning her keep," Roman suggested, gesturing to the animals.

Claire had been with them ever since Abel took her from the streets. Her ex was proving hard to pin down, having seemingly dropped off the face of the earth. With no guarantee for her safety, no job, and no home, Roman had agreed to allow her to stay. Besides, the woman was still afraid of her own shadow. He felt bad, knowing firsthand what domestic violence could do to a person's soul.

"You have a problem with her staying?" Abel asked sharply.

"I don't, no," Roman responded slowly, eyeing his friend curiously. "I wasn't implying that at all."

"Awfully touchy there," Salvatore commented to Roman conversationally.

"Kind of like how you were with Luca," Roman pointed out.

Abel glared at both of them. He punched Roman in the shoulder as he stalked past, rounding the SUV to the passenger side with the two dogs trailing after him obediently. "More like how *you* are with Angela," he yelled back.

Roman grinned at Salvatore. "Definitely touchy."

CHAPTER TWENTY-THREE

Morrigan and Luca were waiting for them as the three men got out of the elevator on the fiftieth floor. None of them had ever had any pets in the building, so the medical suite was set up for humans only. But Roman figured it was better than nothing.

"Oh my god," Luca gasped, hands flying to his mouth when he got an eyeful of the dirty, undernourished Pitbull mixes. "Poor babies. Roman . . ."

"I dealt with it," he promised his kindhearted brother. "Is Claire inside?"

"She is," Morrigan confirmed. Her jaw was clenched tight, and her eyes were like flint as they took in the dogs.

"Good." He was eager to get them seen to, and the

kittens as well, which were wrapped in his jacket. He was unsure how the dogs would react to the babies, but so far, they had shown no interest. They hadn't shown any interest in anything at all. They certainly weren't acting aggressively towards the humans.

Claire was pacing when Roman and the others pushed their way inside the medical clinic. She jumped when the door banged against the wall, but quickly got over her automatic fear. "What happened?" she demanded, striding over to them.

"Dog fight," Abel clipped.

"You had them in a fight? How could you?!" Claire shot Abel a horrified look. "You asshole!"

It was the first time Roman had ever heard her swear. He was gratified to see she had some spine beneath her soft demeanor. Especially if his best friend was interested in her for more than a quick lay.

"It wasn't me!" Abel protested vehemently. "We rescued them."

Claire glowered at Abel for a moment longer, clearly suspicious. "Let them go," she instructed Abel, who released his hold on the leads. The dogs didn't move. Claire made some kissy noises, holding her hand out. It was steady as a rock.

"Here, boys. Come here. Good boys, such good boys," she praised them when they tentatively sniffed her hand. Claire let them sniff her until they chose to wander off on their own. She watched them carefully from where she stood, but made no move to initiate contact.

"Are you going to do something?" Roman asked when all she did was stand there.

Claire narrowed her eyes at him. "I *am* doing something. I'm giving them time. Both are limping and clearly malnourished. There are a few cuts I can see from here. But you have to understand, I'm an animal nurse. Not a vet."

"But you can still help them, right?" Abel asked anxiously.

"I'll do my best." Her eyes shot to Roman's jacket when the two kittens began to squeak. "Who else do you have?"

"Kittens. They were using them as bait," Roman explained.

Claire's face flushed, and she cursed low again. When she reached for the kittens, her hands were gentle. She cupped them close to her chest and walked to one of the private rooms. "I'll keep them in here. No use waving a red flag at a bull," she said, lifting her chin in the direction of the two roaming dogs.

"They've been super calm," Abel said. "They haven't so much as growled—at us or each other."

"*Yet,*" Claire corrected him, focusing on the white kitten. "They haven't growled or attacked yet. Chances are they will at some point, depending on what they've gone through and what kind of life they lived before the dog fights."

"You're giving up on them already?" Roman wasn't impressed with her attitude at all.

Her gray eyes flashed to his. "That's not what I said. I'm giving you realistic information—not dreams and rainbows. If they can be saved, I'll work night and day to rehabilitate them. I give you my word. I'm no quitter."

Roman grunted, mollified by her promise. "What do you need?"

"Let's start with the kittens. Let the dogs calm down a bit longer and see if we can get them to understand we mean them no harm. They're disassociating in the corner right now," Claire pointed out.

Everyone turned to where she was staring with a sympathetic gaze. The two dogs were curled up in a ball together, quite literally on top of each other, and visibly trembling. They were staring at the wall, not even blinking, and Roman wished he had done more to Louis than just shoot him in the foot.

"They were fine before," Abel said, looking mad.

"They were *not* fine before," Claire corrected him

firmly. "That's what I'm trying to get you to understand. Trauma manifests in many ways. Right now, the contrast in their environment is likely hitting them. They were there, on the verge of death. Now they're here, warm and safe. It's too much to take in. Too much to trust."

Abel drew in a deep breath, holding it for a second. His expression lost some of its malice, and he nodded at Claire. "We give them time."

"We give them time," Claire confirmed, then turned to Morrigan.

"A few T-bones wouldn't go astray, either."

Morrigan looked behind herself comically for a second before it clicked. "Are you ordering me to do your bidding?"

"I'm simply saying that most dogs are food orientated. It would be a good way to begin to build trust," Claire lectured, checking the white kitten's ears with a small light.

"And you expect me to do it?" Morrigan sounded scandalized.

"Unless you don't care about traumatized animals," Claire replied casually. She didn't even look at the assassin.

"Oh, guilt. Not bad, Mouse. Not bad at all. I'll get the steak," she said, disappearing in the next instant.

Claire sighed, turning the kitten over and examining his belly. "I wish she wouldn't call me Mouse."

"You do kind of act like one," Abel pointed out truthfully.

"I was in a nightmare of a relationship, stalked, had my home and my job taken from me. Then I was kidnapped after having a man almost beaten to death in front of me. My apologies if I've been a little upset," Claire said with some fire.

Luca snickered from the dumbstruck look on Abel's face. He leaned in close to Roman, whispering, "Another one bites the dust, huh?"

Roman withheld comment. Although it appeared Abel liked Claire, he knew his friend too well. Abel was the king of love 'em and leave 'em. If he were a betting man, he would bet on his friend nailing the pretty brunette and then losing her number. Mind you, that was difficult to do when she was living in the same building.

It took Claire four hours to be satisfied her four patients would make a full recovery. "Physically, that is," she warned them all. "Mentally, I can't say."

Everyone was still there—Roman, Sal, Luca, Abel, and Morrigan. None of them wanted to leave until they knew the animals were going to be okay. The kittens were found to be in good health, suffering dehydration and fleas, but thankfully nothing else. They had been sleeping on Roman's lap for the last hour.

"These boys need antibiotics, food, fluids, rest, and time. They are miraculously docile, but don't be fooled. It's likely shock holding them back. They could snap at any moment," Claire warned.

"Or they might not," Abel grumbled.

Instead of correcting him again, Claire acquiesced. "Or they might not." She patted the dogs gently, crooning to them and giving them lots of praise and love. She looked at Roman. "I'll write a list of supplies, if someone will go and grab it all?"

"Do that. I'll see to it," Roman assured her. "Thank you for your help."

"Thank you for saving them," she said quietly. She met the eyes of everyone in the room before returning her attention to the canines. "And for saving me."

CHAPTER TWENTY-FOUR

"I have a surprise for you."

Angela glanced at Roman from the corner of her eye. "A surprise?" she asked cautiously, wondering if it was his dick.

She was just leaving after a visit with Claire. Angela really liked the younger woman and made a point of seeing her at least once a week. So far, Claire had said no to Angela's offers to get her some professional emotional support. She claimed to be dealing fine after her ordeal. But Angela wasn't convinced. She had barely left the Omertà building since arriving three and a half months prior. She did hang out with some of the others, but Angela was worried about her being so isolated.

But that could be changing, Angela thought

happily. Because she had seen a noticeable difference in Claire's demeanor ever since taking on the responsibility of the two fighting dogs. They had been there two weeks, and Angela had only just met them that day. They were sweet, with sad eyes and bodies that looked as if they had been in a war. Which they had been.

"Not that kind of surprise," Roman promised, chuckling. "Though I could be persuaded."

"No persuasion happening," Angela replied. *More's the pity*, she added. Keeping her hands to herself was becoming harder and harder. But if she couldn't commit her mind—or her heart—she wasn't going to commit her body. It was unfair to both of them. Plus, things were going so well between them now. She even maybe, possibly, kind of thought of Roman as a friend now. It was miraculous.

"Have it your way," Roman said, shrugging one shoulder. "Follow me. The surprise is in my private office."

Angela walked with him, discussing how her past couple of weeks had been at work. For some reason, the amount of overdoses decreased in the last few days. It was a welcome relief. She didn't attend the ER often, so she didn't need to deal with it as much as some of her fellow doctors and nurses, but it was still a burden.

Walking into his office, Angela gasped when two

little balls of fluff came charging over. "Kittens!" she exclaimed, bending over to stroke them. They were extremely soft. "They're adorable. Where did you get them?"

Roman explained how they were about to be used as bait when he and his men had arrived at the fighting ring, and Angela fumed. Tears pricked her eyes, and she scooped both babies up. "People really are the worst."

"Not *all* people," Roman told her softly. He reached, scratching first the white kitten, then the black kitten behind the ears. "A few months ago, you told me you were wanting someone to come home to, well . . ."

Angela's eyes widened when she understood what he was saying. "You're giving me kittens?"

To her surprise, Roman ducked his head, looking a little embarrassed. "Well, one kitten. I, ah, thought I might keep one too."

Her lips twitched. He wasn't fooling her. He had fallen in love with one kitten—if not both. "I couldn't possibly split them up," she said.

"That's just it—they don't need to be split up. Not permanently anyway," Roman said quickly. "When you have your twelve-hour shift, you could drop him off on the way, so he isn't home alone all day. That way, he could visit with his brother. Or Abel or someone could pick him up and drop him off."

She couldn't believe her ears. "You're going to send your second-in-command to my place almost every day so two kittens can have a playdate?"

Roman shrugged his broad shoulders. "Sure. If you want to look at it that way."

Angela snickered a little, rubbing her chin over the top of the white kitten's head. "What other way is there to look at it?"

"Shared custody."

Angela let out a startled laugh, but her response was very firm. "No."

"Yes," Roman retorted. "Look at them. Just agree. They don't want their parents to fight."

"Roman . . ." Angela pursed her lips in exasperation. The man was damned hard to say no to.

"They've been here for two weeks. Claire wanted to make sure they were healthy and happy before they went anywhere. Which they are. They're ready to spread their little kitty beans," Roman said, tickling the kittens on their paws until they began to make biscuits on her sweater. "Well, what do you say?"

The tiny little paws with the tiny little claws were already comforting. And it had only been five minutes. She knew exactly what she was going to say. "I say, thank you, Roman. This could just be the best gift anyone has ever given me."

Roman's smile lit up his entire face. "Wonderful. Here, take a seat." He helped her sit down on the couch, his knees touching hers so the kittens could move between them easier. "You don't receive a lot of gifts?" he asked carefully.

Roman rarely asked her any personal questions. A few months ago, she would have balked, but that reaction was more muscle memory than anything else now. Still, she needed to take a breath before she was able to answer. "No, I don't. I remember my grandmother used to spoil me on my birthday when I was little. She knew me—really listened to me when I spoke—so she knew just what to get me to make me smile. And when I was older, when I told her I wanted to be a doctor, she gave me this old-school medical bag. You know those leather ones with the top latch? She even had my name burned into it."

She saw Roman look to the door where she placed her bag down. She never went anywhere without it, especially to Omertà. It didn't matter if she was only there for a social visit, she invariably needed her bag for something. It was black leather and very functional, looking more like a thick briefcase than a medical bag. It did what it was supposed to do but lacked the charm of her old bag. Not to mention the good memories.

"How come I've never seen you use it?" he asked when he faced her again.

"I left it at my parents' one day when I was visiting," was all she said. It was the truth. But not the *whole* truth.

Roman nodded his head easily enough, but there was a slight frown on his face. "And you didn't go back for it?"

"No," she responded flatly. "I didn't go back for anything. My grandmother would have understood."

Thankfully, Roman didn't press, even though he had to be curious. "Your grandmother sounds like a good person."

Angela smiled a little, stroking the soft fur of the kittens. "She was. The best. I called her Grom because I couldn't say grandma when I was little. It stuck. She died when I was fifteen," she added sadly.

"*Mi dispiaci.* I am sorry," Roman said, bowing his head respectfully. "Did she know you were going to be a doctor?"

"Yes." Angela paused, then cleared her throat. "She was proud."

"Naturally. You are a wonderful doctor," he complimented her. "And what about your parents? Don't they ever send you gifts? Christmas presents?"

She stiffened. She didn't want to invite any more

questions about her parents. But he didn't seem to be fishing for information. It was just a friendly conversation. She unclenched her hands and responded evenly, "No. We're estranged."

"Fair enough," Roman said, moving on quickly. "I don't exactly receive gifts from my remaining family, either. Nothing that doesn't tick, at least."

"Roman!" she gasped. Here she was, thinking they were enjoying a nice conversation. She nudged him with her shoulder.

"What?" he said innocently. "It's the truth."

"That's what bothers me," she informed him. "Now, I assume the little midnight dude is staying with you?"

The black kitten had climbed his way to Roman's shoulder and was draped around his neck like a furry scarf. Roman reached up, dislodging the kitten, who gave a cranky mewl, and he chuckled. "I guess so."

He placed the kitten on the carpet, and Angela followed suit. She bit her lip when they started to play happily with each other. "Do you really want to break them up? They love each other."

"We're not breaking them up," Roman reminded her. "They're just having some alone time, so they don't annoy each other to death." She nodded, still not convinced. Roman placed a hand on her lower back, leaning in close. "How about this? We do a trial. Just a one-day trial. And if either kitty gets depressed, you take both."

"I couldn't do that," Angela denied quickly. "I'm not going to take your kittens away from you, Roman."

"They are not my kittens," Roman refuted. She shot him a look, and he had the grace to look sheepish. "Fine. Maybe I've gotten used to having the little fur balls around. But that just proves I know what good company they are. Give them a chance."

It felt like a huge decision. So much bigger than it likely was. But she had never had a pet before. Not so much as a goldfish growing up, and none as an adult. It was a big responsibility. Not to mention, the choice had the ability to break her heart. She would surely fall in love with it, and those kinds of emotions terrified her.

"Okay," she finally decided. "Let's stick with the original plan. I'll take Mr. White and you keep Mr. Black. We'll re-evaluate tomorrow."

Roman's hand squeezed her hip where he was still touching her. "Wonderful. Oh, question: do feet have arteries?"

She thought it was an odd topic change, but she was always happy to educate people about medical issues. "Sure they do. There's an entire web of arteries across the foot that extends down into each toe."

"Huh. You learn something new every day. It's definitely a record," he murmured, then grinned boyishly at her. "Thanks, Doc."

"You're welcome. I guess," she added uncertainly. "Do I want to know?"

"Probably not," Roman admitted.

She sighed, placing the kittens on the ground, smiling when they began to tussle with each other once again. "I won't ask, then."

"Very wise." Roman nodded approvingly—before falling into her.

They stumbled, ending up on the ground in a tangle of limbs. Angela groaned because she was on the bottom. Roman had managed to break her fall, though, wrapping his arms around her and protecting the back of her head. "What the hell?"

"I believe the kittens tripped me," Roman said, his gaze moving worriedly over her face. "Are you okay?"

She *had* been fine until she realized they were now plastered together from head to toe, and she could feel Roman's dick growing between them. She gaped at him. "Really? Already?"

Roman smirked. "I can't help it. He has a mind of his own."

She tried her best not to laugh. And tried even harder to stay still and not arch against him. He felt incredible, and she wanted him. But she had promised herself—*and* him—that she wouldn't yank his chain. And, unfortunately, that included the one between his legs.

Suddenly, Roman jerked and swore. Then he went stiff, not moving.

"What is it?" Angela asked, worried. Then the realization hit her. "Did you cum in your pants? It's okay. Don't be embarrassed. It's completely normal."

Roman gaped down at her. "I did not jizz in my pants. There's a kitten with its claws digging into my ass."

Her eyes widened. "What?" She quickly scooted out from beneath him, giggling when she saw the little black kitten kneading Roman's derriere. She couldn't blame the animal—it was a great ass.

"Allow me," she said, reaching over to unhook the mischievous fluff ball. A blur of white entered her field of vision, and the second kitten pounced on Roman's back. The hiss that came from his mouth told her the kitten's tiny little claws had made contact with his skin.

"A little help here?" Roman demanded, looking over his shoulder at her. "Or do you plan to leave me at the mercy of these beasts?"

Angela rolled her eyes. "Oh, yes. Such dangerous beasts."

"Their claws are like razor wire!" Roman exclaimed,

wincing when the black kitten dug its claws into the meat of his butt. "Ow! Damnit, Angel. Get them off before I fling them off."

She was happy to learn Roman was all bark and no bite. He remained still as she unhooked the two little menaces, making no attempt to roll over or rise, and she knew it was because he didn't want to squash them or hurt them in any way. He could be vicious when it came to people, but he was a softie where animals were concerned. She found it endlessly endearing. She couldn't help but soften a little more towards him as well—and it wasn't the first time. Somehow, over the past six months of her attending to stitches and bruises and gunshot wounds, Roman had stopped being a detested crime boss.

He was simply . . . Roman.

"You never mentioned their names," Angela commented, once she freed him from the evil clutches of the baby cats.

Roman shrugged, reaching over to gently stroke the soft fur between the pair's ears. She was back to holding them again as they stood in the center of his office. "I figured you'd want to name them."

Angela studied his impassive face for a moment. He was very good at that particular expression. But she had gotten better at reading him. Initially, the realization bothered her, but now she kind of liked it. "You did name them. What is it?"

Roman put up a token fight, grumbling for a moment before saying, "Slap and Tickle." He waggled his eyebrows like an eighties pornography producer.

Angela laughed. He looked ridiculous. But oh, so handsome. How had she not noticed how fun he was before now? She'd been so focused on finding reasons to push him away, that was why. He might kill people as easily as blinking, *but* he was a funny guy. *And kind*, she added, thinking of the way he was allowing Claire to stay there rent free. "I'm not calling them that! Can you imagine me saying those names when I have the windows open? What would the neighbors think?!"

"That you're a lucky, lucky lady," he said with a smirk.

She snorted in good humor but shook her head. "Come on. Tell me."

Roman rolled his eyes as if he was irritated and the whole thing was no big deal. "Smith and Wesson. I've been calling the white one Smithy and the black one Wes."

Angela scrunched her nose. "You named them after a gun?"

"I named them after *your* gun," Roman corrected her. "You know, the one you threatened me with the day after we met? The one you held onto the entire time we fucked against your kitchen wall?" he asked rhetorically. "*That* gun."

Angela's throat suddenly went dry, thanks to the images bombarding her mind. Roman's words painted a very accurate picture of what had occurred over six months ago now. She had to clear her throat before she could talk. "Umm, why would you do that?"

"Because it's one of my favorite memories of all time," Roman replied.

"Of all time? Seriously?" she asked, thinking he was making another joke.

"I am being serious. You were angry and hurt and scared. You were vulnerable and raw and wide open. I saw it on your face. In those beautiful eyes of yours. And still, you gave yourself over to the pleasure—to *me*. You hated me, but you still gave yourself to me. You hated being so attracted to me—a criminal and a *mafioso*. But at that moment, you hated yourself more. You hated whatever past was coming back to haunt you."

He stepped closer, cupping her cheeks with his palms. "I was happy to be the one you took out your punishment on. And honored. So, yes. It is one of my best memories. And I hope, one day, you'll be ready to make many more memories with me."

CHAPTER TWENTY-FIVE

"Angel agreed to a timeshare type of arrangement for Smith and Wesson," Roman revealed.

Luca's eyes lit up, and he clapped. "Yay! I'm so happy she's taking one. I think the little guy will be good for her." His excitement dimmed a little, and he frowned. "But why didn't you give her both? I thought that was the plan."

Instead of heading straight home, Angel was taking a detour with Morrigan. His cousin had challenged her to a duel—her words, not his—upon hearing Angel was trained in Krav Maga. The headstrong doc had been putting it off for months, but she happily handed Smithy back to him just moments ago and followed

Morrigan out of his office with a radiant smile on her face.

He had a hard time wiping the grin off his face as well. And it wasn't because he had two sleeping kittens in his lap. It was because Angel had shared something about her past voluntarily for the very first time. He wanted to fist-pump the sky but didn't want to wake Wes or Smithy. He wondered why he was so happy over something so small. And why he was settling for crumbs when he had never settled for anything in his life.

Shaking off the disillusioning thoughts, he focused on Luca. "I had intended to give her both, but she noted Wes seems attached to me. It was her idea that I keep him." He left unsaid how he had fallen for the mischievous little cat in return.

"Uh-huh. It has nothing to do with the fact that, this way, she has to keep coming around so the kittens can play," Salvatore said from his place beside Luca. "Or that it gives you more liberties to visit her place."

Luca's eyes—the exact same shade as their mother's—widened. "Oooh. Smart."

Roman tipped his head towards his brother. "That's why I'm the boss."

"And as the boss, I think you should see something," Abel said, striding into the office. The two pit bull mixes followed loyally behind.

Roman stood and carefully deposited the kittens into the basket on his desk. Mario and Luigi had proven themselves to be wonderfully tempered dogs who showed no aggression towards the cats. In fact, their tails wagged a mile a minute whenever they saw them. Like now. Mario's butt moved madly from side to side with the force of his happiness. But none of them were taking any chances, and they were still being overly cautious. Triggers were hard to predict. Roman was confident time would take care of the minor trust issues.

"Mario! Luigi!" Luca cried, getting onto his knees so he could hug the big dogs. Claire had been the one to name the dogs. Apparently, she was a closet gaming nerd.

"What do you want me to see?" Roman turned to his second-in-command. "And will you please knock? What if I was doing something private?"

"Like wanking," Luca supplied. He looked up at Abel and Sal. "He does that a lot these days."

"Mario. Luigi. Kill," Roman commanded, pointing at his brother. The two dogs attacked, jumping on Luca and licking his face off. Or so it looked to Roman. But based on Luca's happy laughter, that wasn't the case.

He ignored the subject of his solo sex life and addressed Abel again. "What's going on?"

"Turn on the security feed for the gym," he said, already moving to the large monitor on the office's west wall.

"Angel and Morrigan?" Roman demanded, grabbing the remote and hitting the green button as he walked to the screen.

Abel nodded his head at the video feed now playing. "Yep. Watch."

Roman was concerned Morrigan was kicking ass and doing what he had told her not to do: hurt Angel. But within moments, he learned he was wrong. "Whoa..."

"Is it wrong to be really turned-on right now?"

Roman turned to his brother with a scowl. "You're gay!" he snapped.

Luca shrugged, his gaze pinned to the scene on the monitor. "Maybe I used to be. But not anymore."

Salvatore nodded vigorously. "I agree, babe. Who knew, huh?"

"Those women are dynamite," Abel added, just as riveted.

Roman didn't answer. He was too busy adjusting his stiff cock where it was pressing uncomfortably against the metal of his zipper. "Keep your eyes off Angel."

"I'm trying. But it's a little hard when she's matching one of the best assassins in the world blow for blow," Abel told him.

Roman acknowledged that. Angel's form wasn't as good as Morrigan's, but that didn't mean it wasn't as effective. She was fast and sneaky and totally without fear. It was just the combination needed to defend against any foe.

She was a study in contradictions, he thought, watching her execute a body roll after being thrown to the mats. There was something inherently vulnerable about her, but she also had a take-no-prisoners mindset. She spent her days healing people and was compassionate beyond measure. Yet, he could tell she had no issue with inflicting pain when it was necessary. Proving his point, she grabbed Morrigan by the hair, wrenching her head back.

"Is there nothing this woman can't do?" he wondered out loud.

"Commit," Abel replied blandly.

Roman heard the bite in his friend's tone. "*Scusa?*"

Abel held up his hands. "I agree with you—she's the full package. But there's something about her, Roman . . . She's a flight risk."

361

"I thought you liked her," Luca accused angrily.

"I do like her. Very much," Abel promised. "More than I like most people on the planet. I'm just being honest."

Roman knew his family had his best interests at heart, so he held up a hand for silence before they could start bickering. "I know she's a flight risk. I see it."

Abel nodded. "You've been patient, but it's been over six months since she first got under your skin. It could take another six months. Are you willing to keep being patient?"

"For Angel?" He already knew the answer to that. "Yes."

Ten minutes later, Abel left with the Super Mario Brothers as Roman continued to chat with Luca and Sal. That was, until he heard Angel knock and ask if she could come in. Panicking, he ordered, "Get in the closet."

"The closet?!" Sal exclaimed. "Do you know how long it took me to come *out* of the closet? Now you want me to go back in?"

"Stop trying to be the comic relief. We both know that's Abel's job," Roman replied, pushing Sal in the direction of his large walk-in closet.

"Why exactly are we going into the closet?" Luca asked in amusement.

"Because!" Roman clipped out. He wasn't about to tell them he was still sexually aroused from watching Angel fight and he was hoping for at least a kiss before she left. Fighting had a way of stirring the juices. Perhaps she was feeling *stirred*. But his brother and his best friend were sure to ruin the mood.

Salvatore snorted and snickered, allowing himself to be shoved into the closet. "Oh, this is kind of romantic," he said, snuggling Luca in the darkness.

"Quiet," Roman hissed, hearing Angel knock again.

Sal's hands stopped wandering, and he grimaced. "Wait . . . you haven't jerked off in here as well, have you?"

Roman planted his palm over Salvatore's face and pushed. He slammed the door shut, grinning happily when he heard cursing and the crashing of coat hangers from beyond the door. He walked to the office door, quickly opening it. "Angel. Hi."

She looked at him strangely. "Sorry to disturb you."

"I wasn't busy," he said quickly. *Too* quickly if her suspicious look was anything to go by.

"Right," Angela agreed, looking unconvinced. "I just wanted to see if I could leave Smith here for one more night before taking him home. I need to get supplies: food, litter, a scratching tree . . . all that kind of stuff. I want him to be happy."

"He'll be with you. How could he not be happy?" His eyes widened. He had not meant to say that. What was he, a fricking poet now? What next, he'd start reciting Shakespeare?

"Oh," Angel muttered, her cheeks flushing prettily. "Thank you."

Instead of checking for his balls on the nearest shelf like his brain told him to do, he listened to his heart instead. "You're welcome. It's the truth." He cleared his throat, adding, "But you don't have to leave him here. Claire provided Abel with a very extensive list two weeks ago. Both kittens have everything they need. I'll have one of the men take it all down to your car for you."

"What? Roman, no. I can buy my own stuff. It's the least I can do," she told him firmly. "Especially when you're single-handedly paying for Lighthouse to be restored and supplied."

Roman bit his tongue because he had news about that. But seeing how freaked out she was about a bit of kitty litter, he thought it best to save it for another time. "Angel, I'm a billionaire. Take the scratching post."

She grunted, making her way to the kittens. They were awake and very vocal. "A billionaire. Sure you are."

He raised his eyebrows because the disbelief in her voice was genuine. "You don't believe me?"

"I know you're a millionaire, Roman. I mean, look at this place." She gestured to the view from his office. "But do you know how many zeros there are in a billion?"

He did know. Because he'd seen the zeros the day before during his monthly meeting with his accountant. But he didn't say so. He moved on instead. "Also, you should start to see a decrease in overdoses soon."

She shot him a look, stroking the kittens. "What makes you say that?"

"I spoke to the man in charge of the city's drug supply," Roman divulged. "He's going to sort it out. Or he'll have me to deal with," he added with a mutter.

"I don't understand." Angela was standing very still. It had him a little worried.

"After you showed up with that bruise, I looked into who's been supplying drugs on the streets and paid him a little visit. He assured me he had nothing to do with these new drug concoctions. I'm inclined to believe him. Which is why he's still alive," he explained.

Angela blinked at him, still unmoving. "You did this . . . why?"

He shifted uncomfortably, looking behind him. Perhaps shoving his brother and Sal into the closet wasn't such a good idea. They no doubt had their ears to the door. "You got hurt because of that shit. It wasn't even a question that I was going after him. Plus, you're tired, Angel. You don't think I've noticed the dark circles recently? No doubt from idiots taking too many drugs and taking up your time. You don't need that shit. You have enough responsibilities as it is."

Angela finally moved, collapsing into his chair behind his desk. His dick perked up again. "I don't know what to say," she replied quietly.

Say you'll be mine, he silently bade. But he had promised not to pressure her. He wanted her to want him for the same reason he wanted her: because she saw him. Really saw him and wanted him anyway. The tension that rose between them was different. It wasn't sexual, but it wasn't entirely comfortable either. "It's no big deal," he said, breaking the silence. He wondered how to get them balanced again and blurted, "You can thank me in orgasms if you want."

She gasped, chiding, "Roman!"

Her resulting laughter was the best thing he'd heard all day. Luca and Sal must have thought so, too, because there was a loud thump behind the closet doors.

Angela narrowed her eyes. "Do you have someone in there?"

"What?" His laugh was stupidly fake. "No."

Her expression turned sour, and she leaped up. "Oh, really? Sorry to interrupt your interlude."

"My . . .?" That's when it hit him—Angela thought he had some skank in there. "Are you jealous?"

"Of course not." Her nose shot into the air with a huff. "You're free to fuck whoever you want. Just don't come to me when you get chlamydia."

More rustling. No doubt his brother and Sal trying to keep their laughter in.

Angela picked up Smithy, walking to the door. "Angel, wait," Roman called, collecting Wes. "It's just Luca."

Angela stopped. "Why would Luca be in your closet?"

"Exactly!" Luca's voice could be heard loud and clear through the wood.

Angela's eyes widened. She walked over and opened the door. "It really is Luca. And Sal. What are you guys doing?"

"I have no idea," Sal answered. He glared at Roman. "It's really fucking dark in here."

"I'm not even going to ask," Angela said. He saw her shoulders relax and her back lose its rigidity. "I better go. I've been here longer than I planned, thanks to Morrigan's version of *Mortal Kombat*. I'm going to need to soak in the tub. My muscles are already screaming."

"We saw you with her—just a little. I didn't know you could fight like that. You're awesome," Luca enthused with a clap.

Angela smiled at him. "Thanks. But I don't think I'll be doing it again anytime soon. She's brutal." She said goodbye one last time and walked out.

Roman hurried after her, pausing just outside the doorframe. "Angel," he called. "You don't like the thought of me with other women." It was a statement.

She halted her retreat, remaining silent for a moment before she turned and gave a single nod. "That's an accurate assessment."

"Good." Satisfaction ran through him. "But, baby, you don't need to worry. This"—he palmed his crotch —"is all for you. Whenever you're ready, just give me the word."

Her eyes locked onto the location of his hand, and while she didn't say yes, she also didn't say no. It was a definite step in the right direction. "Thank you for the kitten. And the drug lord. And anything else you've been doing."

She ran back to him, blushing prettily as she kissed him on the cheek. And before he could even react, she was gone.

He walked back into his office in a daze, cupping his face where it still tingled from her lips.

"Wow, bro. That was really frickin' romantic."

Roman didn't even look, just shoved Luca with his hand on the way past. He heard the collective *oomph* as his brother and Sal landed back in the closet, and he grinned. His ice Angel was thawing. He just knew it.

CHAPTER TWENTY-SIX

"Isn't he adorable?" Angela asked Finn, showing him a picture of Smithy.

"He's so cute!" Finn enthused. "And a gift from a friend, you said?"

"A rescue," she confirmed, nodding her head. "This is his brother, Wes. They still see each other every day."

"That's so great. There are so many animals in need," Finn said, thumbing through the dozens of photos on her phone.

"I agree." She didn't know why she hadn't considered adopting animals before. Why had it taken a crime boss to show her the way? It was ridiculously ironic.

He was making it hard for her to stay distant. With every new thing she learned about him, the more she fell. Not in love, she told herself, but fell from her initial thinking. She knew he wasn't a mindless criminal or thug. He wasn't a monster—not to her anyway. And she was strangely okay with that.

He was a good man. And, she was beginning to think, perhaps the *best* man.

His words to her from a week ago, when he had confessed to naming the kittens Smith and Wesson, had echoed in her skull ever since. He wanted to make memories with her. Making memories had never been high on her priority list. Mainly because they were a form of torture more than anything else. But the way Roman said it had her thinking it could be nice, and that was just crazy, wasn't it? No matter how sweet, funny, kind, or sexy he was, he was still Vincenzo Romano, heir to two crime families with an extremely dangerous past. A past she knew practically nothing about.

Wow, way to be a hypocrite, her inner self piped up. She promptly told herself to shut up. She knew her secrets could very well outweigh every one of Roman's. And that was another reason why she was holding back from him. He wanted her to accept him for who and what he was. But would he be able to return the favor when he finally learned about her past?

Finn handed her cell back, and she bid him good-night. It was only early evening, but it was the first day of her weekly rotation, so she had three more days to go. She wanted to get home to her kitten, her bed, and her dreams. Which were filled with Roman.

"Angela, hi," Brian greeted her, stepping out from the male change room.

She paused. "Hi." She'd had very few words with him over the last few months. Nothing that wasn't professional, anyway. She was relieved when he hadn't brought up Sal or Roman again.

"I was wondering if you'd like to go for a drink?" he asked her, falling into step beside her.

She did her best to smile as she turned him down. "Thanks, but I'm exhausted. I think I'll just crash."

Brian's smile dimmed a little. "There are a bunch of us going to celebrate Paulie retiring."

"Oh." She knew Paulie, one of the janitors. He was retiring after working there for thirty years. She had spoken to him earlier that day and wished him all the best. He would be taking a well-earned vacation to Bermuda with his wife. "I could spare a few minutes," she agreed.

"Great. How about you go home and change, and I'll pick you up in, say, thirty minutes?"

Before she could argue, Brian was walking away. She looked down at her black slacks and pink button-down shirt. It was fine for casual drinks with colleagues. "I need to change?" she asked Finn, who was watching the show with amusement.

He winked at her. "I think you look great."

"Hmm . . ." Angela was annoyed, but that wasn't Paulie's fault. He deserved a nice farewell. Thinking of the timeline, she shrugged. "I may as well. My friend will be dropping Smithy off soon. I can get changed and put in an appearance for Paulie. And then curl up with my kitten after."

After a second goodbye to Finn, she left the hospital quickly. She wove her way through traffic easily—and happily. Happily because she was going to see her new furry friend—it really was wonderful to have someone to go home to. But also because she was feeling good. And she knew just who to thank for her newfound good mood.

She was still shocked to learn the lengths Roman had gone to in order to stop the drug problem in the city. Of course, he hadn't shut down that operation, or any others, for good. That was impossible. Drugs were always going to be a part of society. And it was better to have someone like Roman involved than some drug lord who didn't give a shit about what they did or who they hurt. She wasn't suddenly wearing rose-colored glasses. She knew Roman was a criminal and made choices she never would. But she now had a better understanding of perspective.

"It's all relative," she murmured as she got out of her car and entered her building. She decided to walk up the stairs, rather than take the elevator, which she liked to do whenever she had the energy.

She said hello to a neighbor and was about to unlock her door when she noticed it already was. She groaned, banging her head against the wood. She didn't know if it was in annoyance or resignation. Walking in, she found Abel sprawled on her couch with a white kitten on his chest. "Stop breaking into my home," she told him, putting her stuff on the kitchen island.

"Your home security is shit," Abel told her—not for the first time. "Why won't you let Roman install the security he wants? Luca knows the best systems on the market. We literally have a security business at Omertà."

"Because there's nothing wrong with the locks and cameras I have now. At least, there wasn't. Not until a bunch of criminals began breaking in semi-regularly." She walked over and plucked Smith from Abel's broad chest. She nuzzled his head, grinning when he immediately started purring. He sounded like a little motorboat. "Thanks for bringing him back," she said to Abel.

"No problem. He and Wes had heaps of fun today. They visited Mario and Luigi. We didn't leave them alone, and we didn't allow them to jump on each other, but I swear they wanted to wrestle."

"The kittens or the dogs?" Angela asked, smiling.

Abel laughed. "Both. Which is great progress. For all their sweetness, the dogs still won't play."

Angela rocked Smith against her chest. "How are the dogs doing overall?"

"Really well. They are calm, sweet, and love pats. But they never play and can't cope on walks yet. They don't like the noise of the city or the crowds. They really only like a few people, to be honest. But I can't blame them. Most people are assholes."

"And you're one of the few people, I take it?"

"I am. So is Claire. And Morrigan, Abel, Sal, Roman, you . . ." He flashed her a grin. "The dogs have good taste."

"Claire is doing an amazing job with them," Angela said. "I'm so glad she was there to take care of them."

Abel nodded, picking at his jeans. "So am I."

Angela eyed him for a moment. His reactions whenever they discussed Claire were fascinating. "So, is she living there now or what?"

"She's still too skittish to be out in public. She's been out a few times now, thanks to Mario and Luigi. But other than that, she still goes nowhere. I'd be crazy by now, but she seems content to remain a hermit," Abel told her with a concerned frown.

"Insulated," Angela corrected him. "Claire is content to remain *insulated*. There's a difference. She feels safe for the first time in a long time. She doesn't want to let that security go. I don't blame her."

Abel was silent for a moment before meeting her eyes with his stunning blue ones. "You sound like you can relate to how she's feeling."

She ducked her head, nuzzling Smithy. "I can," she responded quietly.

When Abel got up and wrapped her in his arms in a giant bear hug, she allowed it. She leaned into him, accepting his support and affection, and taking comfort. Once, she would have battled against it. Now, she embraced it. She started crying before she even registered the tears.

Abel pulled back, gripping her shoulders. There was a look of panic on his face. "Angel! What is it? What's wrong? Did I squeeze too hard? Did I crack a rib? Oh god, I'm sorry. I don't know my own strength. I really *am* the Hulk!"

Angela laughed, wiping her eyes. "I'm fine. You didn't squeeze too hard. See." She held up a still furry, purring kitten. "Smithy isn't a pancake. These aren't sad tears. Well, not really," She amended. Because it was complicated. They were sad tears, but they were also healing tears. And that made all the difference.

Abel eyed her like she was crazy or maybe about to blow. "Whatever you say. Women are weird."

Angela laughed, the last of her tears drying. "Well, thanks again for bringing Mr. Smith home. I'll see you tomorrow."

Abel narrowed his eyes at her suspiciously. "Are you trying to get rid of me?"

"Yes," Angela stated readily. "I am. I'm going out, and I need to get changed."

"Out? Out, where? With whom?" Abel fired back, following her into her bedroom.

She placed Smithy on her bed, grinning when he began to pounce on his tail. She couldn't blame him—it was incredibly fluffy. "Just to a local bar. And with some work colleagues," she replied to Abel. "Brian is picking me up in ten minutes. I really need to get changed."

"Brian? Who the fuck is Brian?" Abel demanded, yelling far more than necessary.

Angela rolled her eyes, moving to her walk-in closet. "He's a cardiothoracic surgeon. He works at the hospital with me."

Abel crossed his arms, planting his feet shoulder-width apart. "Is this the same guy Salvatore told us about?"

"He told you?"

"Of course. He told Roman as well. Luca performed a background check on him months ago," Abel revealed.

"Oh, my god!" she exclaimed. "You roped poor Luca in on this too?"

"He gave Sal the willies," Abel declared, as if it made all the sense in the world. Angela gaped at him. "The willies?"

Abel nodded. "Yes. You know, his gut. Sal's gut is never wrong."

She pursed her lips, tapping her foot. "And what exactly did Luca find?"

Abel's look turned disgruntled. "Not much," he admitted. "He's living within his means, has no extra cash flow or hidden bank accounts. He has no arrest record but was present one night when a domestic altercation took place with a neighbor."

"Present? As in, he helped?" Angela pressed.

"He and the woman had coffee one day. She woke up outside in her garden after having an argument with her boyfriend. Dr. Brian Mathers found her and called an ambulance," Abel explained.

Angela relaxed completely, returning to sifting through her clothes. "So, he helped her. Give it a rest, Abel."

"Maybe," Abel grumbled. "Sounds suspicious to me."

She found a cream satin top with sequins along the neckline and some dark skinny jeans. "I'm getting changed. Get out."

"Ain't nothing I haven't seen before," he said with his trademark grin.

"You haven't seen *mine*." She paused for a moment, considering her words, but finally decided to go with the threat. "I'll tell Roman you saw me naked."

Abel stumbled back a step, clutching his chest. "You are a vicious, evil woman. Are you trying to get me killed?" But at least he stepped out and shut the door.

When she walked out five minutes later, Abel was still standing in her living room. Pouting. "How do I look?"

Abel grunted. "Beautiful, of course."

Angela grinned, walking over to pinch his cheek. "You're just the sweetest."

He swatted at her hand but smiled. It didn't last long. "This is not wise."

"What isn't?" she asked absently. She was trying to find a smaller purse in the drawer in her cabinet by the door.

"Going on a date with another man," Abel clarified. "Roman isn't going to like this."

"Firstly, Roman has no right to dictate whom I do and don't date," she said, wondering why the words felt like a lie. "He's not the boss of me," she added for good measure. She pointedly ignored Abel's rude snort. "Secondly, it is *not* a date. It's a retirement party for a very hard-working man."

"Does dipshit know that?"

Angela sighed. "Don't call him dipshit."

"Fine," Abel snapped. "Does fuckface know it isn't a date?"

She shot him a frustrated look, adding her ID, a credit card, and some bills to her purse, along with her apartment keys. "Of course he does. Brian is a colleague. Nothing more. Besides, he's not my type."

"No," Abel shot back. "We all know what your type is: brown hair, brown eyes, a dangerous aura, and a take-no-prisoners attitude."

Angela donned an amused smirk. "Careful. With such a poetic description like that, I'll start thinking *you* want to date Roman."

Abel puffed out his chest. "He should be so lucky."

Now that she thought about it . . . "Why don't you date?"

"Nope," he said simply and began heading to the door.

"What do you mean *nope*?" She chased after him with a laugh.

"I'm not doing this." He waved his hand back and forth between them. "I'm not discussing my love life with you like some gossiping twit."

"Does that mean you have a love life?" Angela pressed, enjoying the panicked look on his face. "I've never seen you with anyone."

Abel huffed, bending over to pat Smithy, who was winding around his ankles. "Angel, any woman who is dumb enough to have me is too dumb for me to be with."

"You're not *that* bad . . ."

"A glowing testimonial," Abel replied dryly.

Angela snickered and thumped him on the biceps. "Don't be so sensitive."

"You know who is sensitive? Roman is. When other men touch what is his. Be careful, Angel. Be very careful."

Before she could refute Abel's claims that she was Roman's woman, he walked off. She ignored the way the words resonated in her skull—and in her heart.

———

The party was boring as hell. She had spoken with each of her colleagues, sincerely wished the retiree well in his future endeavors, and now she was ready to go home.

She smiled and excused herself from an ER doctor she was talking with. She was feeling a little off, a small headache creeping in and some nausea in her belly. Finding a quiet table in the rear of the bar, she sat down for a moment, taking small sips of her water. She'd had one glass of champagne thirty minutes ago and had no intention of having more.

When her stomach rolled, and she was forced to swallow her rapidly forming saliva, she bolted into the restroom. She pushed her way into a stall, leaning over the toilet bowl. She stayed that way for a few minutes, until she was confident she wasn't going to barf everywhere. Her stomach really wanted to, but it wasn't happening. And that made her feel even worse. Oftentimes, once she vomited, she felt much better.

Groaning, she went to the sink, cupping her hands under the cold water. It felt nice. She watched, frowning when the water started to look a little funny. She tilted her head to the side to get a better look, but that made her feel dizzy. Very dizzy. She stumbled a little, gripping the vanity to keep her steady. That's when it hit her.

She'd been drugged.

It had been a long time, but she recognized the signs for what they were. With the room now spinning, she fumbled for her phone. It took her three tries to press the right button. She called the only person she knew she could trust completely.

"Roman . . ." she rasped when the line connected within a single ring.

"Angel? You don't sound right. What's going on?"

His voice soothed her fear but not the rising dizziness. She was struggling to focus. "Roman . . . drugged."

When her fingers went lax and she dropped her cell, she tried to retrieve it but no longer had the dexterity. She was also quickly losing her concentration. Trusting that Roman would find her and make everything okay, she stumbled to the restroom door. One of her colleagues would help her.

"Angela. There you are," Brian greeted her as soon as she pushed her way out of the restroom. He must have noticed how she looked because his face turned worried. "Angela? Are you okay? You look sick."

She managed a wonky nod, and he jumped into action, gripping her gently but firmly and leading her to a private room down the hall. "Here, sit down. I'll check you out. Do you need an ambulance? What's happening?"

"Dizzy ... sick ..." she slurred.

"Oh dear, you really don't look well. Can you follow my finger?" he asked, holding up a finger and moving it from side to side.

She tried but ended up groaning and listing to the side. It made the dizziness worse. "Drugs," she mumbled.

"Yes." Brian nodded his head, looking serious. "I know. Nasty things. But also very useful. I mean, where would we be as surgeons without drugs?"

Something in his tone set off her inner alarm. She squinted, focusing on his face. A face that looked satisfied—and more than a little mean. "You!" she accused.

"Now, Angela, it's only to get you feeling a little more compliant," Brian said, as if that made it okay. "I've been chasing you for a long time. But did you notice? Did you even give me the time of day? No. You were in your oblivious little bubble."

Angela pushed herself off the seat, but her knees collapsed. She had no strength left at all.

Brian clucked his tongue, reaching down and yanking her up. He held her close, taking all her weight when her legs didn't hold her up. "Perhaps I added a bit too much flunitrazepam to your champagne. Oh well. We'll manage. You ignored me for years," he continued on. "Yet you somehow manage to find time to be with criminals. I know you've been consorting with Romano and his men. Tell me, Angela, have you let him fuck you?"

Angela groaned, her stomach roiling. She hoped she vomited all over Brian's ugly, crazy face. "Go . . . to . . . hell," she managed.

Brian chuckled, dragging her over to the sofa along the far wall. He was stronger than he looked. "Hell? Why, Angela, I'm planning to go to Heaven." He dropped her down, arranging her onto her back. His eyes glowed with a sickly fervor. "I can't believe it's finally my turn. Don't worry, this won't hurt a bit. And I have it on good authority that you won't remember a thing."

Angela wondered how many times he had done this in the past. How many women he had drugged and raped. Because she had no doubt that was his intent. She also knew she would never allow that to happen. Such an act would send her spiraling into her past, and she was just beginning to envisage a future.

A future where she wasn't alone.

A future where she had friends and family and kittens.

A future with a man in it that not only talked the talk, but walked the walk.

A future with a *Roman* in it.

She'd be damned if she would allow some sick, rich doctor take the promise of all that away. She launched herself off the couch, missing him completely and falling onto the floor. She landed on her face and couldn't even roll over.

"You want it dirty, huh?" Brian cackled. "Why am I not surprised? If you want it on the ground like a dog, I'm happy to oblige you."

He placed his shiny shoe on her hip, using it to roll her over. Then he bent over and lifted up her shirt, tearing it at the seams a little in his haste. The look of crazed lust on his face as he took in her lace-clad breasts made her stomach roil. She tried to lift her arms, sweep her foot out—anything from the training she had demonstrated she knew with Morrigan and Roman. But she couldn't move anything. Her whole body felt like lead.

Brian's hand cupped her breast, and she flinched. "Come now," he said. "If you let a criminal's hands on you, surely mine aren't so bad." He held them up. "Do you know how many lives these hands have saved? You should be thanking me."

He patted her cheek before standing up again. She did her best to roll over, managing a pathetic twitch of her finger instead. She watched him hum a tune as he pulled his brown sweater over his head, untucking his shirt from his pants. He paused when he saw her watching and grinned at her.

Patting his crotch, Brian said, "Do you want to see, Angela? Do you want to see the treat you're about to get?"

The urge to throw up increased, especially when he undid his button and lowered his fly, revealing his erection.

"Isn't it a beauty?" Brian smirked, kneeling down next to her. "What if I were to put it in your mouth?"

Brian's revolting flesh was a mere inch away when the door crashed open. Feet thundered on the floor, and Brian was yanked off her. Angela saw Roman punch Brian over and over again, only dropping him when Salvatore forced him to. Abel and Morrigan were already kneeling next to her, asking her questions. But she only had eyes for Roman. When their gazes met and he rushed over to her, barreling past Abel and Morrigan, her throat constricted with overwhelming emotions.

The last thing she saw before she passed out was Roman's face hovering close to hers. And the last thing she heard were his murmured words. "I've got you. I've got you, Angel. You're safe."

She succumbed to the darkness, knowing it was the truth.

CHAPTER TWENTY-SEVEN

Roman answered the phone on the first ring. It wasn't often that Angela chose to call him. "Angel?"

"Roman..."

Her voice was unsteady and had him standing up immediately. He clicked his fingers at Abel and strode from the room, his second-in-command falling in beside him. It was Friday night—family dinner night— and it was his turn to host. He and Abel had been going over a few accounting issues in his office while Luca, Salvatore, and Morrigan bickered in the kitchen.

"Angel? You don't sound right. What's going on?" he demanded. His words brought Sal and Morrigan running, followed closely by his brother, all having heard him. He was now in the living space, and it was open plan.

"Roman . . . drugged," he heard Angela rasp.

His blood turned to ice in his veins. "Where are you?" But he got no response. "Angel? *Angel?!*" He looked at his cell, noting the line was still open. But he couldn't hear her.

"What the fuck is happening?" Abel growled from beside him.

Roman's hand started to shake as he stared blankly at his cell. "Angel needs help. She's been drugged."

Chaos ensued for a moment, everyone yelling and questioning him. "Quiet!" he roared, coming back to himself. He had choked for a second there, but his rage helped focus his attention where it was needed. "Luca, find where she is." He passed his brother his phone. "We're still connected."

Luca didn't ask any questions. He ran to Roman's office, where Roman knew Luca could access anything he needed.

"She was going to a farewell party with that doctor," Abel revealed, looking sick. "But I don't know where."

Roman growled. "Brian Mathers? The doctor Salvatore told me about?"

When Abel nodded silently, Roman's blood began to boil. If the man was behind this—whatever *this* was —then Roman would skin him alive.

Two minutes later, he and a large portion of his crew were getting into cars and speeding off. Luca had stayed, but everyone else was with him. He felt like he was going to be sick, and he wanted to pound something badly, but he didn't have time to lose his shit. Angel had called him when she needed help. And he was going to provide it. One way or another.

———

When Roman broke down the door and saw Brian on his knees with his dick out, and Angel's shirt ripped off, he lost his mind. He discovered that seeing red was not just an analogy. His vision turned hazy, and his hearing switched off for a moment, a loud ringing taking it's place. He didn't recall beating the man's face in, only the rage he felt.

It was only when Salvatore peeled him off the sick fuck, and told him Angel needed him, that Roman came back to himself. Stepping over the piece of shit, he ran to Angel, dropping onto his knees. The tear rolling down her cheek nearly ended him, but he did his best to smile reassuringly. "I've got you. I've got you, Angel. You're safe," he vowed.

His heart stopped when her eyes closed. "Angel!" he shouted.

Salvatore knelt on her other side, checking for a pulse and listening to her breathing. "She just passed out."

"She said she was drugged. What kind of drug?" Abel wanted to know. "What do we do?"

Roman didn't reply. Because he didn't fucking know. He heard Morrigan giving orders to the men, telling them to take Brian back to the penthouse pit. "No!" he said sharply. "I don't want that scum anywhere near Angel. Take him to the docks." He had plenty of properties where killing could be done. He didn't want Angel to wake up and discover Brian was within spitting distance of her. No matter what condition he was in.

His men nodded, hefting the unconscious soon-to-be-dead man and walking out. Roman trusted them to get out of there without anyone from the party in the front of the bar seeing them. They had come through the back in the first place and not seen a soul. This was the second room they'd checked.

"Maybe we should take her to the hospital," Abel suggested, wringing his hands.

"The hospital where she works? Where dozens of people she works with are just feet away partying while she's lying here unconscious from being drugged under their noses? Hell no," Roman snarled.

"Take her home, Roman," Salvatore said quietly. He placed a hand on Roman's shoulder and squeezed. "As long as she hasn't had an overdose, I can treat her there. I swear I wouldn't put her at risk, Roman."

Roman knew that, so he thanked his friend and scooped Angel into his arms. She didn't wake up during the drive back, but she did moan a few times. Luca was waiting for them anxiously when they arrived in the medical suite. Roman moved past him, placing Angel on the bed. He thanked Luca when he covered her with a warm blanket.

"What happened?" Luca asked, smoothing hair back from Angela's face. "She doesn't look so good."

No, she doesn't, Roman silently agreed, afraid to speak in case he screamed until his throat bled. There were some red marks on her nose and forehead that could have been scratches or perhaps carpet burn. Her skin was pale, bordering on green, and she was starting to shake.

Salvatore shone a light in her eyes, asking if she

could hear him, then checked her heart rate again and blood pressure. "It's fast. And her BP is up. I'll push fluids to get the drugs out of her system faster. But it would be better if we could pump her stomach," he admitted.

"The . . . drawer . . ."

Roman wheeled around. Angela's eyes were half open, and she was looking at the large supply cabinet. "Angel." Roman took her hand in his, bringing it to his cheek. "I'm here. Everything is going to be okay."

She smiled a little. "I know." She looked across the room again, stammering, "Ch-ch-charcoal . . ."

"Good girl," Sal murmured, kissing her on the forehead quickly before heading to where Angela was looking. He rummaged around, pulling out a bunch of shit that Roman had no clue about. "Get Claire," Sal ordered nobody in particular.

Roman frowned. "Claire?"

"She's a nurse. For animals, sure, but the mechanics of it are the same. She can monitor Angel's vitals, do IV lines, and assist me as I administer the activated charcoal," Sal explained. "In fact, *I* should probably be the one assisting her. She's technically more qualified."

"I'll get her," Abel said, rushing off before Roman could say anything.

"Activated charcoal?" Roman questioned Salvatore, eyeing the crap in his hands warily.

"It will get the drugs out of her system quickly." Sal blanched, looking apologetic. "It won't be fun. But it will work."

"What happened?" Claire asked, rushing to Angela's side the moment she saw her.

"She was drugged," Salvatore replied.

Claire smiled comfortingly at Angela, glancing up at Sal. "Do you know what with?" When they all shook their heads, she looked at Angela once again. "Angela? Do you know what drug was used?"

"F-f-flu . . ." Angela groaned in frustration. "Fluni . . ."

"Flunitrazepam?" Claire supplied.

When Angel managed a tiny nod, Roman was glad Salvatore suggested Claire's presence. She was already helping. "You know what it is?" he asked.

Claire nodded. "I'm sure you do too. It's also called Rohypnol."

"What?!" Abel shouted. "That's a date-rape drug."

"She should go to the hospital," Claire advised, holding Angela's wrist and counting her pulse.

"No. No hospital," Roman bit out. "It was one of the fucks that work there that did this to her."

Claire didn't respond to him, speaking to Angela instead. "Angela, do you want to go to the hospital?"

"We can help her here," Salvatore told her.

"I wasn't asking you," Claire snapped, showing the spine Roman had seen before when she'd treated the animals.

"Here." Angela said the one word stronger than any since Roman found her. It was slurred, but it was clear.

"Okay," Claire said, patting Angela's arm. She turned to Salvatore. "What do you want me to do?"

Claire and Sal worked together to get Angela hooked up to an IV, as well as electrodes to monitor her vitals. It was hard, but Angela was able to drink down most of the nasty cup of thick blackness Sal gave her. Roman held her upright, coaxing her to swallow, hoping she was able to finish the cup. Otherwise, Claire said they would need to move to more invasive techniques.

There were a few mouthfuls left when Angela began to moan pitifully. She vomited within seconds, the blackness returning just as thickly as it had gone down. Roman stayed where he was, supporting her back and making sure her hair didn't get in the way. She wretched so long and so hard that Roman was afraid she was going to crack a rib.

It was a miserable and painful experience—and not

just for Angela. Everyone in the room winced and cringed right along with her. Every time Angela moaned in pain, Roman added to the ways he was going to make her attacker pay. Killing his father and uncle had been a very personal type of vengeance. It had pushed Roman to his limits. He knew this time, with Brian, would be no different.

———

Hours later, Roman gently deposited an exhausted Angel in his bed. She hadn't vomited for a while, her vitals were stable, and she'd already slept for five hours.

He had to go out, and he didn't want her anywhere else but in his personal space. She would be safe there, and he wouldn't have to worry about her while he was taking care of business.

Pulling the covers up to her chin, he reached down to pick up Smith and Wesson. He'd asked Abel to go and fetch Smith a few hours ago, knowing the kittens would bring Angela comfort. "You two be good," he warned the fluffy pair. They mewled at him, curling up close to Angela's shoulders.

"They're always good," Angela told him softly.

The hoarseness of her voice had his fists clenching. Her poor throat was sore from all the vomiting. He reached out, smoothing her thick blonde hair over the pillow. It looked incredible against his dark green pillow slip. "I'll be back," he said, kissing her gently on the lips. It was brief and chaste and likely unwanted given the circumstances, but he couldn't help himself.

When she sighed, he felt it against his lips, and he sighed in return. *This here. This right here is what I needed,* he thought. A moment to share her breath. "I won't be long," he promised, moving away.

"Roman," Angela called. "Don't kill him."

Roman stopped in the center of the room. "There are many things you can ask of me, baby. But this isn't one of them. He's already dead."

Angela was silent for a moment. She didn't look away or block out the image of the man in front of her who was about to go forth and kill. She simply stared at him until a soft expression took over her still-pale face, and she relaxed back against the pillows. "Don't get caught."

Roman closed his eyes as his foundations rocked. They were three small words, but they changed his world. They weren't the three he hoped would come with time, but they were the ones that told him his woman accepted him. He was truly hers. And, as of this moment, she was truly *his*.

When he opened his eyes again, Angel was still watching him, a small smile on her lips. He cleared his throat. "You know I love you, right?"

Her smile grew. "I know."

"And you're the most important thing to me on this whole fucked-up planet," Roman continued.

"I know that too," Angela confirmed.

He grunted, lifting his chin in her direction. "Good. When I come back, we'll talk more."

Angela nodded, reaching out to the kittens with an unsteady hand. "Okay."

"Rest," he commanded before leaving the room. After closing the door quietly, he leaned his back against it, his legs a little wobbly.

"Roman? Are you okay? Is Angel sick again?" Luca asked worriedly, coming down the hallway.

Roman shook his head. "She's fine. Resting with Smithy and Wes."

Luca released a sigh of relief before frowning. "What's with the look then?"

"She's mine," Roman stated.

Luca rolled his eyes. "Duh. We all know that."

His brother's bratty ways made Roman feel better, and he pushed himself off the door. His arms snapped out in a flash, grabbing Luca and yanking him into a headlock before he even had a chance to yelp. "Yeah, well, now she knows it too."

Luca stopped struggling, meeting Roman's gaze as much as his current position allowed. "She does?"

Roman gave Luca one last noogie with his knuckles against his scalp before setting him free. "She does," he confirmed.

"Oh, Roman. I'm so happy for you." Luca launched himself at Roman, hugging him hard.

Roman hugged him back. "Thank you."

He patted Luca on the back before releasing him and walking down the hall to the living space in his wing. When he got there, he found Abel, Salvatore, Morrigan, Claire, Mario, and Luigi. *It's nearly enough to bring fucking tears to the eyes*, Roman grumbled silently. Out loud, he announced, "Time to get to work."

"We're all coming with you," Salvatore said.

Roman shook his head, already stalking past them. "No. I need you to stay here with Angel. She might need something. I can handle this."

Morrigan blocked his path. "She's not just yours, Roman. She's family. She belongs to all of us," she pointed out in a low voice.

"Luca and Claire will stay in your wing with Angela," Abel told Roman. "Alaric and Teague and a dozen other men are spread out in your apartment and at all elevator entrances. Plus, Sal got a few of his bodyguards up here as well. She's safe."

"We do this together," Morrigan said, hazel eyes flashing with the promise of retribution.

"Together," Roman agreed.

CHAPTER TWENTY-EIGHT

Roman nodded silently to the handful of men as they filed out of the room. They'd brought Brian to one of Roman's properties at the marina—an empty boathouse close to the docks. It wasn't much to look at from the outside, but it had a large, walk-in freezer that was completely sound-proof. Security was also top-notch.

When the heavy door closed, trapping Brian in with Roman, Salvatore, Abel, and Morrigan, the man's head swung their way. He was tied with his hands behind his back to a chair in the center of the otherwise empty space. His face was bloody and swollen and bruised, but Roman could still make out his features. And Brian was still capable of talking. Which he did the moment he saw them.

"Mr. Romano! You need to let me go. This is all a big misunderstanding," the doctor said, pleading with his eyes.

"My reputation precedes me, I see," Roman commented, moving further into the freezer. It wasn't turned on. But it could be if needed.

Brian nodded shakily. "I know who you are. I've worked with a few of your colleagues. I-I-I've always found the transactions easy."

"Is that so?" Roman inquired mildly. It was news to him. And news that made his blood boil. "In what way?"

Brian looked from one pissed off, intimidating face to another, swallowing audibly. "Drugs. I have access at work to all kinds of medicine. I've swapped some products a few times."

"Swapped with whom?" Salvatore asked, coming to stand by Roman. He glared down at him from his considerable height.

"Gentry," Brian replied.

Salvatore nodded, a tick forming in his jaw. "I know Gentry," he allowed.

So did Roman. He was a mercenary who contracted with Salvatore. And he would be getting paid a visit by his friend before the day was out.

Brian looked relieved. "Good, good. So, we're cool?

You'll let me go?"

Roman looked at his friends in shock. The man thought they were going to let him go because they had a mutual acquaintance? "I don't think you realize the severity of your predicament," Roman informed the surgeon.

"I made a mistake," Brian said. "It won't happen again."

"You made a mistake," Roman confirmed, stalking closer. "The worst mistake of your miserable life."

"Please, I-I can pay," Brian offered.

"Pay?" Roman asked incredulously. "You think I want or need your money? I'm a fucking billionaire!" he roared into Brian's face.

The man was startled so badly his chair almost toppled over. Roman blew out a breath, getting himself under control. *Just a little longer,* he promised himself. He needed to keep it together just a bit longer because he had questions he wanted answers to.

"This is how this is going to work," Roman began. "I'm going to ask you questions, and you will answer them promptly and truthfully."

"And then you'll let me go?" Brian asked hopefully.

Silence met his moronic question for a few tense moments before Roman and his family burst into laughter. Brian's eyes widened, and he looked around fearfully. When they all quieted, after sharing amused looks, Roman told Brian, "No. I will not let you go. I'm going to kill you, Dr. Mathers."

"Ki-kill?" Brian looked around frantically. "You can't do that. I'm a surgeon!"

"What the fuck does that have to do with anything?" Abel wanted to know.

"I'm important!" Brian shouted. "I'm well known. You can't kill me."

Morrigan circled Brian slowly, tapping her knife against her palm with every step she took. "You are no more important than any other person on the planet. A job doesn't dictate your worth . . . you fucking piece of shit." She kicked him in the chest, sending him and the chair flying.

They all left him where he landed for a few moments. He was on his side and crying. It was pathetic. Roman motioned to Salvatore, and he sighed, reaching down to yank the chair back into place. But before he moved back to his position beside Roman, he elbowed Brian in the nose, causing it to gush blood.

Roman smirked to the sound of pitiful whimpering. It seemed his friends were short on control this evening. Roman knew just how they felt. He wanted to let loose on the man. But he really did have some things he needed to know. The first being . . . "How many women have you tried this with?"

"Better question: how many women have you *succeeded* with?" Morrigan questioned, her hazel eyes narrowed dangerously.

"Why do you care? I know who you are," Brian spluttered out through his messed-up face, looking at Roman. "I know what you've done. You're worse than me!"

Roman looked at the disgraced surgeon in disdain. "You have no idea who I am. You have no idea what I've done. As for being worse than you? You can be the judge of that after I'm done with you. But know one thing . . ." He backhanded the man, unable to keep his temper in check. "I don't rape. That act is reserved for the lowest of the low."

Brian swore, but Roman figured it was more automatic than anything else because he also resumed whimpering about how hurt he was. Roman shook his head; the man had no idea how much hurt he was about to feel. "You didn't answer my question. How many?"

Brian licked his bleeding lip. "I-I don't know."

"Bullshit!" Morrigan swore. "A man like you keeps count. You probably even have a little black book of horrors."

Roman saw Brian lower his eyes and knew Morrigan was correct. The sick fuck had kept records. He looked at Sal, who nodded back. Salvatore would find it. "How many?" Roman demanded again.

Brian's eyes jumped around the room. "Angela was the first. I . . . I'm sorry. I don't know what I was thinking. Too many long hours. I made a poor choice."

"Oh, you've made a poor choice, all right," Abel agreed, walking into Brian's line of sight. He was holding an innocuous-looking, plain mug. "You chose to lie. *After* needing to be asked more than once." He shook his head sadly. "Poor choice, man. Close your eyes."

Brian's eyes did the opposite—they widened, as much as the swelling and bruising would allow. "Why?"

"Okay," Abel shrugged. "Don't." He tossed the mug filled with salt onto Brian's face.

The man screamed so loud that Roman winced, and Morrigan actually covered her ears. "Fuck, man! What's wrong with you? Have some self-respect," she admonished.

Because his hands were tied behind his back, Brian was unable to rub his stinging eyes, let alone the scrapes and cuts on his face. Roman had no sympathy for the man. After all, Abel had told him to close his eyes.

"I ask a question, and you answer it. Do you understand? If you don't, you get more pain," Roman informed Brian evenly. "It's interesting, isn't it, how something as easy as table salt can be turned into a weapon?" He looked around the barren space. "This isn't my usual place for such activities. Most of my favorite toys are in my penthouse. But there is a fully stocked kitchen, so I'll make do."

"W-why are you doing this?" Brian asked, his eyes streaming from the salt and pain.

"He can't be this stupid?!" Morrigan exclaimed, looking dumbfounded.

Roman knew he *was* this stupid. The man still thought he'd be walking out of there after they were done. His brain couldn't compute that death was coming. But it would before they were finished with him. In fact, he would beg for the mercy of death."Let's try this again. How many women have you drugged?"

He wanted to lie; Roman could see it on his smarmy face. But in the end, he confessed, "Six. There's been six."

"And how many have you raped?"

"Four."

"We saved Angela in time. Was the other woman your old neighbor?" Abel questioned.

Brian looked surprised. "How did you know about that?"

"It doesn't matter how I knew." Abel glared at him. "Just answer the question. Or I'll get my salt back out."

"Yes. Yes, she was the other one," Brian said quickly. "She'd been flirting with me for months. Even when she had a boyfriend. When they fought, I figured it was my chance. She turned me down." His face darkened, and his voice turned harsh. "They *always* turn me down."

"And you don't like taking no for an answer," Morrigan concluded. "I'm going to enjoy slicing your dick off."

"My . . ." Brian's eyes bulged. He looked at Roman, of all people. "She won't really do that, will she?"

Oh, she would, Roman knew. An eye for an eye was big in their world. It was something they had been raised with and witnessed many times as youths. When he turned his back on his blood family, he turned his back on many of their ways. But an eye for an eye wasn't one of them. He fully intended to give Brian as much pain as he dished out over the years. And because that pain included his cock, it would be one of the first things to go.

Morrigan moved her head into Brian's line of sight

like some demented Jack-in-the-box, saying, "She will."
She brandished one of her knives at him.

Brian struggled a little, trying to loosen the ropes
that were wrapped around his chest as well as his
hands. It was entirely pointless. His team knew their
way around rope. Roman let the man cling to his false
hope, enjoying the way he thrashed and wiggled like a
fish on a hook. "I'm going to need a machete or something," he told Abel quietly. "Maybe there's something
in the kitchen, or in the trunk of one of the cars?" he
suggested.

Abel nodded and left the room.

While Roman was waiting for Abel, he squatted
down in front of Brian. "What hand was it?"

"Wha-what do you mean?" Brian looked around a
little, blinking rapidly. His eyes were still streaming
water and incredibly bloodshot.

"Angel told me everything you did to her. She said
you touched her breasts." Roman could barely get the
words out because he was so livid. Saying it out loud
caused him to think about it. And thinking about it
caused him to want to vomit. But not as much as it
made him want to chop up the man in front of him.

Roman leaned in close to Brian's face. "Which hand
did you use to touch that which didn't belong to you?"

Brian looked petrified. "Wh-why?"

Salvatore moved swiftly, smacking Brian up the back of the head. "Are you fucking stupid, or what? Didn't you learn anything from the salt?" He gripped Brian's hair, wrenching his head back. "*Answer the fucking question!*"

Brian cried out again, like the little bitch he was, but he finally stammered, "Ri-right. It was my right ha-hand."

Roman glanced at Sal as he rose to his feet. "Would you please untie Dr. Mathers?"

Brian looked confused as his hands were untied first, followed by the ropes around his chest. He slumped forward, breathing heavily and rubbing his wrists. He looked at the door, which Abel had left open a crack. Roman smiled unpleasantly. "Oh, I dare you to try."

In the end, Brian disappointed them all by staying put. Roman could see the regret in his eyes, though, when Abel walked back in carrying an axe. "Other than a meat cleaver, this was the best I could do," Abel said, passing the axe to Roman.

Morrigan raised her hand as if they were in a classroom. "I'll take the cleaver."

"It's dull as hell. That's why I went with the axe from beside the fireplace," Abel explained.

Morrigan shrugged negligently. "Dull won't be a problem to deal with his cock. In fact, it will be better."

This time, when Abel left, Brian's fight-or-flight response took over, and he charged from his seat. He ran with his head down like a linebacker, aiming directly for Roman. Unfortunately, he was *not* a linebacker, and he ended up on his back on the ground when Roman easily side-stepped and Salvatore moved in front of the stupid fuck. Salvatore wasn't as big as Abel, but he was damn close. He didn't even need to use his arms. He simply allowed Brian to crash into him, resulting in Brian rebounding backwards.

When Abel stepped in a minute later, he looked at the three of them standing in a circle around Brian as he moaned and whimpered on the ground. "What did I miss?"

Roman hefted the axe, his eyes pinned on the prize in front of him. "Nothing, brother. Nothing at all."

He signaled the others with a lift of his chin. Abel and Salvatore pinned Brian's arms and legs to the ground with their body weight as Morrigan removed her belt and tied it around Brian's upper right arm. The man bucked, but it was useless. Sal and Abel were too strong.

"What are you doing? What's that?" Brian bellowed.

"It's called a tourniquet." Morrigan shot him a dirty look as she stood back up. "I thought you were a mighty surgeon. You don't recognize it?"

"I don't want you bleeding to death too soon and missing all the fun," Roman said. Then he swung the axe without further preliminaries.

His aim was a little off—probably because he was tired and running on pure adrenaline—and instead of slicing through Brian's wrist, the axe chopped cleanly through the center of his palm. Four fingers and half of Brian's hand detached, blood flowing out as if a bottle of water had been tipped over. The man screamed, his eyes pinwheeling in their sockets. He choked on his saliva as his head thrashed from side to side.

"You missed," Abel pointed out. He squinted at Roman in concern. "You feeling okay?"

Roman smiled. Abel really was a considerate guy. "I just want to get back to Angel."

Abel nodded slowly, ignoring Brian's pleas and cries like the rest of them were. "Then let's get this done so you can go home."

Roman nodded, watching dispassionately as Morrigan tugged Brian's pants down. If they thought the man's scream was shrill before, it was nothing compared to what he sounded like when his cousin went to work on his scrotum. After she had her fun, Roman cracked his neck and stepped up to the plate.

It was time to unleash the monster his father had created.

————

B rian had lasted a pathetic forty-two minutes before he succumbed to his injuries. Roman didn't think it was long enough to feel the pain and the error of his ways. But he didn't have the power to resurrect the bastard and do it all over again.

He and the others cleaned up in the bathroom, taking turns to wash the blood off and change clothes, before they ushered Roman out, promising to deal with the body and all the evidence of what had gone on inside the freezer. Roman trusted them implicitly, so he agreed, getting in his town car and heading off.

He surprised himself when he didn't head directly to Omertà. He made the detour without conscious thought. He spent ten minutes sitting alone in the garden before a voice had him looking up.

"Roman?" Sister Philomena inquired, walking over to him slowly. "What are you doing here?"

"I don't know," he told her truthfully.

She nodded even as she smiled. "Well, this is a good place to seek illumination."

When the nun sat next to him on the bench, Roman allowed it, finding a strange comfort from the older woman. Eventually, he confessed, "I don't want to drag her down." He didn't think it was necessary to say who he was talking about. The nun surely knew.

"And why do you assume it is *you* who will do the dragging?" Sister Pip inquired.

Roman frowned at her in shock. And insult. "Angel is one of the best human beings on the face of the Earth. She—" He broke off when the Sister chuckled, holding up her hand for silence.

"Your immediate defense of her is endearing. But that is not what I meant. I meant that perhaps *she* would be the one dragging *you*," she clarified. "*Up*, that is. Not down."

He thought about how he'd just spent the last thirty minutes or so and could only shake his head. "I am what I am, Sister. The things that I've done? They can't be undone."

"And why would you want them to be?" she asked briskly. "Those choices got you to where you are—in this very moment."

Roman opened his mouth, only to close it with a snap. He wasn't sure what the correct answer was. He had many regrets in his life, but meeting Angel would never be one of them.

"Do you know why I chose the name Philomena when I entered the convent?" Sister Pip went on. Roman shook his head silently. "Because Philomena is the Patron Saint of lost causes. I've always been drawn to the underdog and the downtrodden. Those lost souls who feel unseen and unlovable."

Roman scoffed in a self-deprecating way. "That certainly fits me."

"But do you know what I've discovered, sharing my mission here at Lighthouse and on the streets?" she asked, continuing on before he could answer. "There is no such thing as a lost cause. Only those still seeking the light."

"Seeking the light . . ." Roman murmured. "My mother used to tell me the same thing. '*Follow the light, and you'll never be lost*,' she would say."

"Such a wise woman, Luciana was," Sister Pip concurred, patting his knee in a maternal way.

Roman lowered his head, blinking rapidly. It took him a moment before he was able to reply, "She was."

"Oh, will you look at that." Sister Philomena pointed to the small outbuilding at the rear of the courtyard. It had a stained-glass window. "The sun is rising on another day."

Roman looked up, finding the first rays of the sun shining through the red and purple glass. It created a beautiful pattern on the pavement. Perhaps it was the unevenness of the stones, or just his tired brain, but the shape the sunlight made looked very much like an arrow. "It looks like an arrow," he murmured out loud.

Sister Pip made a sound of agreement. "Funny about that. I wonder where the light is pointing?"

It was pointing directly east, where he knew Omertà was. And where Angel was resting in his bed. He looked apprehensively at the older woman from the corner of his eye. "You're a scary woman."

Sister Philomena laughed. "Oh, my boy." She stood up and patted him on the cheek. "You have no idea. Now, scoot. Follow the light. And embrace your woman wholly, just as she has embraced you."

"Wait, how did you know she . . ." But she was already gone.

Roman shivered. *Yep, she is one scary-ass nun,* he decided and hightailed it out of there fast.

CHAPTER TWENTY-NINE

When Roman returned, he nodded to his men in thanks, sending them away to guard the entrance rather than the interior of his apartment. He wanted to be alone with Angel. He made his way to his personal wing, finding Luca and Claire still there, along with the two dogs.

"Everything okay?" Luca asked, coming to give Roman a hug.

Roman returned the affection. "Everything has been sorted," he replied vaguely. "How is Angel?"

"She got up a little while ago. She was steady on her feet. I tried to get her to eat, but she said she wasn't ready. She has been drinking water, though," Claire reported.

Roman released a pent-up breath. "Okay. Thank you."

"She's in the shower," Luca added, looking worried. "But she's been in there for a long time."

"I'll handle it. Thanks for staying with her." It was a dismissal, and they knew it. They mumbled a few more words before leaving quickly, taking Mario and Luigi with them.

Roman went into his bedroom to find his bed unmade and the sound of the shower running in his ensuite. Smith and Wesson were curled together in the soft cat cave in his walk-in closet. They looked very comfy.

He knocked on the half-closed bathroom door. "Angel? Can I come in?" When he received no response, he pushed his way inside. He found Angel sitting on the floor of his shower, her arms wrapped around her knees and her long, wet hair plastered to her body.

He quickly opened the glass door, checking the water temperature. Thankfully it was still warm. Squatting down, he spoke quietly. "Angel? Let me get you out of there."

She didn't respond.

He reached in, his arm getting wet as he tilted her face to his. She had dark smudges under her eyes and was very pale, but her eyes weren't red. She wasn't crying. He wished she would because the vacant look in her eyes was far worse.

Instead of trying to get her out, he went in. Heedless of his clothes, he sat down next to her, close enough so she could feel his presence, but not close enough to touch her. Then he talked. He talked until the water turned cold, wrapping a warm towel around her from the heated towel rack. She didn't move, she didn't so much as twitch. He wasn't even sure she was hearing him. But still, he talked.

He spoke of his mother and her beautiful garden. He spoke of how he and Abel had met when they were eight years old, when Abel's mother had joined the household as a maid. He told her that Salvatore's family had been a part of the Romano crew for generations and that they had literally grown up together from birth, having been born two weeks apart. He told her stories about raising Luca, and how hard it was to become a father and a brother to a traumatized ten-year-old at the age of twenty-two. He told her how he shunned his family, creating a new one just for himself.

"And for you," he told her. "This family is yours as well."

"Roman..."

Roman jolted, turning his head to find Angela's eyes

focused on him. "Angel . . ." he murmured. "You're back."

She frowned. "Where was I?"

He smiled gently, reaching out to cup her cheek. "It doesn't matter. You're back now."

Angela looked around, taking stock of their surroundings. Her pale cheeks flushed, and she looked embarrassed. "How long have I been in here?" She ran her eyes over his wet form. "Roman! You're soaking."

"It's okay," he promised. But apparently, she was well and truly back because she scowled at him.

"It is *not* okay. You'll catch a chill. Get those wet clothes off," she ordered.

Roman's smile grew to a grin. He loved her bossiness. He ignored her grouchy swearing as he helped her back to bed first, making sure she was tucked in warmly. He averted his gaze from her nakedness, not wanting her to feel exposed or uncomfortable. Next, he stripped his wet clothes off in the ensuite, leaving them where they fell and threw on some sleep pants. Angela was watching him as he walked back into the bedroom. He checked on the kittens once again; they were still sleeping.

"Do you want to know what happened?" he asked, scared of her answer. He wouldn't lie to her. Angela shook her head in the negative, drawing his attention to her wet hair. "I didn't dry your hair. Here, let me get the dryer."

"I don't want a hairdryer, Roman," Angela said firmly.

Roman paused. "What *do* you want?"

"I want you to make love to me."

Her words shocked him. They also hit him like a lightning bolt. She was naked and in his bed for the first time. He didn't need her to be using words like *making love*. Not after what she had just been through. "I don't think—"

"I'm not asking you to think, Roman," Angela interrupted him. Her emerald eyes met his. "Do you love me?"

The answer was easy. "Yes. I love you. You're my light," he confessed.

"And you're mine," Angela told him. "Make love to me."

Roman didn't question her further. He simply walked to the bed and joined her.

———

ngela watched Roman as he lifted the comforter and slid in beside her. He opened his arms, and she scooted into them quickly. She closed her eyes, her legs tangling with his, and just allowed herself to be held for a while.

She could feel Roman's hardness between them, hidden behind the fabric of his sleep pants. But he didn't seem to be in any rush to take her up on her demand. And neither did she. This close, she was able to properly study his tattoo. She was curious about it. She knew he had gotten it in memory of his mother, hence the lovely flowers. But . . . "Why the two skulls?" she asked, tracing the bigger one, followed by the smaller one next to it.

"The bigger one is for my mother. The small one is for Luca."

The words rumbled low in his chest, Angela feeling the vibration due to their closeness. She looked up. "For Luca? But he's not dead." She cringed at how insensitive that sounded. "I'm sorry." She still wasn't feeling the best—physically *and* emotionally—but that was no excuse to be indifferent to Roman's grief.

Roman smiled at her, twirling her damp locks around his hand. "It's fine. Truly. I know what you meant. I got the first part of the tattoo when I was sixteen. At the time, I believed both *Matri* and Luca were dead. I've added flowers to it over the years, but I've had the skulls and the red rose for a long time."

"Sixteen? That's young," Angela said.

Roman shrugged, drawing her attention to his muscled shoulders. "Age didn't mean much where I grew up. I'm grateful for this tattoo, actually. My getting it is what prompted my father and uncle to talk about what they had done. And for me to overhear them."

"Divine timing?" Angela suggested.

"Perhaps," Roman said with a small smile.

The look in his eyes damn near took her breath away. He was in love with her. And she was in love with him. She had no doubts about that. But why couldn't she tell him? She wanted to. Now was the perfect opportunity to tell him how wonderful she thought he was. How brave and kind and strong. But her tongue felt glued to the roof of her mouth.

"I'm sorry I can't say it," she whispered, ducking her head like a coward.

Roman surprised her by chuckling. "I don't need words, Angel. Not when I have this. You. Right here in my arms." He smoothed his hand over her back, hips, and ass, leaving it there to rest.

"How are you so perfect?" Angela asked, sniffing a little. She was feeling rather emotional.

"I'm so far from perfect that it's laughable, Angel," Roman told her dryly.

She raised her head, tracing his frown lines with two fingers until they disappeared. "How about a compromise? Perfectly imperfect."

Angela kissed him, giving Roman all her weight when he rolled so she was on top of him. Heat built slowly, a gentle burn rather than an inferno, but it was no less intense. Roman mapped her body with his mouth and hands, using Italian and Sicilian interchangeably to tell her how much he loved her and wanted her and how sexy she was to him.

Angela yanked on the waistband of his pants, her hand delving inside to play with the metal bars at the head of his cock. Wetness began to trickle between her thighs because it really was erotic as hell. The memory of what the magic crown could do had her impatience rising to the forefront. "Off. Now," she commanded, tugging his sleep pants off.

Roman helped her, pushing the covers to the bottom of the bed. Then he returned to his spot, laying on his back with his stiff dick jutting from his crotch like a flag. "Go ahead. Do what you will," he invited.

Angela grinned at him. "Is your safeword still

stegosaurus?" she teased. She gripped his shaft, jacking it slowly from root to tip before she straddled his thighs.

Roman groaned, his neck straining as his head pushed into the pillows. "Safeword be damned. I'm always safe when I'm with you."

Angela stopped playing, staring at the man in front of her. "The things you say to me . . ."

Roman was breathing hard, clearly extremely turned-on, but when he spoke, it was easy and unrushed. "It's all you, baby. I only say these things because of *you*. You make me weak and yet powerful at the same time. Weak because I love you, and that is a target on both our backs. Whether I want to admit it or not. Yet powerful because, well, I love you. And nothing is stronger than love. I will always protect you. I will always be here for you. You can count on me. Always."

"I know I can." She wanted to say more, but there were tears welling in her eyes, and she wanted to take the man before her in the worst way. She wanted him to feel what he did to her—feel what he did *for* her.

She stood his erection up straight, moving from his thighs to his hips, and lowered herself down slowly. Her hands immediately clenched, as did her pussy, and she sought out something to stabilize her. Roman, of course, reached for her, linking their hands together as she started to rock.

She moved slowly at first, watching the way joy ran over his face. But she was unable to keep up the steady rise and fall for long because her pleasure was increasing rapidly. She released his hands and planted them on his pecs over the stunning tattoo and rocked back and forth, grinding her clit against his pelvis. The dual stimulation of her clit and his cock inside her was astounding. She cried out and moved her hips faster, loving the way Roman bared his teeth in an almost snarl.

"Fuck!" he shouted, his hands tightening on her hips for a moment before they traveled to loop over her shoulders.

The action forced her body down until her chest was touching his, and he captured her lips, kissing her with passion . . . with *love*. When his hands smoothed back down to her ass, she braced herself on her hands, lifting up and falling back down onto his cock. She gasped, tossing her head back, and noticed the mirror above his bed for the first time. It was dark, clearly made from smoked glass, but it was on the ceiling directly above them.

She kept up her movements but asked, "How did I not see that before?"

Roman grunted, following her gaze with his until they clashed in the mirror. His hips surged harder, faster as they watched the scene together. "You are fucking gorgeous," he told her. "Look at your tits bouncing and your hair touching my thighs while my dick moves in and out of your sweet hole." He followed up his naughty words with a literal growl.

Angela moaned, closing her eyes. "Stop," she admonished him. He was going to make her come, and she wasn't ready for the moment to end.

"Open your eyes, Angel," Roman bid her. "Open your eyes and watch. We were made for each other. There will be plenty more moments for us. Come for me."

She opened her eyes again, looking up. She saw Roman's hands cup her breasts and felt them squeeze her until she lost the rhythm of her hips. He then gripped one of her thighs, planting his feet flat on the mattress and using it for leverage to pound up into her.

"Roman!" she shouted. "Yes! Right there!" His cock piercing was hitting her sweet spot perfectly.

"Right here?" Roman's voice deepened seductively. "Or right *here*?"

Angela didn't know what he meant until he used his free hand to touch her clit. But not just touch—he pinched it, then tugged on it in time with his hips. It

was too much. She screamed, her already raspy voice—
thanks to the charcoal—turning hoarse. She screamed
and shuddered, bucking against his restraining hands.
She was glad he didn't let her escape because she didn't
really want to. But her body was so overstimulated that
it didn't know what to do.

When she fell onto his chest, twitching and panting, he rolled her, swapping their positions. She blinked
blearily at the mirror, seeing Roman's ass flex as he
drilled into her with abandon. His head was buried in
the crook of her neck as he fucked her hard. It didn't
make sense, but she had never felt so loved, or so cared
for. He didn't treat her like she was battered or broken.
He treated her like a woman.

Like *his* woman.

Angela wrapped her legs around his waist and
gripped his head, tangling her fingers in his disheveled
hair. She met his thrusts again and again, as well as she
could, telling him, "I love you. I love you, Roman. So
much."

He stiffened immediately. "Goddamn it, Angel," he
rumbled, his warm release spurting inside her. "I
fucking love you, too."

He pushed inside her a few more times, and the
sound of their bodies coming together—all wet from
sweat and cum—was the most erotic thing she had

ever heard. When she felt his cock flagging, she tightened her internal muscles around him, angling for another orgasm of her own.

He glared at her playfully. "Quit that. You'll break it."

Angela grinned, doing it again. "I doubt that. Not with all the steel that's in it."

He shook his head, slipping free. But he replaced his cock with his fingers, pushing into her with three of them. "Yes," she moaned. "Please."

Roman obliged her, finger-fucking her into a second orgasm, using his cum as lube. He swallowed her shouts of completion, kissing her breathless.

But not breathless enough that she couldn't tell him again, "I love you."

CHAPTER THIRTY

Roman stared at the ceiling, holding Angel in his arms. They had made love twice, Angel had told him she loved him, and he was feeling happier than any man had a right to. She was perfect to him. And perfect *for* him.

The knowledge filled him with apprehension rather than peace, and he admitted to her, "I almost didn't do this."

Angela glanced up from her position on his chest. "What do you mean?"

"After I killed Brian, I had second thoughts about this. *Us*," he clarified.

"Second thoughts?" Angela asked hesitantly. She removed her hand from his chest.

Roman grabbed it, returning it to his tattoo. She had been tracing it with her fingers, and he could stand for her to do it every day for the rest of their lives. "Not about loving you. I could never regret that," he assured her. "But about claiming you as mine officially. Angel, I'm not a good man. No, let me speak," he said when Angela opened her mouth. "I'm not a good man. I don't think I ever really had the chance to be a good man. But my upbringing can't hold all the blame. I've made choices that have shaped me into the person I am today. Choices that I don't want to rub off onto you. Brian said some things . . ."

"And you listened to him?" Angela asked incredulously. "He was full of shit."

"He was. But some things he said were true." *Like me being worse than he was,* Roman thought. "I don't want you tainted by me, Angel."

"Roman, I'm not worried about you tainting me. I never was," she told him earnestly. She sat up, taking the sheet with her and covering her delicious breasts. "My denial of you was all about me. I accept you just as you are. What's more, I know who you are."

"Do you really, Angel?" Roman pressed, propping himself up on some pillows so they were eye to eye. "I spent part of the night torturing a man to death."

"And I've burned dozens of people alive," Angela stated. She paused for a moment, holding his eyes so he saw the truth. "I liked it."

That gave Roman pause. "Tell me."

———

"I t was a long time ago," Angela began. "Not that it makes it okay. Time doesn't erase what I did."

She was terrified to open herself up to Roman—to *anyone,* really. But it was tougher with him because his opinion mattered to her the most. Only one other person on the planet knew all the details of her past. And that was her therapist. Angela hadn't wanted to speak of it to anyone. But now, with hindsight, getting therapy and speaking her truth at least once had been the correct choice.

"I was eighteen," she said. "And I'd just spent the past two years being sold to the highest bidder."

Roman went so still she wasn't sure he was breathing. "A trafficking ring?" he asked, lips barely moving.

She hated to resurrect memories that were surely terrible due to Luca's history, but it was time Roman got to know the *real* her. And it was time for her to be free. "Not exactly," she replied. "You know I attended Granger boarding school for the last two years of high school? Well, that was a lie. My parents were in debt. They were on the brink of bankruptcy. They signed a six-month contract for my *services* in exchange for being bailed out."

"Your parents *sold* you?" Roman snarled.

Angela nodded. "They did. After the first six months, I was supposed to go home. But I was . . . popular. The people in charge offered my parents more money. Not just enough to get them out of debt this time, but enough to set them up for life. My mother and father were both born into money," she explained. "Generations of millionaires. They blew it all before I turned fifteen."

"And used you to make up for it," Roman stated.

"Yes," she confirmed. "My grandmother, the only person in my life who cared about me, died when I was fifteen. But instead of leaving them her modest fortune, she left it to me. It could only be accessed when I turned twenty-one. It was ironclad. My parents couldn't get around the measures Grom had put in place."

"Are they the ones you burned?" Roman asked, brown eyes like flint.

Angela shook her head. "They're still alive."

"Not for long," Roman growled. "They're dead. So dead."

When he went to get up, she pulled him back down. "Don't. Roman, please."

He looked at her like she was mad. "You don't want them punished?"

"Of course I do," Angela replied fiercely. "In fact, I spent years trying to do just that. But they have too many ties to the community. They're too wealthy. Even evidence sent directly to the police yielded nothing."

"*My* actions won't yield nothing," Roman vowed to her.

"I don't doubt that. But their deaths won't go unnoticed or unexplained. You can't kill them. I won't risk you like that," she said.

Roman still wasn't backing down. "You don't think I'm more powerful than them?"

"I won't risk you," Angela repeated sternly. "They are already dead to me. I haven't seen them in years. I don't even think about them. Truly."

Roman stayed stiff and unyielding for a moment longer before relaxing back against the headboard and pillows once more. "It's not enough, Angel. But I'll let it go for now."

It was all she could ask of him. "Anyway, I stayed with The Foreman—that's what he called himself—for two years. He never used me personally, but he was the one in charge of arranging my services. There were auctions and parties, as well as private viewings." Angela blanched. "I had no idea there were so many ways to turn a human being into a commodity before then."

"Angel . . ." Roman murmured brokenly, tugging her against his chest.

She hiccuped, sucking back her tears. Once they fell, there would be no stopping them, and she wanted to finish her story. "Not everyone wanted me for sex. Some wanted me to clean and cook. Others wanted me to do degrading, dehumanizing things like eat out of a dog bowl while wearing a collar and lead. There was this one man who liked to throw parties and invite his guests to play roulette with the bodies of the males and females in his service."

Angela recalled the night when Jedidiah had passed her around on the whim of a roll of dice. Her body felt broken, and it had been hard to move. She was bleeding from multiple orifices and had been ready to launch herself off the balcony. Unfortunately, he kept the place too well guarded for that. She, and others like her, were insured at a high price. Jedidiah and the other bastards that hired them didn't want to have to pay out the exorbitant death clause.

She explained all this as dispassionately as she could to Roman. When she looked at him, she found tears running down his face, and her heart lurched in her chest. "Roman. I'm sorry. This is hurting you. I'll stop."

"You—" He broke off, looking incredulous. He wrapped her up tightly, his head resting between her neck and shoulder. She stroked his back as he shuddered. "You really are a miracle," he told her. "So much compassion for someone shown so little."

Angela allowed herself to fall against him, so they were holding each other up. "The next morning, I was in the bathroom, and I found an envelope with Jedidiah's name and address on it. We never knew where we were. We were also transported blindfolded or with a bag over our heads."

Roman made a sound of distress and reared back. She knew what he was going to say before he opened his mouth. So she beat him to it. "Don't tell Abel. Promise me. I know him well enough to know he would never forgive himself for putting that bag over my head. Don't tell him."

Roman ran his fingers through his disheveled hair. "No wonder you didn't give a fuck when we abducted you. No wonder you were such a mess the following day. That look in your eyes . . . I'm sorry, Angel. I'm so sorry. And I used you against the wall." He looked devastated.

"Hey, I'm okay," she said. "I'm okay because it was you."

"That's not good enough for me," Roman told her, still looking guilty.

But she didn't want him to be guilty. Not for that. "Listen to me," she ordered him, tugging his chin so he faced her once again. "You were right. Using you that day gave me my power back. It helped sandblast some of the triggered memories away. It also felt damn good." One side of her mouth quirked. "I have learned not to deny myself things that feel good. That includes your dick with its jewelry."

Roman was startled into a laugh, and it was music to her ears. He looked so much younger and carefree when he laughed. "I really do love you," she told him.

He stopped laughing and cupped her face with his hands. "I really love you, too."

Their kiss was brief but filled with warmth. When she pulled back, she returned to her tale. "After that event, I was sent home two weeks later."

"What?" Roman asked with a shocked frown.

Angela gave a short laugh. "Right? I was just as confused as you. But my contract was up. The Foreman is a man of his word and runs an honest and ethical service. Or so he told me when he dropped me back at my parent's house."

"Who the fuck is this guy?" Roman wanted to know.

"I have no idea. I don't know his name or where he lives, or even what he looks like. He always wore a mask. Like a masquerade ball-type mask. His eyes and hair changed color all the time. Clearly, he wore colored contacts and dyed his hair." She went on to tell him everything she knew of The Foreman.

"I will find him," Roman vowed. "I promise you."

Angela swallowed hard, nodding silently. The thought of The Foreman finally getting his comeuppance both thrilled and terrified her. He would be an older man by now, given she estimated him to be in his forties twenty years ago. "Thank you."

Roman leaned forward to kiss her chastely on the lips. She chased his lips, extending the kiss but not deepening the contact. "Do you want to hear the rest?" she asked him. When he nodded, so did she.

"My parents had the audacity to pretend that they didn't know what happened to me. They acted as if I had been away at school, just like they told everyone I was. But they couldn't look me in the eye. They knew," she said flatly, her heart breaking a little bit more. "They knew, but they didn't want to. I couldn't stay there. I packed a bag, and I left. I only had a few clothes, but I had memorized the details on that envelope. That was better than clothes or money."

She stared straight ahead now, not seeing Roman's bedroom but the glass house on the hill. "He was in Vermont. It took days for me to get there. But when I did, I found a party in full swing. There were so many people there. At least twenty. Men and women. When I saw two girls stumble outside and turn on the hose, something in me snapped. Jedidiah would make us wash off outside. I picked up a rock and smashed it against the head of the one guard. Over and over, even when he was no longer moving. The girls didn't scream, thankfully. I shoved my bag at them and told them to run. They listened."

"Do you know who they are?" Roman asked quietly, picking up her hand and holding it tightly.

Angela shook her head. "I never saw them again. But I like to think they're okay—that they made it. Anyway, I searched the guard, hoping for a weapon. I was going to go inside and shoot as many of them as I could. But I found a lighter instead. Jedidiah had a private gas pump, so he could fuel up his cars whenever he wanted. It was on the side of the house, away from the crowd. I knew it was there because I saw it when he fucked me against one of his convertibles. I used it to douse the house as much as I could, along with the grounds. I snuck around to the front and barricaded the doors by knocking over a statue. Then I used the lighter."

Angela blinked at Roman's soft-gray walls, seeing glass and flames instead. "The house went up quicker than I thought it would. Flames reached from the ground to the roof in seconds. When I heard the first screams, I smiled. I should have left, but I stayed. I stayed to watch the place burn. And I stayed to watch the *people* burn. No one escaped."

"Thank fuck for that."

She turned back to Roman. "There were innocent people there, Roman. Employees who didn't take part in Jedidiah's games. Cleaners, cooks . . . And I killed them all."

"Do you really think they didn't know what was going on?!" he questioned loudly. Roman snapped his mouth shut, taking a deep breath. "I'm sorry. I didn't mean to yell. They knew, baby. They knew, and they did nothing. Don't feel bad about anyone who died in that hellhole."

Angela nodded but wasn't sure she could take his advice. "So, there you have it. I'm an arsonist and a mass murderer."

"You're fucking incredible, is what you are," Roman

corrected her with a growl. He lifted her hand, placing it over his chest. "Thank you for surviving. Thank you for surviving so you could make your way to me."

Angela sobbed, her hand flying to her mouth. It was one of the only things in the world he could have said to make the cruelty in her life mean something. "Roman, thank you for waiting for me. Even since I met you, you've been waiting. It was exhausting, denying you— denying *myself*—for so long."

"*Mio angelo* . . . my angel," he repeated. "I would wait a lifetime for you."

Angela half-laughed, half-cried. "That's not going to be necessary."

Roman held her while she cried, whispering to her in Italian and Sicilian the entire time. "Thank you for loving me," she said when she had quietened down.

"I don't have a choice," Roman admitted, wiping her face with the sheet. "I don't think I ever did."

"That makes us even," she told him, kissing him with passion this time. When she pulled back, she licked her lips. "I'm glad your cold feet didn't last long."

Roman looked surprised before he laughed. "Well, you can thank Sister Philomena for that."

Angela frowned. She was confused. "Sister Pip?"

Roman looked adorably sheepish as he explained, "I went to her for advice."

Angela laughed, ignoring the irritated growl that rumbled through Roman's chest. "You, a mafia prince, went to a nun for advice about your love life?" Angela cackled. "That is gold."

"*Ex-mafia* prince, thank you very much," Roman told her with a light smack to her butt.

Angela jumped, finding the way her stomach quivered to be interesting. "That's right. You're a businessman now. Mafia for hire."

"There's a big difference," Roman informed her with a sulky frown.

"Of course there is," she soothed him.

Roman narrowed his peepers at her. "You're placating me."

"Of course I am," she answered in the same tone.

He mock-growled at her before pinning her to the bed with her hands above her head. He watched her carefully for signs that she may be uncomfortable with the more dominant position, but she remained relaxed and smiling. She trusted him. Even with everything she had just disclosed.

He squeezed her wrists and placed a kiss on the tip of her nose in acknowledgment of her bravery but didn't push her boundaries further. Releasing her hands, he levered himself onto his forearms by her head, allowing his cock to nestle between her legs. "You're going to be trouble, aren't you?"

"Oh, my sweet, bad boy," Angela crooned, lifting her hips to rub her clit against his magic crown. "Only in the best possible way."

EPILOGUE

Angel stopped at Roman's private office door and stepped back without knocking on it.

It was closed, so she assumed he was still in his meeting. She didn't know what the meeting was about or whom it was with. She hadn't asked that morning when he'd kissed her before dashing from the shower, claiming he was going to be late. Again.

She snickered to herself, thinking about all the times Roman had been late thanks to her in the past two months. She checked her smartwatch, thinking the same thing was going to happen to her if the meeting didn't end soon. Roman's lovely personal assistant, Marcia, wasn't at her desk, so Angela couldn't ask her how long Roman was going to be. Angela knew it all depended on whom he was meeting with.

She knew Roman would tell her about it in a heartbeat. He trusted her. He *loved* her. She knew it. What's more, she trusted it. The knowledge was liberating in a way she hadn't expected it to be. It had only been two months since committing herself fully to Roman, but she was the happiest she had ever been. She still had hard days, and there were times when she got in her head and panicked, but Roman was always there for her. The man had the patience of a saint. And a heart of gold. Both attributes were surprising, but very, very welcome.

Checking the time again, Angela decided to head off. She had a meeting with Sister Philomena to discuss the next stage of the renovations at the resource center. She would send Roman a message instead of the goodbye kiss she originally intended.

She made it partway down the corridor when she heard her name being called. Angela stopped and smiled. "Claire, hey." She hugged her new friend warmly.

She was so glad Claire had decided to accept Roman's offer of a permanent apartment. The other woman had become much more open and outgoing with the promise of a home. But it wasn't just the security of having somewhere to live, Angela knew. It was also the promise of friends. Of family. *And of pets*, Angela added silently.

The two rescue dogs and two rescue kitties had free reign of the complex and were officially little Omertà mascots. Everyone adored them, and they were spoiled rotten. It was wonderful.

"Dinner tonight is lasagna," Claire said. "Roman said you'll be back in time."

Angela nodded. "Yep. Family dinner night is a go. I don't start my hospital shift until eleven." Turned out, Claire wasn't just good with animals but was also an amazing cook. "Lasagna, huh? You like to live dangerously. Cooking lasagna for an Italian family," she teased.

Claire rolled her eyes. "Tell me about it. I've had Abel breathing over my shoulder all day, asking what I'm adding to the sauce and why."

"Are you sure that's the only reason?" Angela asked slyly. The chemistry between the pair was growing. And so was the tension.

Claire rolled her eyes, backing away towards the elevator. "Nope. I'm not doing this."

"Doing what?" Angela asked innocently.

"Discussing this with you. There is no me and Abel. There never will be."

Claire fled before Angela could question her further. She shook her head in amusement because the conversation was reminiscent of the one she'd had with Abel a few months before. Her smile dropped when she recalled that was the same day Brian had drugged and attacked her. His murder was still a hot topic at the hospital, with his mutilated body having been found one week after the incident. She didn't know what kind of person it made her, but she didn't care too much. Her main concern was for Roman and the others. But their names hadn't so much as been breathed in the same sentence as Brian's in any official— or unofficial, thanks to Luca's sneakiness—reports.

Angela heard masculine voices growing louder, and she turned, happy for the distraction. There were three men heading her way, their heads down as they spoke to each other quietly. One was a little further behind the other two, and Angela recognized him as one of the bodyguards working in Sal's company. She smiled because it meant Roman was now free, and she could steal that kiss. But as she nodded politely to the men, her whole body froze. Every single part of her locked up, from her feet to her head, including her breath. The first two men didn't appear to notice. They kept walking to the elevator. But the bodyguard frowned at her in concern.

"Dr. Hawthorne, are you okay?"

Angela didn't answer. She couldn't.

"I'll get Roman," the man said, walking away quickly.

Angela jolted and backed away as if there was a ticking bomb about to blow. And there was. Inside of her. Or so it felt. Her back hit the wall, and she slid down it until her ass touched the ground. She heard running feet but didn't look away from the broad-shouldered older man with the silver at his temples.

"Angel. Angel, what's wrong?" Roman asked worriedly, dropping to his knees beside her.

But she couldn't answer. All she could do was stare at the man who had helped change her life forever. Just as the doors were closing, their eyes met. She saw recognition flash over his face, even though it was a face she technically hadn't seen before. Then the doors closed, and she was left with Roman. The man she loved.

But was no longer sure if she should.

The Mafia For Hire series continues in *One-Way Ride*.
OUT NOW!

WANT MORE?

Do you want to find out what happened when Abel was delirious with chickenpox? How about when Roman called in reinforcements because of the *ahem* location of his?

Simply head to my website to claim your FREE bonus scene.

Claim Bonus Content

Do you want to receive news, exclusives, and giveaways? Join me for a monthly playdate by subscribing to my newsletter, The Halifax Herald.

Sign Up For The Halifax Herald

ABOUT THE AUTHOR

Darcy Halifax writes dark(ish) contemporary romance with anti-heroes and happily ever afters. Why? Because sometimes psychos need hugs too! Her book ingredients include a pinch of violence, a dash of psycho, and an abundance of spice.
Darcy lives in Australia with her two spawn, several pets, and multiple book boyfriends.

You may already know Darcy's paranormal romance alter ego – Montana Ash.

Darcy loves to hear from readers! Email her: contact@ darcyhalifax.com

Visit Darcy's website:
www.darcyhalifax.com

ALSO BY DARCY HALIFAX

The Mafia For Hire Series

(This is a series of duets. All books are in the same world/same series. But every couple gets two books of their very own.)

Silver Or Lead (Book One)

OUT NOW

One-Way Ride (Book Two)

OUT NOW

Kiss Of Death (Book Three)

PRE-ORDER COMING SOON

PAPERBACKS

Special edition discreet, foil covers can be purchased
directly from my website. Along with signed copies of
the yummy Roman cover.
www.darcyhalifax.com

Made in the USA
Columbia, SC
02 September 2023

22402558R00259